INTO THE FLAMES

KNOXVILLE FBI - BOOK ONE

Into The Flames

Knoxville FBI - Book One

Liz Bradford

Copyright © 2021 Liz Bradford
All rights reserved.

Stand on the Rock Publishing
Lizbradfordwrites@gmail.com
Lizbradfordwrites.com

Print ISBN: 9798736123209

Cover Design by Alyssa at Alyssa Carlin Designs
http://www.alyssacarlindesign.com/

Comprehensive Edit by Teresa Crupmton at AuthorSpark, Inc.
authorspark.org

Copy Edit by Sharyn Kopf
https://sharynkopf.wordpress.com/

Formatting by Kari Holloway at KH Formatting.
khformatting.com

Scripture quotations are taken from the *Holy Bible,* New Living Translation, copyright © 1996, 2004, 2007 by Tyndale House Foundation. Used by permission of Tyndale House Publishers, Inc., Carol Stream, Illinois 60188. All rights reserved.

Scripture quotations are also taken from The Holy Bible, English Standard Version. ESV® Text Edition: 2016. Copyright © 2001 by Crossway Bibles, a publishing ministry of Good News Publishers.

Scripture quotations are also taken from Holy Bible, New International Version®, NIV® Copyright ©1973, 1978, 1984, 2011 by Biblica, Inc.® Used by permission. All rights reserved worldwide.

This novel is a work of fiction. Names, characters, businesses, places, events, locales, and incidents are either the products of the author's imagination or used in a fictitious manner. Any resemblance to actual persons, living or dead, or actual events is purely coincidental.

Isaiah 43:1-3 (ESV)

*... Fear not, for I have redeemed you;
I have called you by name, you are mine.
When you pass through the waters, I will be with you;
 and through the rivers, they shall not overwhelm you;
when you walk through fire you shall not be burned,
 and the flame shall not consume you.
For I am the Lord your God,
 the Holy One of Israel, your Savior ...*

Romans 2:29b (NLT)

... a person with a changed heart seeks praise from God, not from people.

Chapter One

The candle flame flickered. Dylan leaned his elbows on the table and let his mind drift from the conversation that circled around the room to the images of the eight girls he and his team had extracted a few years ago from a burning house. They had been from all parts of the world. They had been so young.

He reached out and swiped his finger through the yellow flame.

"Dylan" —his mother's voice was stern—"you'll burn yourself."

He stifled an irritated groan and sat back in his chair. He had wrinkled the linen tablecloth, so he ran his hand across and smoothed out the cloth his mom had no doubt freshly pressed this morning before church.

Like always, she had gone all out for this Sunday dinner. Her grandmother's china, in addition to the crisp tablecloth and candles, adorned the table. But this Sunday afternoon dinner was nothing more than an accolade to his older brother.

"Chadwick, we are so proud of you!"

His mother's gushing was excessive today.

Chad *had* done well. He was a big-shot lawyer in their hometown of Knoxville, Tennessee, and he *had* won a big case last week. But having a brother as a defense attorney was not easy for Dylan, whose very purpose as an FBI agent was to put criminals behind bars. Thankfully, Dylan's disdain for defense attorneys did not inhibit his relationship with his brother, and they had never had to sit on opposite sides of the aisle. Dylan's times on the witness stand had never required his brother to cross-examine him. But it was bound to happen eventually. Though he hoped it wouldn't.

Dylan peered down the table past his mom, dad, sister, and sister-in-law to where his brother sat with a confident look. Dylan did love his brother but living in the shadow of his spotlight was tiresome.

His sister, Scarlet, who was three years younger, kicked Dylan sideways under the table. "How's work?"

Chad leaned forward. "Good question. Were you all able to catch that drug dealer you were pursuing?"

Dylan sat up. "Actually—"

"That is not dinner conversation." His mother looked as if she would devour someone.

Scarlet gave him a half-shrug, and he shook his head. He really wasn't surprised his mom cut him off.

A little hand tugged on his sleeve. "Uncle Dylan."

Dylan turned and found his six-year-old nephew, Isaac, standing before him with a toothy grin.

"Come play," the boy whispered.

"Sounds like a plan, buddy." He was thankful for the reprieve from the adults. "Please excuse me," he said to his family. He neatly laid his cloth napkin next to his plate.

Isaac grabbed Dylan's hand and tugged him into the living room where the boy's brother and sister were playing on the floor. Dylan plopped down on the floor by his ten-year-old niece, Anna, and two-year-old nephew, Peter.

"Whatcha playing?" He tickled Peter.

Peter laughed and squirmed away.

Isaac pushed his sister. "Anna! Get your stupid dress off the train track!"

"It's not my fault!"

"Yes, it is. Get it out of the way."

Dylan stuck his hand in between them. "Knock it off, you two. Isaac, there are nicer ways to ask your sister to move."

Isaac met Dylan's eyes as if to stare his uncle down. Dylan raised his eyebrows, careful not to let his amusement show. He'd make this kid crack. After all, Dylan had made that drug lord crack two days ago … Okay, that took more than a stare down.

"Fine. Sorry, Anna," Isaac said. "Could you *please* move your dress?"

"Sure," she said with a snooty head-bobble.

Dylan stifled a laugh. This girl was like her father in more than looks. Was it an oldest child thing?

Dylan grabbed a black and red engine from the floor and raced it along the wooden track behind Peter's eight-car train that lacked an engine entirely. In his best conductor voice, Dylan said, "I think you forgot me back at the station, Peter."

Peter sped his train up.

Dylan bumped Peter's back car.

"Hey!" A glint flashed in Peter's eyes, and he looked at his brother.

"Let's get Uncle Dylan!" Isaac shouted.

Both boys jumped off the floor, ran around Dylan, and pounced onto his back. He flipped Peter over his shoulder and tickled the boy again.

"Noooo!" Dylan put his hands up in mock surrender. He gracefully fell to the floor, and all three kids, even Anna in her poofy Sunday dress, joined in.

"Dylan Andrew Harris!"

He looked up.

His mom stood in the arched doorway with her hands on her hips. "Kids, go wash your hands. I've got cookies for you."

The kids ran off, and Dylan picked himself up. He ran his hands down his disheveled dress shirt in an attempt to smooth it out. His mom hated even the slightest thing out of place.

"Dylan, will you ever grow up? You really should seek Melanie out again. She was so wonderful. You need to get married or move forward in your career like your brother."

His insides wound up tight. *But Mom, if you'd ask, I'd tell you how I broke a case and took down that drug dealer last week.* But he kept his mouth shut.

She turned and walked through the dining room into the kitchen. Dylan constricted every muscle in his hands.

Scarlett came into the room and took his elbow. "You have to stop letting her get to you."

"I know. But I'm so tired of listening to how Chad does everything right, and how nothing I do matters. You know, I helped crack a big case last week."

"That's awesome, Dylan. I'm proud of you. Does that count?"

"Definitely. Thanks." He put his arm around his sister's shoulders.

"But Mom is right about one thing."

"What's that?" He dropped his arm and squared himself with her.

"You need to find yourself a nice girl and settle down. Thirty-three isn't a spring chicken, ya know."

He shook his head. "I'd love to, but a few months ago, I went out with this really sweet girl a buddy from work set me up with, but as soon as she found out who my brother was she said—" He went into his best "girly" voice— "'Oh, you're Chad Harris's brother. Oh my word. He's so amazing.' Real buzz-kill."

"I bet. But you have to stop living in his shadow. Be your own person." She smacked his arm.

"Easy for you to say. You've never had to live as his little brother."

"No, but I'm his sister. You know I still have to prove myself every turn I take. Why do you think I moved out of town?"

"I tried that."

"Too bad you got transferred back here." She giggled. "Didn't you have any say?" She raised a single eyebrow.

"Well, yeah, but I love this city."

"I know. I kinda miss it." She cast a longing gaze out the front window. "But Raleigh is almost as awesome."

"I missed the mountains too much in St. Louis."

She swept her arm out in front of herself. "Hence why you took the assignment here."

He nodded. "And can I say, if I do find someone, you better believe I'm not ever bringing her here? Why would I ever want to torture someone who's into me with this?" He waved his arm toward their family in the other room. "Anyway, enough about me. You look great in that exquisite blue dress."

"Thanks. And it's periwinkle—my favorite color. You should know that one by now." She adjusted the thin black belt that sat high on the waist of her dress.

"Somehow you still manage to fit Mom's ideal."

She let out a dry cackle. "But don't be fooled, I only wear a dress when I'm home." She lifted her hand to direct her voice and whispered, "Don't tell Mom, but I wore ripped jeans to church last week."

"You rebel!"

They both laughed, and Dylan drew Scarlett into a hug, thankful for his sister's camaraderie.

Monday morning, Jacq Sheppard knelt on the carpet in the babysitter's living room and wrapped her arms around her almost three-year-old daughter. Her heart quivered as little Harper's arms circled her neck. "You are going to have a great day with Ms. Rachel."

A few feet away, Rachel sat on the edge of the couch. "We sure are."

Harper pulled out of the hug. "Momma go to work."

"Yep, and then I'll be back."

"Uh-huh." Huge tears pooled in the corners of Harper's eyes, but she stood in front of Jacq with a tough little face.

Jacq swallowed hard. She needed to not start crying too. The last two weeks of settling into their new home in Knoxville had been delightful. Between unpacking and setting up their spacious two-bedroom apartment, the two of them had spent time reading and playing. Jacq hadn't wanted it to end, but it had to. Duty called.

Harper took the sides of Jacq's face in her tiny hands. "Momma help people. I be fine." Two enormous tears rolled down Harper's cheeks and dropped onto Jacq's blouse.

She wiped her daughter's face. "You are so brave. I love you."

"I yuyou too. Momma brave."

Jacq chuckled lightly. "I'm going to go now."

Harper threw herself against Jacq, gave a great big squeeze, and then let go. "Bye, Mommy."

"Goodbye, Harper." Jacq kissed Harper's head and stood.

Harper darted to the toys in the corner.

Jacq tried to steady her breath and turned to Rachel, the wife of a fellow FBI agent. She understood the life of an agent and the crazy hours that could ensue. But more than that, Rachel was a believer who had quickly become Jacq's friend. Harper didn't often take to new people but had connected with Rachel right away. Jacq had dropped Harper off a few times while she ran errands, but this was the first full day—Jacq's first full day at the Knoxville field office.

"She'll be fine."

"If by fine you mean she'll forget about her mom in about—"

"You know she won't."

Jacq met Rachel's eyes. "I know. She'll be fine. Although, I'm not sure I will be."

Rachel rested her hand on Jacq's shoulder. "You will. I've seen you talk about your job. God put you in this place for this time, so He will take care of you both."

Peace flooded Jacq's heart. "True. Call me if—"

"You know I will."

Jacq nodded and said goodbye. She walked out the door and down the front steps. Her heart was heavy. She wished it wasn't so hard to leave Harper. When she had been assigned to the field office in Pittsburgh, it had been simple; her mom watched her daughter.

That was the only thing Harper had known, but life would hold new adventures here in Knoxville. And at least Rachel was close to the office and so wonderful. Harper should be safe and happy. Jacq needed that confidence as she started at a new field office.

She climbed into her car and sent up a little prayer for Harper to have a good day. And then one for herself too. She was ready for this change. She had been to Knoxville a few times in college, and she had loved the city then, so when she received this assignment her heart had quickened at the prospects. Even if her nerves set her stomach on edge since a piece of her past, one she'd rather forget, lived here. But she shook that out of her head and drove the five more miles to work. She parked, took a steadying breath, and pushed open the large glass doors to the big stone building.

"Jacquelyn Sheppard?"

She turned at the sound of her name. "That's me."

A stocky Black man with a scar along his left cheek grinned at her and reached out his hand. "Special Agent Warren Bridges, at your service."

She returned his smile and shook her new supervisor's hand. "Nice to meet you face to face."

"Likewise. I hope you like it here in Knoxville. Great city. You settling in?"

"Getting there."

"Good. Well, let's get you settled here too. Let me show you around first." He waved his arm for her to join him.

She followed Warren through the lobby toward the elevators. This man was as kind as he had sounded on the phone. She was off to a good start.

A few minutes before nine, Dylan pulled open the door of the courthouse and held it for three of his fellow agents. All four of them had testified in the case that had brought them back to court today, but after being sequestered all weekend, the jury had reached a verdict.

"Thanks." Aliza Blake nodded. She was the newest member of their team, though not after today. A new guy was joining them. Dylan didn't like that they weren't all there to welcome him, but that would come.

Matt Olsen came through, followed by Gio Crespi. These two were like brothers to Dylan. Working together for the last three years in Knoxville had given them plenty of opportunities to have each other's backs. Gio shared Dylan's faith, and with their gentle nudges, Matt seemed to be opening up to the truth.

Dylan fell in step beside Gio, behind Aliza and Matt, and the four strode down the hallway to the courtroom.

Matt spun around and walked backwards, staying in perfect rhythm with Aliza beside him. He shot the guys a mischievous smirk, imploring them to pay attention.

Gio shook his head. "Don't, man—"

Matt ignored him. "So, Aliza, trouble with your boyfriend? You don't smell like horses today."

Dylan chuckled.

Aliza's head jerked toward Matt. Midstride, she put her foot in his path, and his heal caught it. Anyone else would have toppled onto the floor, but Matt, with his athletic prowess, managed to almost hover while he twisted his body and caught himself on the other foot facing forward.

"We're fine, thank you very much." She raised her head a little higher.

Dylan laughed again.

Aliza spun around and put her fists on her hips, stopping right in front of him.

Dylan lifted his hands up in surrender. "I'm laughing at him, not you."

She looked at him sideways before turning and continuing.

Dylan exchanged a chuckle with Gio. They rounded a corner and entered a crowded hallway. Dylan's eyes landed on his brother.

"Great. Mr. Know-It-All is here."

Gio stepped a little closer. "Where else would you expect to find an attorney?"

"In jail for helping guilty men walk."

Gio let out a loud snort. "That would be fitting. But he's here, and you don't tend to have a problem being cordial with him."

"I'm still irritated about yesterday's lunch."

Chad spotted him and opened his arms. "Agents! How are you all this fine Monday morning?"

Gio shook Chad's hand. Matt did the same and said, "We'll be great once we hear a guilty verdict."

"Ah, yes. Pedophile, correct?" Chad turned to Dylan.

He nodded and grasped his brother's extended hand.

"From what I heard about that case, pedophilia was the least of the charges." Chad pulled on the bottom of his suit jacket.

Least? Dylan's gut burned. *Anyone who would hurt a child …* "He deserves a lot worse than Tennessee law will allow."

Aliza was the final one to shake Chad's hand. She opened her mouth as if to say something but snapped it shut.

The four agents said a round of "have a good days" and continued their way down the hall. Dylan let out a tense breath.

Aliza nudged him with her elbow. "He really gets to you, doesn't he?"

"Only if we aren't hitting balls at the batting cage."

"That's because you are actually better at that." Matt pointed at him.

Dylan let a smile creep in. "True. It'd be nice if he'd for once acknowledge that we did a good thing getting a dirtbag off the streets."

Gio's pensive expression made Dylan slow his steps. "What?"

Gio stopped. "Whose 'well done' are you working for?"

Dylan stopped. His insides prickled. He wanted to blurt out the obvious answer. Wasn't all he did for the glory of God? He wanted it to be.

Gio resumed his course with Matt and Aliza leaving Dylan to

ponder the question.

The last two hours had been overwhelming for Jacq as Warren had whisked her around the building introducing her to dozens of new people. This was her third transfer in the last ten years of being an FBI agent, so she knew the routine. Finally, Warren showed her to their team's office space. They entered a room measuring about thirty-by-sixty feet. Warren directed her to the left half, where six desks faced each other between two cubical-style half-walls.

"This is our team's bullpen. Here's your little corner of the bench." He led her to the empty desk at the far end near the windows that lined the outside of the building. "I'll be in my office if you need me." He pointed to the office past the half-wall behind her space. "Make yourself at home; there'll be work soon enough." He walked between her desk and the windows and disappeared.

She dropped her backpack and sat. Her feet were tired from being on them so much, especially after that exceptionally long conversation with Janice from forensics about the best places to eat in town. Warren and Janice both had strong and opposing opinions on the matter. Good thing she had gone practical instead of cute in her footwear choice for today.

The office was mostly empty. Three people sat silently working around another half-dozen desks on the other side of the room, but her team was conspicuously absent. Where was everyone? Warren had pushed his door mostly shut, so she didn't feel comfortable bothering him so soon.

Jacq picked up her backpack and removed the few personal effects she had brought for her desk—a picture of Harper, the mug her team in Pittsburgh had given her after Sean died, and the Bible she liked to keep in her desk. She'd probably add a few more things over the next few weeks, but these were the items she had to have.

The door to the office opened and a tall, curvy woman in a tailored, dark suit entered. Her short, silver hair bounced as she strode toward Jacq. "Hey, it's the new agent on the block. I'm Sabrina Fitz. Welcome to Knoxville."

Jacq stood and extended her hand. "Nice to meet you. Jacq Sheppard."

"I have to say when Warren said our new team member's name, I didn't expect a young woman with bright red hair."

"It's Jacq with a 'c-q.'"

"Love it. Aliza will be glad we're even now. Three guys. Three women. Not that that girl can't hold her own with a dozen guys. She'll also appreciate not being the short one anymore. Two of the guys are always givin' her grief."

"Good to know. I'll be ready for them. Being five-three has never bothered me one bit. Speaking of our team, where is everyone?"

Sabrina smiled. "They're bummed they didn't get to greet you, but there's a big case wrapping up in court. The other four had to testify, and the verdict came in this morning."

"Ah. But you didn't join them?"

"Nope. It was an ugly case; more than I can handle. Give me the numbers, and I'll crunch them. I leave the violence to the men."

"And Aliza?"

Sabrina nodded her head to the side. "Some days I think she *is* one of the guys."

Jacq chuckled. She already liked Sabrina, even if Jacq would rather kill a chicken with her bare hands than have to do anything with math. She had the analytic skills for the job, but she was an agent because she longed to slap cuffs on the criminals.

The glass door to the room opened again, and a stout older woman made a beeline for Warren's office. She moved at a much greater speed than Jacq would have thought possible.

"Uh oh," Sabrina said.

"What?"

"That's Tina from dispatch. It's never good if she feels the need to storm in here. Might as well gear up; we're headed out."

Jacq picked up her backpack and set it in her chair while Sabrina did the same. A few moments later, Warren came out and said, "Fitz, Sheppard, gear up."

"What's the case?" Sabrina asked.

"Suspected kidnapping at the mall. Possible victim is a white female, approximately thirteen years old."

"Possible?" Jacq slung her backpack onto her shoulder.

"Witness spotted a girl being shoved into a car. I'll call Harris and tell the rest of the team to join you. Local PD is already onsite."

Jacq's heart stopped. Harris? No, it wasn't him; she didn't need to worry about that. She knew with confidence *he* wasn't an FBI agent. And Harris was a common name; she didn't have anything to worry about. Right?

Chapter Two

On Interstate 40, Dylan swerved around a slow-moving sedan.

Matt braced his hand against the dashboard. "Harris, you don't have to drive so fast."

Aliza and Gio were in the backseat. It was her turn to give Matt a hard time. "How do you call yourself an FBI agent if you can't handle a little crazy driving?"

In other circumstances, Dylan would have been amused. "A child has been kidnapped, and it's our job to save her. I'm sorry, but I do have to drive fast."

"Well, you're going to make me sick."

Dylan glanced over at Matt Olsen. He did look a little green. Dylan quickly darted around another car as he sped down the highway in his Dodge Charger. He really wished they had taken an FBI vehicle to court so he would have lights and a siren to turn on to get people to move out of his way.

He had been an FBI agent for the last nine years and had seen more than his fair share of kidnappings go sideways. The sooner the team got on the scene, the sooner they started searching for her, and the sooner she'd be home. He'd drive as fast as necessary to make that happen.

God, please be with this girl. Keep her safe and help us find her as soon as possible. Give us wisdom and discernment. Point us in the right direction.

Thankfully, they arrived at the mall on the west side of town ten minutes later without Matt tossing his cookies all over Dylan's clean car. They pulled up to the mall entrance near JCPenney's, which the local police had cordoned off with crime scene tape. Dylan cut the engine and jumped out and ducked under the yellow tape, the others on his six.

Sabrina strode toward them. "Hey, guys."

"Hey, Fitz. What do we have? Bridges didn't give us much detail on the phone."

She adjusted her large, black-rimmed glasses. "Possible abduction of a young teenage female."

"Possible?"

"We only have one witness, and no one's been reported missing. We've only been on scene for about ten minutes."

"We? You brought the new kid?"

"Yes, and Jacq's no rookie. Transferred from Pittsburgh and is specialized in working kidnappings."

"You seem to have learned a lot about him in the last couple hours."

"Try thirty minutes. Warren gave Jacq the whole tour of the building."

"Oh boy. Where is he now?"

"You mean she." Sabrina pointed toward the mall entrance. "Talking with the witness."

"She?" Dylan looked in the direction Sabrina pointed. Sitting on a bench right outside the mall door with an older lady was a woman with flaming-red hair that cascaded over her shoulder. Her face was turned away from him. She listened intently to the woman sitting with her, but then she turned. When he caught sight of her face, his breath got stuck in his chest.

Her eyes made contact with his, and he couldn't fight smiling. Her eyes grew wide, and she moved toward them.

"Jacqui." He could hardly believe his eyes. She was every bit as gorgeous as he remembered her being more than fifteen years ago.

"Dylan. Hi."

He could barely get his mind to think straight. "Good to see you. You're our new teammate?"

"I am."

Sabrina's voice brought his eyes away from Jacq. "Apparently no introductions are necessary here. Jacq, this is Matt Olsen. Matt, this is Jacq Sheppard."

Matt shook Jacq's hand. "You look nothing like the Jack Shepard from the TV show."

She laughed. "Not hardly."

"Sheppard? Married?" Not the last name Dylan expected, but he didn't see a ring on her finger. Some agents chose not to wear jewelry, but the small hoops in her ears and the simple silver cross around her neck indicated that wasn't the case for her.

"Widowed almost four years ago."

"Sorry to hear that." He turned to introduce her to Gio and Aliza, but they were nowhere in sight. "Where'd the other two go?"

Matt pointed in the other direction. "They saw Gabe"—he turned to Jacq—"Aliza's boyfriend and local LEO. They went to help the search over yonder. So, what did you learn from the woman?"

Jacq perked back up. "She said she came out this entrance just in time to watch a man she described as Latino and about mid-twenties push a teenage girl into the backseat of a black sedan. She couldn't get any details on the car—black, four doors, and very dark-tinted windows. The man got into the car and it sped away. She didn't see the driver. She described the girl as probably about thirteen, give or take, with long blonde hair pulled back in a ponytail. The woman called 9-1-1 right away, which is how we got to the scene so quickly."

"No idea who this girl is?" Dylan asked.

Jacq pursed her lips and shook her head. "Local LEOs are keeping their eyes out, and patrols have been increased, but we don't even have enough for an Amber Alert."

"Agents!" A mall security officer jogged over to them. "I think we have something."

"Excellent."

Jacq pivoted toward the mall security officer. "What do you have?"

"Come with me. We may have an ID."

Dylan came up next to her and matched her stride. She couldn't believe Dylan was the Harris on her new team. Her heart sank the moment she made eye contact with him, but, at the same time, the familiarity was comforting, and a touch of attraction flared up inside. The dichotomy of the emotions she felt was unnerving, especially in the middle of a case. She needed to keep her own emotions turned off so she could focus. She would not let a Harris ruin her first day.

She shook her head to clear it and followed the officer inside the mall. They walked through the dark entryway, where the rental carts and strollers were parked along the center, before stores began appearing on either side. A chill tickled the back of her neck. She turned her head and slowed.

"What is it?" Dylan slowed with her.

"Got that feeling like someone was watching me." She scanned all around but saw no one.

They continued to the main thoroughfare of the mall and to three hysterical teenage girls, who barely looked thirteen. Jacq picked up her pace and passed the officer. She placed her hand on the back of the closest teen. "I'm Special Agent Jacq Sheppard with the FBI. And this is Special Agent Dylan Harris."

The girl fell into her arms and another one said, "Is it true? Did Marrissa get kidnapped?"

Jacq rubbed the sobbing girl's back. "We're trying to figure that out. Is Marrissa your friend?"

She lifted her head. "Yes." She sniffed. "I thought she went with us into the store, but we can't find her anywhere."

"We're searching the mall for their friend," said the officer who had led them over.

Dylan nodded at him and turned to the girls. "Tell us what

Marrissa looks like." His voice was kind and gentle as he leaned in slightly to reduce his height.

"She's about as tall as me."

"Long blonde hair in a ponytail. She always wears her hair in a ponytail."

"She's really skinny, like Kylie." The girl indicated one of her friends.

"Yeah," Kylie said. "She was wearing black skinny jeans and a blue t-shirt."

"How old are you all?" Jacq asked.

"Twelve," they said in unison.

"But Marrissa's going to be thirteen in a month."

Jacq's heart sank. So young. This sounded like a match to the girl the older woman saw taken. She met Dylan's eyes. He nodded slightly. Jacq swallowed hard. "Let's go sit on the bench and call your parents."

While they shuffled over to the bench, Dylan asked, "Does Marrissa have a cell phone?"

They nodded. "We tried calling, but she didn't answer."

"Can you give me her number?"

Kylie gave him the number, and he left. Matt came in and joined Jacq. They would help the girls call their parents.

Kylie paused before hitting send to call her mom. "What's he going to do with Marrissa's number?"

"We can track it."

Dylan pushed the mall door open and stepped outside, stomach unsettled. Twelve years old. So innocent and young. He didn't want to think about what could happen to the girl if they didn't find her.

Gio and Aliza had joined Sabrina. Dylan said, "We have an ID."

The others followed him to his car. Aliza said, "And?"

"Marrissa Highwater. Twelve."

Aliza gasped.

Dylan grabbed his bag out of the trunk, extracted his laptop, then tossed the pack in the backseat. He opened the computer and logged in. In a matter of moments, he was connected to his hotspot and found the Highwater's information.

Gio pulled a notepad out of his pocket and wrote down their address. "Aliza and I will go."

Aliza put her hand on her hip. "How? We rode with Dylan."

Sabrina produced a set of keys from her pocket and dangled them in front of Gio. "It's over there."

Gio and Aliza left to make the dreaded notification. How do you tell a parent their child has been abducted?

Dylan shook his thoughts free with a quick snap of his head and opened the application to track the cellphone.

A little dot bleeped on the map. "I got it!" But then his heart dropped. The dot wasn't moving, and it wasn't far away.

Sabrina hovered near his shoulder. "What is it?"

"Marrissa's phone, but I'm guessing it was ditched."

"Well, go find it. Maybe there'll be a clue of some sort. Olsen and I will take care of interviewing any more possible witnesses and then move toward getting the security footage."

"Perfect." Dylan didn't envy that job. An abduction from a mall would be an interview nightmare.

Jacq joined him. "Did you find her phone?"

"Yep, going to look for it now. Want to come?" His heart skipped a beat.

"Definitely." Jacq grabbed her backpack, and once they were in the car, Dylan handed her the laptop.

He pulled away from the curb. "Which way?"

Jacq folded the computer back into tablet mode and zoomed in with her fingers.

"Turn right here and then left out of the mall's drive."

He wanted to ask her a zillion questions, to get to know her, but now wasn't the time. The time for that would come after they got Marrissa home.

"Go straight at the light."

He slowed down for the light, but it changed to green. "Has it moved?"

"No …" Her voice was soft. "Take the onramp to I-40 East."

He followed her directions.

"Looks like it's on the entrance ramp to eastbound I-640."

"That's what I was afraid I saw."

They were both silent for the next four miles. He put on his flashers as he drove around the eastbound entrance ramp.

"To the right up there."

He pulled the car onto the shoulder, and they both jumped out.

There was no car parked along the side of the road, and no sign that Marrissa herself was here. Her captors probably realized she had a cellphone and ditched it out the window. Dylan paused before he began his search. If he had thrown a phone from a presumably moving vehicle, where would it have landed? He probably would have chucked it as far as possible and aim for the shrubs and trees. He kept his eyes trained on the ground and walked toward the brush.

"Oh, this is silly." Jacq headed back to the car.

He turned toward her. "What's silly? Looking for a missing girl's phone? It could prove helpful in finding her."

"No. I know *that*. We have her number." Jacq pulled out her phone and dialed the number.

He dropped his shoulders. *Duh!* He turned his head to listen. He could hear the cars whizzing by on the highway and on the overpasses in front and behind them, but he listened a little closer as he slid down the embankment behind the guardrail.

"Anything?" Jacq came closer and pressed the end button on her phone.

"No. Try again."

They both wandered toward the shrubs. "Wait." Jacq grabbed his elbow sending an unexpected electrical current up his arm. "I think I hear something. Shoot." She ended the call and tried again.

They both stood still and listened intently.

"There!" He moved into the budding brush.

Jacq came behind him. "I see it."

His eyes fell on the white phone in a bright pink case. He trudged a little deeper into the brush and pulled the branches back. He took several pictures with his phone. Then Jacq came in close to him and snapped on a latex glove. At her closeness, his lungs seized. She reached past him, their bodies nearly touching, and grabbed the phone. She grinned up at him, and the noise of the cars vanished. He smiled back.

"We got it."

He snapped out of the trance she had put him in. "Yes. Let's get it to the lab techs."

Chapter Three

Jacq ducked under Dylan's arm that held the door to the police station open. He'd been tall at eighteen, but now he stood nearly a foot over her. And he had filled out from the lanky teen she remembered. Was it possible that he had gotten better looking too? *Jacq, get your head in the case!* She was growing irritated with herself.

Stopping just inside the station, she closed her eyes. She took a deep breath, let it out, and opened her eyes. The building was buzzing with activity. She had no idea which way to go.

"Nothing like a big case on your first day." Dylan's hand came to rest on her upper back.

Jacq met his eyes. "No kidding. I must say, having a familiar face around is nice, even if it's been fifteen years."

His smile grew, and his cheeks flushed ever so slightly. "I'm glad."

Her heart fluttered. Why was she reacting to him this way? It was insane. "So where do we go?"

"Follow me." He pointed to their right. Dylan flashed his badge at the receptionist, who nodded in response. Down a hall, up an elevator, and around a corner put them in a busy squad room.

"Sheppard, Harris." Warren waved them over.

They crossed the room and joined him. He stood next to a table where a map of the area had been spread out.

"You found the phone?"

"We did," Dylan answered. "And handed it off to CSU."

"Excellent. Crespi and Blake are with the parents, and I'm assigning Crespi as the family liaison. I want the two of you to go over and interview the parents. Also, do extended interviews with the friends to get a whole rundown of their interactions this morning."

"Will do."

"Here's the parents' address." Warren picked up his phone off the table and pushed a few buttons. Seconds later Dylan's phone buzzed.

"Got it."

Warren turned to Jacq. "Sheppard, are you surviving diving in today?"

"I am."

Warren pointed at Dylan. "And this guy's treating you all right?"

Jacq chuckled. "Yes. We actually sorta knew each other in college."

"Oh, you went to Duke?"

"No, actually, I went to University of Dayton."

"Oh, isn't that where Chad went?" Warren looked at Dylan.

"Yeah," Jacq and Dylan said in unison.

"Nice. Go find out what you can and keep me in the loop, of course. Olsen and Fitz finished up with the canvas of the mall and are moving on to the video surveillance. If they get anything, I'll send it to you immediately."

"Perfect." Dylan turned to Jacq. "Looks like you're stuck with me. Ready?"

She nodded and suppressed a grin.

His eyes smiled, and he ever-so-slightly raised his eyebrows. She must not have done enough suppression.

They moved toward the door. Dylan said, "Sorry you don't get to have girl talk with Sabrina or Aliza."

Jacq let out a slight chuckle. "I'm not real good at girl talk. Back in Pittsburgh, I was the only female on the team for a long time."

"How is a woman not good at girl talk?"

She chuckled. "I'm not a girlie-girl at all. Never have been. I don't have 'girlie' things to talk about."

"Nothin' wrong with that."

Once they got in Dylan's car and drove to the Highwater's house, the conversation lulled.

"Looks like we're in the right place." Dylan pulled the car up to the curb in front of a modest ranch-style home with a black FBI SUV sitting in the driveway.

Jacq got out and waited for Dylan to come around before heading up the driveway to the front door. "Any particular way you want to approach this?"

Dylan straightened his tie. "Let's see how it goes, but we should definitely talk to Mom and Dad separately at some point."

"Okay, I'll follow your lead."

He nodded. "Praying we'll get something that will help."

"Me too."

Dylan knocked on the door, and a man who looked almost exactly like Tony DiNozzo from NCIS answered the door. "Hey, Gio."

"Hey, Dylan, come on in. Who's this, and where's the new guy?"

"Jacq is the new guy. Jacq Sheppard, Giovanni Crespi."

"Nice to meet you, Jacq." Gio extended his hand.

She shook it. "Likewise."

Dylan looked past him. "Where's Aliza?"

"She caught a ride to the police station about ten minutes ago with Gabe." Gio motioned for them to follow him. "The parents are in the kitchen."

Jacq didn't move. "Hold up. How are they handling it? What's your impression of the situation?"

"They're pretty messed up. I'd say they're handling it as would be expected. Nothing seems out of place."

"Thanks." Jacq nodded. He had understood the meaning behind her question.

"Gio's got a good gut for these things." Dylan reached across and patted the man's stomach.

Gio quietly chuckled and rolled his eyes before leading them to the kitchen. "Mr. and Mrs. Highwater, these are my colleagues,

Agents Harris and Sheppard. They'd like to speak with you."

"And ask the hard questions, huh?" Mr. Highwater, a balding man in his mid-forties, leaned back against the counter and crossed his arms.

Dylan answered, "Unfortunately, yes. We want to make sure we don't miss any potential leads. That way we can get Marrissa home as soon as possible."

Mrs. Highwater dabbed her makeup-less eyes with a tissue. "Thank you, we'll tell you what we know, but I can't think of anything."

Jacq took half a step forward. "Why don't we sit down? We'll ask you some questions and just talk. Helping us get to know Marrissa will make a big difference."

Mrs. Highwater's short hair bobbed as she shuffled out of the kitchen.

The five of them went into the living room. Mr. and Mrs. Highwater sat on the loveseat and Gio took the armchair, leaving Dylan and Jacq to sit on the couch.

Dylan pulled a stylus out of the side of his phone and took the lead in asking questions. "Tell us about your daughter." His voice was soft and caring.

Jacq retrieved her notepad and pen from her pocket.

Mrs. Highwater told them how Marrissa was a bright and kind girl. She enjoyed playing volleyball and singing in the school choir. Her favorite subjects were math and science, and she hoped to be a veterinarian when she grew up. She loved her friends, and the four girls had been inseparable since first grade.

Mr. Highwater added, "She's always trying to figure out how things work. She has an amazing knack for seeing the reasons behind how things function, especially things biological. Despite having gone to medical school myself, she was teaching me how the digestive system worked better than I've ever understood it."

Jacq asked, "You're a doctor?"

"An ophthalmologist."

Jacq turned her attention back to Marrissa's mom. "Mrs. Highwater, do you work outside of the home?"

"No. How is any of this helping you find her?" Mrs. Highwater pleaded. "Shouldn't you be out there searching?"

Dylan sat forward. "Please trust us. Learning about her helps in ways I'm not sure I can explain. And know that there are agents and police officers out there searching right now."

Mrs. Highwater shook her head. "But won't we get a call for a ransom? Isn't that how this works? Why haven't we gotten a call yet?"

Jacq said, "It's possible you'll get a call, but it may not be for a while. Is there anyone who would specifically target your family and Marrissa?"

Jacq couldn't come up with an obvious reason an ophthalmologist and his stay-at-home wife would have enemies. On the outside, this family seemed normal and well-balanced. The crucifix on the wall next to the front door and the picture of Mary on the bookshelf indicated they were probably Catholic. *Lord, help them to lean on you in this.*

Mr. Highwater answered, "I can't think of anyone. We're your average American family. There's nothing nefarious about our lives."

Dylan asked a few more questions that didn't lead to anything, and the conversation died. He met Jacq's eyes, and she nodded slightly. "Mrs. Highwater," Jacq said, "could you show me Marrissa's room?"

"Sure." The woman suppressed another sob.

Walking down the hallway, Jacq asked, "Was Marrissa having any trouble with anyone at school?"

"Not that she told me."

"No problems with boys or teachers?"

"Again, not that she's told me. Here's her room."

Mrs. Highwater pushed open a door revealing a classic junior-high girl's room. The walls were a bright lavender and covered with pictures. A large poster from a TV show and another of a popular teenybopper movie were next to a giant collage of photos of her and her friends and pictures of celebrities cut from magazines and printed off the internet. Jacq's heart warmed. Some things never changed. Teenage girls would always be teenage girls. Even non-girlie Jacq had had cut out celebrity pictures on her wall.

Jacq crossed the room and ran a finger along a photo of Marrissa and Kylie. "She's beautiful." Jacq touched the M-shaped necklace around Marrissa's neck.

"She wears that necklace all the time. We bought it last summer." Mrs. Highwater's voice trailed off.

"Was she wearing it today?"

"She never takes it off."

Jacq stepped away from the wall. "Do you know if Marrissa has a diary?"

"I don't think so, but she was always typing away on her computer."

Mrs. Highwater grabbed a MacBook with a purple skin from a desk under the window and handed it to Jacq.

"I don't know what her password is, though I should. What if something was going on, and I didn't even know about it? Do you think someone she knew took her? Was she having problems at school I didn't even know about? Why did I let her hole up in her room so much? Why would someone take my baby?"

The woman collapsed into the desk chair.

"I don't know, Mrs. Highwater. I wish I had answers for you." Jacq spotted a box of tissues and handed Marrissa's mom a fresh one.

"I want my baby back."

"I know."

Harper. Jacq couldn't imagine losing her little girl. She needed to hug Harper extra hard, but she wasn't even sure when she'd get to see her. Being on a case like this one would keep her from getting home tonight. Again, she was thankful a fellow agent's wife was Harper's babysitter. Rachel understood the FBI life and had even set up a bed for Harper to sleep in if the job kept Jacq from making it home for bedtime.

"Mrs. Highwater, it's customary for us to get a DNA sample of any kidnap victims. Could we have a toothbrush or hairbrush of Marrissa's? And do you mind if I look around her room?"

"Sure. I'll get her toothbrush."

"Thanks."

Jacq wandered around the room but hadn't even opened a drawer when Mrs. Highwater brought her the toothbrush. Jacq took it and returned to the living room where she had left her backpack and pulled out an evidence bag. She placed the toothbrush inside and wrote the necessary information on the outside. She then placed it inside her backpack.

Mr. Highwater and Dylan had gone outside to talk, but Gio was in the kitchen with Mrs. Highwater. Perfect. She'd rather go through Marrissa's room without her mom hovering. Jacq would be able to analyze things better on her own.

But first she had a call to make. She lifted the phone to her ear; it began to ring.

"Hello," a woman's voice answered.

"Hey, Rachel, it's Jacq."

"You're on the kidnapping case, aren't you?"

"I am."

"I figured. Harper is doing great, and she'll be just fine this evening. You focus on finding that missing girl."

"Thanks, Rachel. Hug her extra tight for me."

Dylan walked back into the house with Mr. Highwater. The conversation hadn't revealed anything that would point them in the right direction. This was looking more and more like a stranger kidnapping, which is hard to solve and too often ends with a body found or no answers at all. He inhaled deeply. Gio was talking to Mrs. Highwater at the kitchen table, and Mr. Highwater sat down next to his wife. Gio glanced up at Dylan.

"Jacq?" Dylan asked.

"Back in Marrissa's room."

"I'll go give her a hand." He strode down the hallway, but when he heard Jacq's voice he slowed.

"Thanks so much Rachel. It helps knowing she's in good hands." She grew silent. The person on the other end of the phone must have been talking.

He hated that he was standing outside the room, but he didn't want to interrupt either.

Jacq spoke again. "I'll slip away for a minute if I can; otherwise, I'll see you tomorrow at some point." There was a pause. "Will do. Thanks, again. Bye."

Dylan searched for a way to categorize the information he'd heard, but he couldn't classify it. He turned the corner, and Jacq slid her phone into her back pocket. He gently rapped on the door frame.

"Hey. Learn anything from the dad?" She pulled a drawer out of the dresser and placed it on the bed.

"No. Seriously, I don't think this family has any enemies or even knows anyone suspicious at all."

Jacq looked him in the eye. "We all know someone who's suspicious."

Dylan pulled back a touch. "Cynical much?"

"Realistic. I've got Marrissa's laptop here, but mom doesn't know the password, so we'll have to get it to someone more techie than I."

"We'll have to take it to headquarters."

She nodded and returned her attention to the drawer. Dylan couldn't get over how Jacq had become even more beautiful than she had been as a freshman in college. He didn't think it was possible, but, somehow, she'd nailed it.

"I haven't gotten very far in here, but nothing indicates anything other than a very normal almost-teenage girl." She reinserted the drawer into the dresser.

"Want a hand?"

She pulled out another drawer. "That'd be marvelous."

He went to the closet and rummaged through the clothes and shoes. But his mind had to fight off thoughts about Jacq while he looked through Marrissa's things. Who had she been talking about on the phone, and who was Rachel? Why was it that the first woman who had sparked his interest in years was completely out of his league? It wasn't fair. Not that he thought life should be fair. He knew it wasn't. He was looking for a missing girl, after all. But man …

Father, I'm going to need your help with this one. I was attracted to her back in the day, and apparently that attraction hasn't changed in fifteen years. Nothing can happen with her, so please take away these feelings and help me focus completely on this case. Please help us find Marrissa.

Finally able to focus on the task at hand, Dylan continued searching the closet. Once he'd finished, he moved on to the bookshelf. He removed an unmarked sketchbook from the shelf, which Marrissa had used as a scrapbook. Movie stubs, zoo ticket, photos. In several of the pictures, an M-shaped necklace hung around Marrissa's neck. She hadn't written anything besides names, dates, and events. He returned the book and finished searching the contents of the bookshelf.

He stood and turned to Jacq. "No diary or hidden anything."

"Yeah, I haven't found anything of consequence either."

Dylan's phone rang. It was Matt Olsen. "Hey, Matt. You guys have anything good? We've got bupkis here."

"Actually, I think so. We have a grainy, half-image of the guy who took Marrissa."

"That's more than our nothing. Send it to me."

"Already done."

His phone pinged. "Apparently, I got it. Anything else good on the tapes?" Jacq stood in front of him, her eyes wide in anticipation of news, so he switched it to speaker. "You're on speaker so Jacq can hear you too. It's just us."

Matt answered, "Hey, Jacq."

"Hey. Anything good?" she asked.

"Not really. We found Marrissa and her friends on several tapes and are piecing together their movements and searching for the guy. Also looking to see if we can find a buddy since there was obviously another one to drive away."

Dylan nodded even though Matt couldn't see him. "You guys still at the mall?"

"No, we brought all the footage back to the office. Bridges would like you guys to interview the friends. He's called the parents and has them coming in. So when you're done there head back here."

Dylan tilted his head. "There? Not at their homes?"

"No, he wants to be able to compare each story to the video immediately."

"Fair enough. We'll share the pic of the perp with the parents and see if they recognize him. See you shortly."

Dylan hung up and looked at the pictures Matt had sent. The first grainy photo was a wide angle of a man talking to Marrissa, but his back was to the camera. The next one showed him holding her arm as they exited the mall, his face obscured by a hooded sweatshirt pulled over his head. The third picture was the one Matt had talked about. Dylan could make out the young man's profile, but it wouldn't be enough for facial recognition. But perhaps, if the parents knew the man, they'd get an ID.

Dylan turned his phone toward Mr. Highwater.

He shook his head. "I don't recognize him either."

Mrs. Highwater grabbed his hand and turned the phone back toward herself. "Maybe—no. I've never seen him before. Why would he take my baby?"

Dylan cradled her hand with his other and pulled his phone away, stuffing it in his pocket. "We'll find out. We will do everything we can to bring Marrissa home."

Sobs overcame the woman again, and her husband drew her against his chest.

After a few awkward minutes, Dylan and Jacq exited the house, leaving the Highwaters in Gio's capable hands.

Dylan opened the car door for Jacq and walked around to the driver's seat. Once in, he pressed the start engine button and pulled away from the curb.

"I'm so disappointed they didn't recognize the guy who took Marrissa."

Dylan looked over at Jacq. "According to what they said."

"My gut isn't lined up with this case yet apparently. I was really thinking we'd be dealing with a known suspect."

"Still could be if it's a hired gun."

"But why go to all that trouble to take her? This family doesn't seem like a good candidate."

Dylan tapped his thumb on the steering wheel. "Yeah, and without a ransom call it really isn't looking like that."

"Dylan, she's been missing for hours already. I don't have a good feeling about it." Her concern wrinkled her brow.

He stopped at a red light. "I thought your gut wasn't working?" He raised his eyebrows.

She glared at him.

He chuckled. "I like working with you, Jacq Schur—I mean, Sheppard."

"I was enjoying working with you too, until that comment."

He laughed.

She smacked his arm. "But in all seriousness, I almost freaked when I saw you."

His heart sank a little. "Really?"

"Yeah, when I heard there was a Harris on the team, I never imagined it would be you."

The light turned green, and he reluctantly pulled away. He wanted to see her expression. "You were afraid it'd be Chad?"

"No. Well, for a micron of a second, but I knew it wouldn't be."

"But instead it was me, his kid brother."

Out of the corner of his eye, he couldn't quite distinguish her expression, but she was watching him. Considering he read people for a living, he was disconcerted that he couldn't read her.

"I'm glad it's you. But hoping I don't run into Chad ... or your mom."

"My mom?"

She shook her head and looked at her hands. "I was always sure she didn't like me."

"You and I are getting along, so I could see that." He rested his left wrist on the top of the steering wheel.

"You and your mom still don't see eye to eye?"

He swallowed hard. "That's one way of putting it. But really it boils down to the fact that I'm not Chad."

"Well, I think that's a good thing."

He let out a nervous laugh. "Thanks, but I think you're the only one."

"Really, Dylan?" She smacked her palms on her thighs. "You seem like a more confident guy than that."

"Only when I'm working." His stomach twisted in on itself, suddenly feeling uncomfortable with this woman. "Wait, how have you managed to get this much out of me? I don't normally unload my secrets to anyone."

"I have a special gift." She reached out and touched his arm.

It was a light, friendly gesture, but he felt it all the way to his toes.

"For what it's worth, from someone who's only been working with you for almost five hours," she continued, "I think you need to stop worrying about what your mom thinks. My memory of her is of an overbearing control freak who favored her eldest son over everyone else in the world."

"Way to say it like it is."

She shrugged. "Also a gift, although that one normally seems like a curse and gets me in trouble."

"I bet." He laughed and hoped it didn't sound as awkward as he felt.

She removed her hand, and his arm immediately missed her touch. Why did it have to be *this* woman who understood him and affected him so.

After a few quiet minutes, they pulled into the FBI field office parking lot. Dylan grabbed his bag from the trunk and stopped when he came around the car and caught Jacq watching him. She smiled. He couldn't help but return it.

They dropped the toothbrush and computer off in the lab and made their way to their third-floor office. He noticed a frame on the corner of Jacq's desk, but he couldn't quite see whose picture it was since his desk was directly across from hers.

Matt walked in. "Oh good, you guys are here. All three girls have arrived and are in separate interview rooms with their parents." Matt handed him a folder. "The pic of the abductor."

"Thanks. We're on it." Dylan met Jacq's eyes. "No rest for the overworked."

"Apparently not. But first I have to eat." She removed a protein bar from her backpack and opened it.

"Seems reasonable." He reached in his desk and grabbed a package of trail mix and poured part of it in his mouth. He hadn't eaten anything since he'd met Gio for breakfast before going to court, and he hadn't realized how hungry he was. Jacq stood, notepad in hand, and he quickly finished the trail mix. Wanting to try and get a casual glimpse of her photo, he jumped up and went toward her, but she was up and away from her desk before he could get close enough for a good line of sight. He followed her out of the bullpen but stepped ahead of her when they reached the door and opened it.

"Thanks."

"My pleasure." Did he *really* say that? He pressed his eyes shut momentarily.

They strode down the hallway to the first interview room. "Ready?" He reached for the doorknob.

"As ready as one can be in a situation like this."

"Indeed." He entered the room. Marrissa's friend Kylie and her parents sat close on one side of the gray table, holding hands, worry lines etched deep in each of their faces. Dylan felt it was appropriate to let Jacq take the lead with the girls. They had seemed to connect with her this morning, and that would help now.

"Hey"—Jacq's tone was very gentle—"thank you so much for coming in to talk to us some more."

Kylie's dad squeezed his daughter's shoulder, and he studied Dylan and Jacq. "We want to help any way we can. Our daughter wants her friend to come home. We realize it could have been Kylie who was taken."

Jacq set her legal pad and pen on the table and took a seat across from Kylie. Dylan sat next to Jacq.

Jacq said, "What I'd really love is for you to walk us through what you and your friends were doing at the mall this morning: what stores you went to, what you talked about, and who, if anyone, you talked to. If you remember seeing anything out of place … You never know what will give us the clue we need."

Kylie told them about her morning. Because it was spring break, she and her friends had decided to spend some well-earned babysitting money. Kylie walked them through everything she could remember.

When the girl was finished, Jacq asked, "Is there anyone in particular you remember seeing who seemed out of place? Did you talk to anyone other than the salespeople in the stores?"

Kylie said, "Well, there was that one guy who tried to talk to us. He creeped me out, so we just kept going. We knew better than to talk to a weird guy."

"That's good," Jacq reassured her. "Can you describe that man?"

"He was old and scruffy."

"About how old?" Dylan asked.

She shrugged her shoulders. "I'm not sure. Fortyish. He had on a sweatshirt and kept a baseball cap low over his eyes." Kylie played with the end of her hair. "We also saw a few people from school."

Jacq asked, "Anyone you girls have a problem with?"

Kylie shook her head.

"You all get along with most of your classmates and teachers?"

"For the most part. We aren't real popular, but we aren't among the outcasts either."

"Did you see any of your teachers at the mall today?"

"No."

"This is going to be a weird question," Jacq said, "but I have to ask. Are there any teachers who have paid any special attention to Marrissa?"

"No. Marrissa's a good student but not that good."

Dylan wanted to smile. This girl was naïve and missed what Jacq was asking. Maybe there was still innocence in the world.

"Anyone else you met at the mall today?"

Kylie said, "We did meet a guy who was nice. He was a little older than us—said he was seventeen—and we talked to him for a little bit, but he left about thirty minutes before we lost Marrissa."

"What did he look like?"

"He had darker skin. I think he was Hispanic. He had a baseball hat on and jeans. Maybe a gray sweatshirt."

Dylan sat up a little straighter. Other than the age, that description was spot on for the guy who took Marrissa.

"Kylie," he said, "I'd like you to look at a picture." Dylan slid the photo of the young man out of the folder and across the table to Kylie. "Is this the boy you met?"

"That's him. I think he said his name was Saul."

He and Jacq locked eyes. Dylan's stomach twisted. This young man had passed himself off as a friendly, safe person, when in fact he had ill intent.

"Could you tell me more about him? More in respects to what

he looked like and what you talked about? Did he say anything more regarding himself?"

"Wait, I don't get it," Kylie said. "Why do you have a picture of him? Did you know we talked to him?"

"No, we didn't, but it's giving us a good clue as to what might have happened to Marrissa."

"Did *he* take Marrissa?" Kylie's mom cut straight to the point.

Dylan wasn't about to avoid the truth either. "We believe so."

The mom gasped, and her hand flew to her mouth.

"But h-how do you know?" Kylie's voice quivered.

Jacq answered, "We have him and Marrissa on the surveillance video leaving the mall."

Dylan leaned forward. "Do you think you could describe him to a sketch artist? We don't have a good picture of his face, and that could really help a lot."

Kylie nodded and raised her shoulders. "I could definitely try."

Dylan left the room to find Aliza. She was skilled with a pencil and would be able to take the three girls' descriptions and give a face to the abductor.

Chapter Four

Jacq walked out of the third interview room and rubbed the back of her neck. They had spent the last two hours questioning Marrissa's friends. Not all their stories lined up perfectly, but that proved that it wasn't rehearsed at all. The interviews had gone well, except at the beginning of talking with the second girl. Her dad had been a little combative, thinking they were interrogating his daughter. Dylan had really stepped up and connected with the man and helped him understand why they were asking tough questions.

Dylan came out behind Jacq and closed the door. His presence unnerved her. It wasn't like her to be uncomfortable around anyone, but Dylan—something about him drew her toward him like a magnet, but she wanted the opposite. *God?*

The door of the second interview room opened. A young woman with a Taylor Swift vibe, long blonde hair pulled into a braid, exited with a large sketch pad in her hand.

Jacq turned toward her. "You must be Aliza."

The woman smiled. "I am. You must be this Jacq I keep hearing about. Matt is still reeling that you aren't a guy. It's so nice to meet you." Aliza extended her hand.

Jacq gripped it. "Nice to meet you too. I'm kind of loving that Warren didn't tell you all that I was a woman. Everyone's expressions have been priceless."

Dylan stepped closer. "I think it was unfair." He winked at her.

She fought the urge to giggle and playfully rolled her eyes instead. She turned her attention back to Aliza. "How'd the sketches go?"

Aliza's expression grew serious. "Not bad." She opened the pad. "This is Kylie's. That kid has a good eye for detail." She flipped to the next picture. "I got a slightly different feel from her." Aliza nodded over her shoulder to the door she had exited. "But they are remarkably similar. Once I talk to the third girl, I'll do a composite of the three."

Dylan squeezed Aliza's shoulder. "Great job."

"Thanks. I'll go talk to the last girl now." Aliza disappeared into the third interview room.

Jacq stepped away from Dylan and looked up at him. "Guess we should—"

Warren came around the corner before she could finish her thought.

"How'd the interviews go?"

Dylan met Warren halfway. "Good."

Jacq followed and let Dylan fill him in. As Dylan spoke, she couldn't help but notice the way he stood a little taller and smoothed his shirt out.

"Excellent. Dylan, relay all that to Fitz and Olsen. Jacq, we have a conference room around the corner—would you see to the families in there? I'm sending up some drinks and snacks. Help them feel comfortable until we know we can send them out. I'd imagine Blake would like to show the sketch to them when she's done."

"Yes, sir."

Warren disappeared, and Dylan turned to her. "Guess I'll see you later."

She nodded, and he shifted to leave. "Dylan, wait."

He pivoted back to her. "Yes?"

"Where is the conference room?"

A grin stretched across his face. Her lungs lost their air, and her cheeks warmed.

He showed her the conference room and left. As soon as he was gone, she said, out loud, "Stop it."

"Stop what?"

Jacq whipped around. Aliza stood in the doorway. Jacq shook her head. "Nothing. Just talking to myself."

Aliza walked over to her. "Dylan getting to you?"

"What's that supposed to mean?" Jacq wasn't sure what to think of this woman. They seemed to have a good connection a minute ago, but now she was uncertain.

Aliza's mouth opened, but her eyes searched the air for words. "I'm not sure." A smirk overtook her face. "He's a nice, good-looking guy. I know nothing, though." Her hands went up. "Came in to see if there were any water bottles. Lainy's mom has a scratchy throat."

Jacq grabbed one off the counter that ran along the edge of the room and handed it to Aliza. "I take it Dylan isn't seeing anyone."

"Ha. I was right, it is Dylan." Aliza gripped Jacq's arm. "It's all good. If my head hadn't been focused on Gabe, I'm sure Dylan would have turned it."

"It's not like that. It's complicated."

"Sure, hon. But for what it's worth, I think I've got a really good idea of what our kidnapper looks like, so hang in there. We'll get the bad guy."

Jacq couldn't resist the smile that overcame her. Aliza had changed the subject mid-thought, and Jacq couldn't be more grateful.

Jacq stepped back into the conference room after escorting the girls and their families to the parking lot. She had sat with them for the last hour and a half while Aliza finished up the sketches and got their final input. Jacq was feeling a bit out of the loop and didn't like it. But more than anything she really didn't want to admit she'd missed Dylan's presence.

He wasn't in the room yet. But Sabrina was.

"Hey, Jacq. Surviving your first day?"

"I think so." Jacq crossed the room and took a seat at the table near Sabrina.

"Well, from what I hear, you're doing a great job. Dylan said you were amazing with Marrissa's friends."

"Thanks."

Warren had asked the team to convene in the conference room to touch base and plan the next action steps. Jacq rested her head against the high-backed office chair. She was tired, and their day wouldn't be done for a long time yet.

The door opened, so Jacq sat up. Matt and Dylan walked into the room. Warmth rushed to her cheeks. She jerked her hands to her face and rubbed her temples. What had gotten into her?

Matt came and sat next to her. Dylan smiled as he rounded the table and pulled out a chair across from her. He had taken off his jacket, rolled up his sleeves, and loosened his tie, making him look much more relaxed than he had earlier. And even more attractive.

Dylan had barely sat down when Warren pushed through the door with two large pizza boxes in his hands and three more people behind him. "This day doesn't look like it's going to be over any time soon, so eat." He slid the box down the table. "But first, get Gio on the line."

Matt reached into the middle of the table to the conference phone and dialed a number. A phone rang on the other end. "Hey, guys. Give me a minute." The other end went quiet, and Warren opened a pizza box and pulled out a slice. Everyone followed suit.

Before Gio came back on the line, five more people came into the room. Aliza was one of them, and she took a chair next to Dylan. Jacq remembered meeting each of the others, but she couldn't remember their names. She only knew they were leaders of other teams.

"Hey, sorry about that." Gio's voice was almost as clear as if he was in the room. "I wanted to make sure Mr. and Mrs. Highwater were okay before I stepped outside. And thanks for the pizza, Warren."

Three more men entered the room and stood behind Warren. Jacq searched her memory. She had seen one of them at the police station.

"Everything going all right there? Anything in particular to report from your end before you hear what's happening with the investigation? And so you know, Police Captain Ward and Detectives Buckley and Martinez have joined us."

"We're doing all right here." Gio's voice echoed over the speaker. "It's been quiet, other than the constant flow of people coming to check on the Highwaters and the press sitting outside. The parents haven't come up with anything new. They truly have no idea who would do this."

"Okay," Warren said. "We have a sketch coming to you of the face of the guy who took Marrissa. He had interacted with the girls about thirty minutes before she went missing."

Sabrina said, "We were able to isolate him on multiple videos, but never once did he look up at a camera or in a direction where we could get anything more than a rough profile."

"He went into a couple of stores," Matt offered. "I went back over there this afternoon and talked to the store managers. Unfortunately, the only purchases he made were in cash."

Dylan added, "Marrissa's friends said he introduced himself as Saul and claimed to be seventeen. I'm guessing that's a fake name, and there's no way that guy is only seventeen."

"I'd tend to agree with the witness and age him at closer to twenty-five," Sabrina said.

"Did anyone ever ask the witness if she would sit with the sketch artist?" Warren asked.

Jacq sat forward in her seat. "I did. She said she didn't get a good look at his face, and he didn't even look around, like he didn't want his face to be seen."

Gio's voice came across the line. "So, we're dealing with someone who knows what he's doing. Someone who's mindful to avoid cameras and possible witnesses. Maybe someone who's done this before?"

Jacq's stomach churned.

Dylan said, "Looks that way. We spotted the 'creepy' guy the girls told us about on the surveillance as well, but, once again, we never could get a clear view of his face."

"You think he's involved?" Captain Ward asked.

"Yes, because—" he pointed to Matt who had a tablet sitting in front of him.

Matt turned on the tablet. "We found him taking pictures of the girls."

Jacq leaned in closer to Matt to see the stills from the surveillance video he had pulled up. The man was obviously holding his phone like he was taking a picture.

Matt turned the tablet for the others to see as he continued. "We believe he may have sent the pictures to the other guy, because if you look in this photo"—he swiped his finger across the screen—"seconds later it looks like the other guy gets a text."

Sabrina added, "They don't appear to look at each other, but they do both check their phones on a regular basis."

Warren turned to one of the other team leaders and asked, "Lawrence, what came up with the outside surveillance regarding the car?"

"We were able to identify it on the tapes, even got the plates, but it wasn't as fruitful as we had hoped. Three days ago, the car had been reported stolen one county over. There is a BOLO out, but so far nothing. We got it on traffic cameras as far as I-640, where Harris said they found the phone. They headed east, but we lost them at the Washington Pike exit and haven't spotted them since. And before you ask, we were unable to get a clear shot of the driver's face."

The conversation hit a lull, and Jacq's eyes fell on Dylan as he reached across the table and grabbed another slice of pizza. When he extended his left arm, his sleeve inched up and, from underneath his shirt, a tattoo peaked out. Dylan Harris had a tattoo? She did not expect that. Jacq could only imagine what his mom's reaction would have been. Jacq wished she could ask him about it, but that would have to wait. It was time to come up with an action plan for the rest of the night ahead of them.

For the next forty minutes they discussed what they should do. The sketch of the suspect was being run through every database they had. Hopefully, they'd have something on that soon, even though it had come up void to this point. It would be hard to do much now that the sun was setting, but the entire team was committed to staying through the night and to keep working the case, ready to jump should a lead come in. Teams were covering the phones, and tips were coming in and being filtered by another team, but nothing worth much had been learned.

Captain Ward and his detectives—along with the other team leaders—left the room as Jacq's team finished the pizza and cleaned up their dinner mess.

Jacq handed her plate to Matt, who was collecting them. "Don't take this as judgmental, because I don't mean it that way, but I can't understand why these girls were at the mall by themselves without their parents nearby."

Sabrina shrugged her shoulders. "It doesn't seem so crazy to me. I used to go to the mall with my best friend all the time when we were that age."

"But that was a completely different time. Back when the internet wasn't a thing, and porn wasn't being streamed into any home. Maybe I've seen too much, but I would never allow my child to wander the mall that young."

"I agree," Dylan said.

Her heart lifted.

Aliza nodded. "Poor Caroline." She looked at Jacq. "My niece. I don't think I'm ever going to allow that girl to leave the house. She's barely younger than these girls, and I feel sick about it."

Matt patted Aliza's back.

She turned to look at her back. "Did you get pizza crumbs on me?"

A ripple of laughter loosened the tightness in the air.

They finished cleaning up and moved back to their office. Warren stopped. "Jacq."

"Yes, sir?" She turned to him, while the rest of the team continued.

"You're doing a great job today. I'm glad you're part of our team; you're proving to be an excellent asset."

Her cheeks warmed. "Thank you."

"And I also understand how hard it is to be on a tough case when you've got a kid at home. Why don't you get out of here for a little bit and at least go kiss her goodnight?"

She let out a large breath. "Oh, that would be marvelous. I'll be back shortly." She practically skipped to her desk, then back down the hallway to the elevator.

Dylan took a swig of his Pepsi as the elevator came to a stop on the third floor. The pizza had given him a hankerin' for a Coke, so he ran down to the vending machines after the meeting. It took a few minutes of debate over Sprite or Dr Pepper, but then he changed his mind completely. Would Jacq think it weird that he called all soda pop Coke? He chuckled to himself.

The doors opened, and he pushed off the back of the elevator with his foot. He found himself walking a little faster than normal. He looked forward to seeing her, and it had only been ten minutes. What was his deal? Why was he so drawn to her?

"Ah, a Coke, that's where you went." Matt appeared from the hall where the bathroom was.

"Yep, Coke and pizza, a perfect combination."

"I think I'll have to follow suit. Be back in a minute."

Matt slapped him on the shoulder and went in the direction Dylan had come from. He chuckled and shook his head. Matt was often one to be easily swayed by someone else's idea, but not in a bad way. Matt Olsen was always ready to listen to others' ideas and weigh their merit. He was an all-around great guy.

Dylan pushed open the door and wound around the desks, scanning the room for Jacq. She wasn't there. He sat down and turned to Sabrina, whose desk was next to his. "Where's Jacq?"

"She went to tuck her daughter into bed."

Daughter? "I didn't realize that she had a kid."

"Really? You two worked together all day, and she didn't talk about Harper?"

"No, but we've been so focused on the case." He spun back to his desk.

"Go look at the picture. Cutest little thing!"

Dylan couldn't resist. He ambled the few feet to Jacq's desk and picked up the five-by-seven wooden frame. Simple and unassuming. The style fit Jacq. The photo inside the frame took his breath away. It was Jacq's mini-me. The little girl had her mom's fiery-red hair and brown eyes, and her smile was just as intoxicating.

"Do you know if this is a recent picture?"

"Must be. She said her daughter was about to turn three."

Dylan looked back down at the photo. The little girl was definitely around three years old. "Adorable."

"Isn't she?"

"Jacq tell you any more about her family?"

"Nope. You'll have to ask her. I thought you two knew each other."

"Sort of, but that was a long time ago." He set the frame back on Jacq's desk right where he found it and wandered back to his own. Something about Jacq being a mom endeared her even more to him. He wanted to be a dad and hoped one day God would bless him with a family. But he still hadn't figured out how he could make that work in the context of his family, especially his mom. He couldn't take a girlfriend home to her, but he also couldn't keep the parts of his life separate. Could he?

Chapter Five

Jacq sprinted up the steps to Rachel's house. She couldn't wait to see Harper. After today she needed to wrap her arms around her little girl. She raised her hand to knock, but before her knuckles could rap on the door, it opened.

"Hey Jacq, heard you pull up. So glad you had a chance to get away for a moment."

Jacq stepped into the house. "Me too. I'm overjoyed she was still up." Jacq had called Rachel when she left the FBI building to be sure.

"Come on in. Stephanie was reading her a book."

Jacq followed Rachel up the stairs and around the corner to the bedroom where Rachel had set up the little toddler bed that had once been her daughter's. The spot was Harper's now, where she would nap and sleep when work kept Jacq from being able to come home. As much as it broke Jacq's heart to have to leave her, she loved that this family had opened their home and given her a little corner to call her own.

"Mommy!" Harper jumped up off the floor, where she was sitting next to Rachel's nine-year-old, and ran to her. Jacq knelt and swept her up into her arms.

"Hey, sweetie! Have you had a good day?"

"Yeah-huh."

"Oh good. I still have to work tonight, but I came over to tuck you in and give you a great big hug."

Harper threw her arms around Jacq's neck and squeezed. Jacq

hugged her back.

"Girl, that is exactly what I needed. I love you, Harper."

"I yuyou too."

"Can we read a few books?"

Harper nodded her head and pointed to the little shelf of books next to her bed. Jacq sat on the floor while Harper grabbed three of her favorites. Harper settled on her lap, and Jacq took the books and read each one.

Harper requested to read *Good Night, Moon* one more time, and by the end she was having trouble keeping her eyes open. Jacq closed the book and set it back on the shelf. Harper curled deeper into Jacq's arms. She leaned her head down and kissed the little girl's forehead, then gently swayed her body. Harper surrendered to sleep in moments. Jacq squeezed her a little more snuggly.

Thank you, Jesus, that I got to rock my baby to sleep tonight. Thank you for Harper. Keep her safe and help her to be okay here. Thank you for Rachel and her willingness to have another little one in her house for unpredictable hours. I can't help but think about Mrs. Highwater right now. I can't imagine what she's going through. Please comfort her heart. And most of all be with Marrissa. Protect her and bring her home safely. Give the team and me wisdom in our investigation so we can find her. Supernaturally protect her from the men who took her and the harm they may be planning. I can't fathom.

Jacq stroked Harper's hair away from her face and kissed her again. "I love you, sweet girl." Jacq sat there holding Harper, soaking her in for a few more minutes before finally relinquishing her to the bed. She tucked her in and, after one final kiss, turned the lights off and left the room. She walked downstairs and found Rachel in the kitchen.

"She's asleep."

"Oh, good. She'll be fine, Jacq. I can imagine how much you're worrying about her, but know that she's in good hands here."

"I *do* know that. I really can't thank you enough for your kindness and help. I was so worried about finding someone who would be willing to have her at crazy hours. But God's hand was on this."

"Most definitely. It's been on my heart for a while now to open my home this way, so when Jeff said there was a single mom coming to the office, I knew this is what God was doing. And Harper—she's a peach."

"Thanks. I think she's pretty great."

"I can see why. Precious little girl. And my daughters adore her!"

Jacq bit her lip. *Thank you, Lord!*

Jacq stepped off the elevator, so grateful to have been able to tuck Harper in, but now it was time to get back into the case. Marrissa had been missing for about ten hours. They needed a lead soon. Jacq hated to think what could be happening to that sweet girl. A teenager being kidnapped by a stranger—her instincts told her this was human trafficking, especially since it was a tag team.

Her smile was gone by the time she pushed the door open to the office. She went straight to her desk.

"Hey!" Dylan gave her a grin that would have melted her if she hadn't been so focused on the case.

Sabrina looked up from her laptop. "Did you get to tuck her in?"

"I did. She actually fell asleep in my arms. That's happening less and less these days, but I needed it tonight."

"I bet," Sabrina said.

Jacq sat and looked over at Dylan. He was still smiling at her. She grabbed the photo of Harper and turned it to face him. "This is my daughter, Harper."

"I saw. She's precious."

"Thanks. I think so. She's a spunky, little not-quite-three-year-old."

"So, the similarity to her mom doesn't end with looks then?"

He winked.

She giggled. "I guess not."

"Lawrence's team has something!" Warren stormed out of his office. The three of them turned. "They found the car. I want you guys to go over and help them out since we aren't on something specific right now."

"You got it," Dylan said.

"Sending you the info. I'm headed down to the tip hotline to join Aliza and see for myself if anything substantial has come in. Keep me in the loop."

They all nodded and stood as Warren left.

Matt crawled out from under his desk. "Let's roll."

Jacq jumped. "I had no idea you were down there."

"Just catching some z's." He stretched. "Four a.m. was a really long time ago."

"Why on earth were you up at four in the morning?"

"Had to put in ten miles." He shrugged his backpack on.

"Ten? Miles? No doubt you're tired!"

Dylan came up next to her. "Yeah, Olsen here is a glutton for punishment. He's training for a marathon."

"You're crazy." She laughed.

He gave her a big grin. "And proud of it."

The four of them made their way out to the parking garage and climbed in a Bureau SUV. Matt drove and Sabrina took shotgun, so Dylan and Jacq sat in the backseat. She leaned her head against the headrest as Matt drove them across and then out of town. She was tired and maybe a few minutes of rest would go a long way to helping, as she needed to be sharp when analyzing a scene. It was still her first day; she wanted to show the team she was capable. She didn't think she had to prove herself, but she did like people to see she was good at her job and to know they could trust her.

A hand came to rest on her shoulder—a strong, comforting hand. She opened her eyes and looked at Dylan. "We're here," he said softly.

She couldn't believe she had dozed off. She stepped out of the SUV. The putrid smell of smoke assaulted her. Lights flashed and sirens blared. Her mind began to spin. *Oh, Jacq, stay here and now.*

But it was too late. Her eyes clamped shut as her vision tunneled.

The heat.

The smoke.

The flames.

The screaming. His screaming.

Pain. The burning.

Her breathing increased as she fought to gain control over her mind. *Jesus, help!* This was not the time or place for flashbacks.

She could hear Matt's voice in the distance. It sounded like he was a mile away. Something about the fire being out. But it was still so hot.

"Jacq." Dylan's voice was close.

Open your eyes, Jacq. She tried to will her body to comply. But her stomach churned.

Dylan's hand came to rest on her left shoulder blade. She jumped. Her mind snapped back to the present.

"Are you okay?" Dylan leaned closer and removed his hand.

Her breathing was heavy and labored. She needed to take a deep breath, but the smoke was too much.

Chapter Six

Dylan removed his hand from Jacq. His heart seized in his chest. Why had she jumped at his touch? She seemed to press into it in the car. "Jacq?"

She coughed. The smoke was still heavy in the air.

He took a step back. "Let's get away from the smoke."

She nodded and turned toward him. He walked around to the other side of the car with Jacq a couple of steps behind him. Her hand gripped his elbow and pulled him to a stop. He turned to her, but she didn't let go, as if to say he wasn't the reason she jumped. There was something more in her eyes.

"I don't do well with fire."

"I can see that. Are you okay? You don't look like you feel all right." Her face was practically green.

She coughed again. "I'll be fine."

"Let's see what we can do to work away from the smoke. Do you have asthma? Do you have an inhaler?"

"It's more psychological than physical. I promise I'll be fine."

Now he had more questions than answers. "If you're sure."

"I am. I just don't like fire."

"I get the sense there's some deeper reason than a simple dislike of fire."

The intensity of her eyes shook his soul. She slowly nodded. "Yes, and one of these days I'll tell you the whole story."

"Can't lie. I'm definitely curious."

She looked off into the distance and opened her mouth as if to speak, but closed it slowly. Her shoulders dropped. She met his eyes again and smiled weakly. But then she turned away.

His heart ached. Something serious had happened, but he had no idea what. He wished he had the option to get back in the car and take her away from the smoke. He wished he could draw her into his arms and sweep away the pain he could see in her eyes. But he didn't have the right to do that.

Yet he couldn't take his eyes off her. She went over and talked to Sabrina. Jacq looked calm and collected, except for her left hand, which fidgeted against her leg. He hadn't seen her do that all day. It was like she was focusing all her nervous energy into her hand. What had happened? And how had she completely captivated him in only one day?

His mind was swimming, and he needed to get out of the pool before he went too deep.

"Hey, Dylan!" Matt called.

Time to get to work. He ran over.

"Jacq ok?" Matt didn't miss a thing.

"I think so."

He nodded. "I was talking to Lawrence. Looks like the whole lead is a bust. The car is a complete loss."

"Arson job, right?"

"For sure. Fire department is already saying an accelerant was used. Took them longer to put it out than they expected."

"Any remains?"

"No."

Dylan breathed a little easier. "They clearly wanted to destroy any evidence."

"My thoughts exactly. Looks more and more like we're dealing with something more sinister than I had thought."

"Yeah…" The air hung heavy in their silence. But Dylan wasn't ready to give up. "Surely there were footprints or something coming away from the car."

"So far they haven't found anything."

Dylan rubbed his chin and stepped toward the remains of the car illuminated by giant floodlights, where a dozen agents and forensic technicians swarmed.

The putrid smell of burning rubber caused Dylan to lift the back of his hand to cover his nose. Nothing was left of the car. The metal was black and curled up. The plastic reformed in malformed drips. All the upholstery reduced to ashes. No hope remained that they'd find any evidence linking this car to Marrissa, let alone her abductors.

Dylan pulled a pair of disposable gloves from his jacket pocket and snapped them on. He reached for the door handle to the backseat, but it fell off. He handed the piece to a crime scene tech, and, with Matt's help, removed the door from the car. The backseat was nothing but ash, yet Dylan combed through it with his fingers. Maybe there would be something, anything.

Matt appeared on the other side and did the same.

Dylan moved to the floorboard behind the driver's seat. His fingers knocked against a small piece of metal, too small to be a seatbelt buckle. He tried to brush the ash off his fingers before he pulled a flashlight from his pants pocket. He clicked it on and aimed it toward the object his hand felt. Sifting through the ash again, he found it and lifted it out of the gray flecks. The stainless-steel M was warped, and its chain cascaded over his fingers.

Chapter Seven

Dylan opened the office door and held it for the team. He checked his watch. Almost midnight. They had returned from the crime scene. Three long hours of breathing in ash and gasoline fumes.

Jacq coughed hard. Again. She'd been struggling since they arrived at the car scene, and he still didn't know why. What had happened? Whatever it was, it had left her with a nasty cough.

They all looked a little worse for the wear. Especially Matt. He was covered in ash and soot.

Dylan brushed the front of his clothes. He wasn't any better.

At his desk, he took off his jacket and hung it on the back of his chair. Apparently, he needed to make a trip to the cleaners soon.

Warren came out of his office. "Talk to me."

Dylan wanted to sit but came around the front of his desk and leaned back against it instead. "We found Marrissa's necklace in the back of the car. I texted a picture of it to Gio, and he confirmed with Mr. Highwater that it was indeed Marrissa's."

Warren folded his arms on the room divider to the right of where Jacq sat at her desk. "I'm surprised they were so careless."

"Guess it didn't matter since we had the identification of the car. We knew it was the same one. They were careful to make sure there was nothing in it that pointed to them, and that's what we needed most."

Sabrina nodded. "With no ransom call this late in the game, guess we can rule out that scenario."

Matt sat on the corner of his desk. "Doesn't mean someone

didn't take her to mess with the family. Only implies it wasn't about money."

Jacq picked up a pen and pointed it in the air. "I'm beg—"

The office door opened, and Aliza entered with Marrissa's laptop tucked under her arm. "Hey, guys. Sorry to interrupt."

Jacq shook her head. "No, go ahead. Did you find anything?"

Aliza held up the computer. "Nothing. This girl is as sweet and innocent as it seems. She had a diary, but it was mostly filled with adolescent musings about her friends and a few boys she thought were cute but wasn't going to do anything about. She wrote about disagreements she's had with her parents, especially her mom, but it was over things like screen time and whether she could dye her hair blue."

Jacq inched forward. "Social media activity?"

"Mostly chatting with her friends and posting duck faces on Instagram. No questionable chat room activity. We did find one follower on Instagram who is sketchy. I'm going to dig a little deeper into him and see what I can come up with. It's possible he's not what he says he is."

Warren pointed at Aliza. "Do it."

"That leads to my thought." Jacq fidgeted with the pen. "We need to seriously consider that this may be a trafficking situation."

Dylan's insides turned over. Images of the past flashed in his mind, but he shook them away.

"You disagree?" Jacq was looking right at him.

"What? I don't know." He had worked trafficking cases, but every time it made him sick to his stomach.

"Based on my experience and my gut"—she shot him a pointed glance—"that's what this is."

Matt rubbed his face. "If that's the case, she could be states away by now."

Sabrina stood. "I'll coordinate a search of the dark web. If she's being sold, we'll find her."

Dylan felt himself shrink back at the idea. Human trafficking, no matter what form it took, was evil. *God, help. Keep my mind focused on finding Marrissa, here, today.* Dylan knew his tendency to focus on his failings in the past would keep him from doing his job today.

He pushed off his desk. "I'll help, Sabrina." He followed her out the door to the cyber-crime unit's office.

Jacq slipped into the dark breakroom and patted the wall until she found a light switch. The florescent lights illuminated the room and blinded her. She shielded her eyes with her hand until they adjusted. She had only briefly seen this room earlier in the day, but now she could take it in. Along the wall to her right was a counter, cabinets, refrigerator and a microwave. Two round tables with four chairs each were in the center of the room. Straight in front of her, a square coffee table sat between a pair of black leather couches, one on the back wall and the other against the wall to her left. Exactly what she was hoping for!

Jacq switched on the small lamp on a corner table before cutting the bright overhead lights. *That's better.*

She was tired. She glanced at her watch: two a.m. Sighing, she sank into the couch along the back wall. She and Matt had been working the tip line phones for the last two hours.

Jacq rested her head against the back of the couch. Nothing worthwhile had come of the car. And nothing good was coming from the tip lines either. In a case like this every tip had to be followed. But of the five calls she had taken, not one of them had led her away from the computer or phone.

Lord, where is Marrissa? Why can't we find her? Why are there no leads? Please give us something.

Jacq's eyes were heavy. As she dozed off, her head bobbed and woke her up, so she lay down with her arm acting as a pillow and allowed her body to surrender to sleep.

A rattle and a creak pulled her from her sleep. Her right hand immediately went to the gun on her side before she remembered where she was.

"Whoa, easy there. It's only me." Dylan stood across the room, grinning at her. "I'm sorry. I didn't mean to wake you. Didn't realize anyone was in here."

"Well, I'm awake now." She smiled at him without getting up. "Any leads?"

Dylan's shoulders dropped. "I wish." He took three steps closer. "Mind if I join you?"

She raised an eyebrow at him.

His eyes slammed shut. "I didn't—"

She giggled. "I know. I'd love the company."

His smile returned, and he shuffled nearer.

Her heart fluttered.

Despite the completely unoccupied couch near her feet, he pushed the coffee table out of his way and sat on the floor in front of her with his back against the couch. He turned his head to look at her. "How long did you get to sleep?"

She uncurled her arm and looked at her watch. Eight after three. "Barely an hour."

"Go back to sleep then."

She propped up her head with her elbow. She wanted to reach out and touch him. She didn't know why, but it was as if her hand was being drawn to him like a magnet. She looked down at him. He had ditched his button-up shirt and was now only in a bright white V-neck. Her eye caught another glimpse of his tattoo. She could see a little more of it now.

"Okay, you have to tell me about this." She let the magnet pull her hand to his arm, and without inhibition she tugged on his sleeve. Her fingers brushed his skin. Lightning bolts shot all the way up her arm. Why had she done that? But she didn't retract her hand.

"My tattoo?"

She nodded.

He lifted his sleeve the rest of the way, revealing a tattoo of a shield. A sword stood behind the shield, reaching from the top of his arm almost down to his elbow, and a red cross filled the shield with the words "I can do all things through Christ" along the bottom edges.

"That's really neat. I bet your mom loves it!"

He tipped his head back and laughed. "Oh my word. I'm pretty sure 'love' is not the word she would use."

"That doesn't surprise me. The Mrs. Harris I knew would have given a nice firm lecture as to the ills of adorning one's skin with such things."

"Oh ... yeah. I really thought I was going to die that day."

"That bad? Come on, you're an adult."

He turned toward her more and rested his arm up on the couch in front of her. "Yeah, but I was only eighteen and still living at home when I got it."

"What?" She moved closer, then pulled back as she realized she was getting too close.

"Well, the story goes like this: it was my eighteenth birthday, but Mom and I had had yet another one of our ... let's say heated discussions about my future. I was so fed up with her trying to dictate exactly what I did with my life, because I knew nothing I did would equate to what Chad was doing with his. I had no desire to become an engineer like she wanted, especially when she'd still be critical. So, I did the only thing I could think of that would make her madder than the Mad Hatter."

"You got a tattoo."

"Yep. Went out on my birthday and got this."

"You got a tattoo of a *cross* to spite your mom."

Dylan laughed. "I did. It wasn't a completely random decision. I had been sketching out my ideas for months. A big piece of wanting it was, in a sense, to claim my faith as my own. I didn't want their stuck-up, fundamentalist faith; I had found a real relationship with Christ. Not that my family doesn't have a relationship with

Christ, that's not what I mean. It's just ..."

"Different."

"Yeah, does that make sense?"

"Absolutely. I only went to your—their church a handful of times, but I remember it being very traditional and even into the legalistic side."

"Oh, yeah."

"I grew up in a slightly charismatic church, so I know exactly what you mean."

He smiled at her. Her heart did a somersault.

"So, you have to tell me how she reacted. How long until she noticed?"

"Three days ... only three days."

"Really? I would have thought you would have kept it hidden."

"Oh, I did. Only it got infected."

"Infected!?"

He nodded. "I wasn't going to let her see it for as long as possible, but I had to tell my dad when it wasn't healing like it should. And he, in turn, told my mom because he wasn't exactly happy about it either."

"I bet."

"But she freaked. My mom's way of yelling at me rarely included her actually raising her voice, but that day ... oh dear. Scarlett said later she thought I was going to die. She even went up to her room and started crying and praying for God to protect me."

"Oh, goodness. I'm surprised Chad never said anything."

"He didn't find out for quite a while."

"Ah. Do you have to cover it up around your mom?"

"I don't know if I have to, but I rarely wear short sleeves when I'm at home."

Jacq laughed and shook her head. "Your family is ..."

"Crazy?"

"I was thinking more like"—she paused for dramatic effect—"special."

He laughed, which was contagious. It felt good to laugh considering the weight of this case threatened to push her deep into the mire.

Gio poured water in the back of the Highwater's coffeemaker. It was five a.m., and he had barely slept at all. He had crashed on the couch when Mr. Highwater finally convinced his wife to go to bed around two. It hurt to be awake, but coffee should help. He had gotten up when he heard the water in the back of the house turn on. Someone was up, and he wanted to be available to them should they want to talk or simply need the company.

He pulled his phone out of his front pocket and opened the Bible app. He went to the plan he was following and read while he waited. Isaiah 43. He couldn't get past verse three. He read the first three verses over and over again.

"… Fear not, for I have redeemed you; I have called you by name, you are mine. When you pass through the waters, I will be with you; and through the rivers, they shall not overwhelm you; when you walk through fire you shall not be burned, and the flame shall not consume you. For I am the Lord your God, the Holy One of Israel, your Savior …"

Prayers for Marrissa, the Highwaters, and the team flowed from his heart to the Lord. God was with them. He would give them help, comfort, and wisdom.

Mr. Highwater came around the corner.

Gio slid his phone back in his pocket. "Morning." He intentionally left out good.

"Good morning." Mr. Highwater pulled a mug out of the cabinet. "Thanks for making coffee."

"Think nothing of it. It's as much for myself as for you."

A kind smile lifted Mr. Highwater's weary cheeks. "I think I'll go have this on the deck. Would you like to join me?"

"Sounds good."

They both fixed their cups of coffee, and Gio followed Mr. Highwater outside. They sat in the wooden Adirondack chairs looking out over the nondescript backyard and quietly sipped their coffee.

"I can't believe she's missing." Mr. Highwater's voice was quiet but felt like it weighed a thousand tons.

"I truly can't fathom what you must be going through."

"Marrissa's such a blessing."

"Kids are."

Mr. Highwater rested his ankle on the opposite knee. "Do you have any children?"

"Not yet."

"Married?"

"Not yet. Haven't found the right woman. I know she's out there, but so far God hasn't let our paths cross."

"One day you'll find her. And then, Lord willing, you can have a whole brood."

Gio longed for the day. "You and the Mrs. didn't want a whole brood?" He lifted the mug to his lips.

"Couldn't. That's why Marrissa is an extra blessing. I can't have kids of my own."

Gio paused before taking a sip. "You aren't Marrissa's biological father?"

"No. Evelyn was pregnant when we met. I officially adopted Marrissa when she was two."

Alarms deafened Gio's mind. "If you don't mind my asking, who is her biological father?"

"Honestly, I can't remember his name. He was some deadbeat. Evelyn has hardly ever mentioned him. They had a falling out, and we've never had any contact."

"Anything else you can tell me about him?"

"No, I never even met the guy."

They could have used this information yesterday, but Gio was careful not to let his frustration show. However, he had to let the team know. "Would you like more coffee, sir?"

"Yes, please."

Gio stood and took the mug.

"Nelson."

Gio turned back to Mr. Highwater. "Excuse me?"

"I think his name was Nelson. L—Lee—no. Lyle—that's it. Lyle Nelson."

As soon as he was in the house, Gio called Matt. "Assemble the team. I have a lead."

Chapter Eight

Dylan stretched his tired body and glanced at the other couch. Jacq was still sleeping. They had chatted for a while before he finally could no longer keep his eyes open. He felt drawn to stay near her but made himself move to the other couch to sleep. He looked at his watch. Five thirty. Not even two hours of sleep. Apparently, his body was more concerned with getting up at its regular time than in catching enough Zs.

But he wouldn't have traded the time he spent talking with Jacq for anything. He couldn't believe how much he had shared with her. It wasn't like him to discuss his family, especially his mom, but Jacq was so easy to talk to. And she already knew and had similar issues with his mom. He had longed to ask her about her reaction to the fire, but he also wanted to respect her privacy. She'd tell him when she was ready, and the last thing he wanted to do was press it and potentially push her away. He already knew she was exactly the kind of woman he had been looking for. Too bad she was out of bounds.

The door swung open and banged against the wall. Matt appeared. "There you guys are."

Dylan sat up. "What's going on?"

Jacq stirred and stretched.

"Got off the phone with Gio. We might have something. Conference room in five."

"Sweet." He stood, and Matt disappeared.

Jacq righted herself and rubbed her eyes. "What's up? Was that Matt?"

He snickered to himself. "Yeah." He repeated what Matt said. "Marvelous." She seemed to click to fully awake. "Five minutes?"

Dylan nodded.

"Okay. Washroom, then I'll be right there."

"Want some coffee?"

"Sure."

"Cream and sugar?"

"Please."

She disappeared out the door, and he wandered over to the counter and turned on the single-cup coffee maker. He definitely required coffee today. They needed this lead to be something worthwhile. *Lord, we could use a break. Please let this be a way to help us find Marrissa. Please protect her and guide us to her.*

The door opened. Dylan grabbed two mugs out of the cabinet and glanced over his shoulder. Matt again. "Hey."

"Spill it."

"Spill what?"

"Jacq. You like her."

"What?" He turned and looked at Matt.

"Don't even try to pretend. We've been friends too long, and it's *so* obvious."

Dylan opened his mouth to protest, but he had nothing to say. Matt laughed.

"Shut up." He pulled two medium roast k-cups out of the basket on the counter. "It doesn't matter if I like her."

"Why not?"

"Because it could never work." Dylan set the first cup under the spout and shut the k-cup in the machine.

"You're worried about FBI policy? You know Warren won't care."

"You're right. But it's not Warren."

"Then what? You two seem to really have taken to each other already."

Dylan sighed. "We have, but it's irrelevant." He removed the first cup and replaced it with the second.

"Why?"

"She's Chad's ex-girlfriend." He looked at Matt.

Matt's eyes grew wide. "Ooooh. Well, then."

"See my problem?"

Matt's face scrunched. "Really? Chad? She seems—"

"Not his type?" Dylan propped his hip against the counter.

"Completely the opposite."

"I guess she isn't his type since it didn't work out, but it was a long time ago. She was only a freshman in college when she dated him."

"If it was that long ago, so what?"

"She dated Chad. Why on earth would she be interested in me?" Dylan pulled the sugar out of the cabinet and added it to both cups.

"Clearly Chad wasn't what *she* was looking for. Maybe you are."

"I don't know."

"Aren't you the one always telling me to trust God?"

Dylan looked up from adding a splash of creamer to each mug. "Yeah, because you should."

"Then shouldn't you too?"

"Not sure I'm not trusting Him."

Matt shrugged. "Just asking. Because, like you've told me over a hundred times, you never know what God's doing, and He's good at doing exactly the opposite of what you'd expect."

Dylan pursed his lips. Nothing like getting your own advice handed back to you. "Point taken."

Matt laughed. "Let's go see if we can find Marrissa."

Dylan grabbed his and Jacq's coffees, and they headed to the conference room.

Jacq slipped into the conference room and took the open seat next to Dylan. He slid a steaming mug filled with liquid that was the perfect shade of tan to her. "Thank you."

"My pleasure." His grin melted her into goo.

She wished she could snuggle on the couch and talk to him all day, but they had more important things to do. As the hours ticked on since Marrissa had been taken, the chances of finding her alive dwindled. She could be anywhere in the world by now.

Warren entered the room. "What's the deal?"

Everyone looked groggy from a lack of sleep but there was still a fire in each person's eyes. They were not giving up on Marrissa.

Matt, who was sitting across from Jacq, said, "Gio called and said he found out something that could potentially be a lead. Said to call when everyone was here."

"Then call him." Warren gestured toward the conference phone.

Matt dialed the number, and Gio answered on the second ring. "Hey y'all. You ready for this?" Everyone stared at the phone. "I'll take that as a yes. I was talking to Mr. Highwater over coffee about fifteen minutes ago. No one's been able to do much sleeping around here. But in our conversation, he said something about not being able to have his own kids. Long story short, apparently he's not Marrissa's biological father."

"What?" She spoke softly, but everyone else had similar reactions.

"You heard me. Mr. Highwater is *not* Marrissa's biological father. He adopted her when Marrissa was only two. Marrissa never knew her biological father."

Warren folded his arms across his chest. "Where is her biological father now? And who is he?"

"Mr. Highwater is a little sketchy on the details. They have had no contact with him since they got married, and Mrs. Highwater hasn't really ever talked about him other than to say he was a deadbeat. He's pretty sure his name was Lyle Nelson. Mrs. Highwater is finally sleeping right now, so I'd love you guys to run the information and see what you can find. I'll let you know as soon as I have more."

Warren leaned on the table. "We're on it. Call us as soon as she wakes up."

"Will do."

Gio hung up and the six of them stared at each other for a moment until Warren said, "I can't believe they didn't think that would be pertinent information." He looked at Jacq and Dylan. "Did either of you get any sense he wasn't her biological dad?"

"No, sir," Jacq said. "She looks so much like her mom, the fact that she doesn't look like Mr. Highwater didn't even register."

Dylan added, "There was no indication."

"All right, let's find out who this father is and what he's up to. Maybe he's got motivation of some sort to kidnap his daughter."

Once back in their office, the team fell quiet after they dispersed the databases to search. Within a half an hour they had confirmed Marrissa's biological father's identity as Lyle Nelson and discovered some rather questionable information.

At nearly eight a.m., Dylan stepped up on the curb in front of a halfway house in the next major town over from Knoxville. Warren's warning echoed in Dylan's head. *"Be careful. Halfway house or not, he's been convicted of gun charges."*

Jacq stepped up next to him, and they strode to the front of the weathered house in what seemed to be a questionable part of town. A protective spirit rose from deep inside him. He always had a passion to guard those around him, but something about Jacq made the desire to protect even stronger.

"Stay close." He stepped a touch nearer to her as they traversed the broken sidewalk.

"Dylan, this isn't my first convict rodeo."

"I know, but..."

She snickered. "Don't worry. I'll stick close." She bumped his elbow with hers.

He waggled his eyebrows at her before he lifted his hand and knocked on the door. They waited for an answer. He let a tense breath out slowly, then grabbed his lapels and adjusted his jacket on his shoulders. Between exhaustion and driving for the last hour, he was ready for a break in the case.

A short, Black woman answered the door. "Can't you see the 'no soliciting' sign?"

"Yes, ma'am," Dylan said. "However, we're not soliciting." He held up his badge, and Jacq did the same. "I'm Special Agent Dylan Harris, and this is my partner, Special Agent Jacq Sheppard. We're looking for Lyle Nelson."

"You're not the only ones. He missed curfew last night. I was giving him a little leeway as he's been doing great and is so close to the end of his time here, but I haven't seen him in almost twenty-four hours."

"The last time you saw him was yesterday morning?" Jacq asked.

"Yeah, he left work a little before nine. Never came home."

Dylan asked, "Where is his place of employment? Do you know if he showed up there?"

"The auto shop over yonder." She pointed down the street. "They didn't call, but most places don't call when an ex-convict doesn't show for work."

Dylan nodded. He was ready to go check whether Lyle had gone to his job, but Jacq wasn't done yet.

"Did you notice anything different about his behavior in the last week? Has he gotten any unexpected phone calls or anything?"

"Not that I can think of. Lyle pretty much keeps to himself. Really trying to turn his life around, or so I thought. I'm not so sure now. He's stayed clean and sober, and we check his room daily for weapons."

"Thank you," Jacq said.

Dylan now had another question. "Did Mr. Nelson ever mention anything about his daughter?"

"Daughter? Nope, didn't even know he had one. Can't say it surprises me, but he's never mentioned her. Why are y'all looking for him anyway?"

"His daughter is missing," Jacq replied.

Dylan pulled a card out of his pocket and handed it to the woman. "Please give us a call immediately if he comes back or you hear from him, Ms. …?"

She reached out and took the card. "Higgs. Loraine Higgs. And I will."

"Thank you for your time, Ms. Higgs."

He and Jacq turned and walked back down the path.

"Do you think Lyle took Marrissa?" Jacq asked.

"I'm beginning to think so. If he left here before nine yesterday, he had plenty of time to make it to Knoxville."

"Unless he did go to work."

"Yeah, let's get that question answered."

They jumped in the car and drove the few blocks to the auto shop Ms. Higgs had indicated. They got out and strode to the front door. The sign still said "closed," but a man was inside putting bottles of motor oil on a shelf in the shop area, so Dylan knocked.

"Not open yet. Come back later."

They didn't have time for that. Dylan pulled out his badge and used it to knock on the door.

The young man looked up. His eyes grew wide, and he dropped the box, sending plastic containers of oil sliding across the floor. He ran toward the back door.

Dylan locked eyes with Jacq and nodded. She bolted to the right, and he went left. Dylan pulled his Glock 22 from its holster and rounded the corner to the side of the building. He slowed when he came around the back.

"Stop. FBI!" Jacq's voice echoed behind the shop.

The man dashed across the street and around a corner. They both gave chase. Jacq was closer and ran like a bat out of the fiery pit on Lucifer's birthday. Dylan darted down an alley. He jumped a chain-link fence and ran around the house. Running up the driveway to the street, he appeared twenty feet in front of the man.

"Stop! FBI!" Dylan kept his gun low.

The man hesitated and turned to run perpendicular to them, but he had slowed enough.

Jacq slammed into him and took him to the ground. She pushed him down, got up, and then pulled his arms back. Dylan, while keeping his gun trained on the runner, grabbed cuffs off his belt and handed them to Jacq. She took them with a satisfied smirk.

He was quite impressed with her athleticism. For a short girl, she was crazy fast.

Jacq stood up, and Dylan reached down and jerked the man to his feet.

"I didn't do it. I swear," the man sputtered.

"Oh, you did something. Otherwise, you wouldn't have run. The only question is what." Dylan pushed him toward where they started. "Let's go back to the shop, and maybe you can answer a few questions while we wait for the local police to show up."

Jacq rested her elbows on her knees and stared down Roger Jones, the runner and son of the auto shop's owner. Dylan, who now paced behind Roger, had called the local PD and the young man's father.

"So, Roger," Dylan said, "why exactly did you run from us?"

"I, I ... I thought you were here for me."

"And why would we be here for *you*?"

Jacq tilted her head forward ever so slightly to emphasize Dylan's words.

"If you don't know, then I ain't tellin' ya."

Jacq snorted and looked up at Dylan, who fake-slapped the

back of the boy's head. She pressed her lips together to stifle a giggle.

The bell on the front door jingled, drawing their attention in that direction. A larger, older version of Roger stepped into the room. "What in tarnation's going on around here?"

Two police officers walked in behind him.

"Hello, sir. Officers." Dylan showed them his badge. "I'm FBI Special Agent Dylan Harris and this is my partner, Special Agent Jacq Sheppard. When we came this morning to make an inquiry, Roger here decided to run from us instead of opening the door to answer a few questions."

"You fool!" Roger's dad said to his son. Then he faced Dylan. "I'm so sorry for the hassle. Could I answer your questions for ya?"

"I hope so."

One of the police officers came over and lifted Roger from the chair.

"We'll take care of this one. We were looking for him this morning after he painted an overpass last night."

"You can't prove it was me," Roger yelled.

The officer replied, "You signed your name."

"Oh …" The officers left with him.

Jacq suppressed another giggle before she stood and strode over to Dylan and Mr. Jones.

"Mr. Jones," she said, "we're looking for Lyle Nelson. We understand he works here."

"Worked. I give guys at the halfway house a chance, but they miss work once, even late by fifteen minutes, and that's it."

Dylan said, "So he didn't come to work at all yesterday?"

"Nope. Didn't even show." Mr. Jones wrung his rough, oil-stained hands. "He was a good worker too. I was really surprised. I honestly thought he was going to be one that stuck around. He has a knack for working with the cars. I had no indication he wouldn't show up. Did you talk to Ms. Higgs?"

"Yes," Jacq answered. "She said he left for work before nine yesterday morning, and she hasn't seen him since."

"He was supposed to start at nine. That's really odd."

Dylan asked, "Does Lyle have a vehicle? Or does he walk to work?"

"His knee bothers him, so I gave him an old beater I let him fix up so he could drive the few blocks and save his knee for work."

"Could we get the make and model and license plate from you?"

"Sure." They followed Mr. Jones across the office, where he grabbed a piece of paper and after looking up the plate number wrote down the information they had requested.

"Thank you very much." Jacq shook his hand. "One more question before we leave. Did Lyle ever mention he had a daughter who lived in Knoxville?"

"Can't say he did. Not to me he didn't."

"Thank you for your time." She turned with Dylan, and they went back out to his car. Once there, she pulled her laptop out of her bag. "This is weird."

"I'd have to agree. It's not looking good for Lyle. I think we might have a suspect finally though."

"So it would seem. But if he was obsessed with Marrissa enough to kidnap her, why didn't he talk about her to anyone?"

Chapter Nine

Dylan stifled a yawn as he turned back onto the highway toward Knoxville. When they left the auto shop, they shared what they'd learned about Lyle with their team, then went to the local police station and gave their report about Roger. Now they were on their way back to the office. An APB had been sent out, and Lyle was currently the most hunted man in all of Tennessee. The vehicle information Mr. Jones had given them coincided with DMV records, and everyone was looking for that car too.

"Dylan?" Jacq broke the silence that had fallen for the last fifteen minutes since they left the police station.

"Yeah?"

"Something's bothering me about all this."

"What's that?"

She shifted in her seat so she was facing him a bit more. "I'm not sure. Maybe I need to talk through it."

"Go for it." He glanced over at her and smiled, but she was too deep in thought to smile back.

"Okay. Lyle had the chance to kidnap Marrissa. If he left the house right before nine like Ms. Higgs said, he could have been in Knoxville by ten thirty, easily. But how would he have known the girls would be at the mall?"

"Well, we have to consider his accomplice."

"Right! The young man who did the actual abducting. So, he had a cohort. Perhaps the cohort was following the girls, and that's how they knew Marrissa was at the mall."

"Seems plausible."

"But why?"

Dylan tapped his thumb on the steering wheel. "Well, because he wanted to know the daughter he'd never met."

"But wouldn't he have tried more conventional methods first? Kidnapping seems a little extreme, especially if he was making the strides toward a better life that people say he was."

"I agree. But what other leads do we have?"

"I know we don't have any, and I'm not saying we shouldn't be pursuing the snot out of this, but I also don't want to miss something else if this isn't it."

"Yeah." He looked over at Jacq.

As soon as they had started driving, she had pulled her hair back into a ponytail and tossed her suit jacket into the backseat. They were both a disheveled mess. Working for twenty-four hours straight would do that to anyone, but she looked even more incredible than when she was fresh yesterday morning. Why was he so attracted to her? This wasn't going to work. She had dated his brother, and there was no way she would even consider him. He was only Chad's kid brother in her mind; he'd be fooling himself if he thought any differently.

"You all right?" Jacq's voice broke into his thoughts.

He shook the distraction from his mind. "Yeah, I'm fine. So, while we pursue this angle, that her bio-dad took her, what other possibilities are there?"

"Well, one is that it was a completely random snatch and grab by a murderer."

"So, she's likely already dead, or soon will be."

"Yeah, but there were two of them, so I'm leaning away from that. I could see a sole kidnapper having that motive more than a team."

"Team leads you to believe this is something bigger?" Dylan asked.

"I'm really inclined to believe it's human trafficking."

"I don't know. Lyle is looking good for this. But if it's not her dad, I guess that's the next most logical possibility given the evidence."

"Yeah …"

Dylan glanced over. Tears were forming in Jacq's eyes. His heart broke at the tenderness he saw in her heart. He reached over and took her hand from her lap and squeezed it. She gripped his back. "I almost hope it was her dad over that."

"Me too," she said. "She could be anywhere by now if it was traffickers. And as much as I think she'd be better off if it was her dad, I don't think that's what happened." She placed her other hand on the back of Dylan's. "We have to find her, Dylan."

"I know." He let his hand linger between hers, even though he knew he shouldn't. It felt so natural, but it wasn't wise.

Several hours later, Jacq slipped into the empty breakroom. She wanted to scold herself considering the case they were working, but something about Dylan had her smiling. Her hands still tingled at the thought of holding his in the car a few hours ago, and then he had treated her to a sandwich from his favorite deli when they got back to Knoxville. Her heart fluttered.

She closed her eyes briefly. What was she doing? What was she thinking? She didn't care that he was Chad's brother; she couldn't care less about Chad, but what if that was a problem for Dylan? She had kissed his brother … But she had always liked Dylan from the moment they met—the first time Chad brought her home from college to meet his family. She chuckled at the memory and crossed the breakroom.

She hadn't met Dylan the first night she had been at Chad's house for Thanksgiving. No, she had met him the next day. She had been helping Chad's mom peel potatoes when Dylan had sauntered into the kitchen. His mom had berated him, albeit the most polite yelling Jacq had ever heard, for being out late the night before.

Jacq's heart had jumped in her chest at the sight of Chad's younger, much better looking brother. Dylan had smiled at her, then invited her to play flag football with him and the rest of the cousins. She couldn't resist and had a blast. Only later did Chad tell her how disappointed his mother was with her. She should have known in that moment things wouldn't work out with Chad. He hadn't stood up for her; he had been as upset with her as his mom.

Jacq shook her head. Chad had expected her to be exactly like his mother, but that wasn't who she was. She wasn't one to hang out in the kitchen when there was a game to be played. Growing up, Jacq's mom had always done as much the day before as possible so she could be out playing with everyone rather than stuck in the kitchen all day. The time with family was more important than a perfect meal. How could anything ever work with Dylan considering his family?

She opened the different cabinets searching for the popcorn Sabrina had promised was in there. On her third cabinet, Jacq found it, but it was on the top shelf barely out of reach, so she pulled a chair over. She reached up and grabbed the box.

What was she going to do about Dylan? Ignore the way her heart fluttered every time he was near? That wasn't going to work. She pulled a plastic-wrapped bag from the box and leaned forward to put it back. Oh, why did she feel this way?

She slid the box back onto the shelf.

"Hey!"

She jumped. Her foot slipped out from under her. She tried to catch herself on the cabinet, but she was going in the wrong direction. Too late. She was going to land flat on her back.

"I gotcha!" Dylan's rich voice echoed in her ear as her body slammed into his. One arm tightened around her back and his other arm slipped under her legs.

"Sorry, I didn't mean to startle you."

"It's okay."

"Is it? You're an FBI agent. Should you be so easy to startle?"

"I'm not normally. Always live on yellow—except when you're in the middle of an FBI breakroom."

Dylan dropped his head back and laughed.

"Snack time?" She held up the bag she was still holding.

"Yep!"

"You'll have to put me down first."

"Oh!" He lowered her feet to the ground.

She immediately missed the warmth of his arms and chest. All she could do was stare at him. He winked at her. Her cheeks warmed, and she forced herself to turn toward the microwave. She unwrapped the popcorn and stuck it inside.

Dylan came over and rested against the counter next to the microwave. He had once again ditched his suit jacket and his rather wrinkled white button-up stretched across his built chest as he placed his palms on the counter.

"Did you only come into the breakroom to scare me so you could catch me when I fell?"

He laughed but looked at his shoes.

What was that reaction?

"I honestly can't remember … oh yeah, a snack. The sandwiches weren't enough, were they?"

"Normally, I think it would have been fine, but I haven't eaten enough in the last day in a half."

"Me neither."

"Are you and Matt having any luck with Lyle's known associates fitting the description of our kidnapper?"

"Not yet. Next up is calling the warden at the jail Lyle was released from. Maybe we'll have a better insight into him after that."

"I hope so." She removed the popcorn from the microwave and gave the bag a few good shakes. "Want some of this?" She opened the bag, and the buttery steam billowed in her face.

"I'm not a big popcorn fan."

She almost dropped the bag. "Who doesn't like popcorn?"

Dylan laughed. "Don't look so cross."

"If by cross, you mean stupefied. Please tell me you like chocolate, because if you don't like either—I don't think we could be friends."

Dylan stepped closer and put his hand on her shoulder. "I assure you. We can be friends."

Something about the way his lip curled up made Jacq feel like her face was on fire.

Daisy closed the door of the pay-by-the-hour hotel behind the trick—client—john—whatever you wanted to call him. He was a regular. Most of her work was at night, but this guy insisted on meeting at a sleazy motel in the middle of the day every other Tuesday.

She scooped up the wad of cash he had left on the table by the window and flipped through it. What she wouldn't give to actually have this much money at once. Maybe then she could escape the game. But she would only be allowed to keep a fraction of it. She grabbed her clutch, slid the money inside, and pulled out her phone. Her closely monitored phone. Two forty-five. She still had fifteen minutes before she was expected to leave. She crossed the room and picked up her tight black dress and slid it on.

Ever since she had seen those guys grab that girl at the mall yesterday, she'd been racking her brain for anything she could do. She recognized those guys. They were Ronan's buddies. She knew better than anyone what was going on here. But what could *she* do?

She sat on the edge of the bed and slid on her stilettos. If only she could tell the cops traffickers had taken the girl, at least they would be able to pursue the right direction. But she had no way to contact them. She didn't know the number to call, and she wasn't about to look it up on her phone.

Reaching to the nightstand, she opened the drawer and grabbed the TV controller. The Gideon's Bible sat there as if to mock her. God had stopped hearing her years ago. Would she still be trapped in this god-forsaken world of prostitution if He listened?

God, I really don't know if You'd listen to me. But that girl needs Your help. She looked so innocent. Don't listen to me for my sake but help that girl.

A whisper echoed in her heart. ***I am the rescuer.***

A shiver pulsed through Daisy's body.

Let me use you.

"Me?"

She stared at the controller in her hand. Was her imagination playing with her? She had felt the Holy Spirit moving in the past, but that was a *long* time ago.

She aimed the controller at the flat screen on the bureau. Click.

The local news station was on, and she listened to the report about the missing girl. Marrissa.

The FBI hotline number scrolled across the bottom of the screen. "If you have any information, please contact the FBI."

Daisy looked down at her phone. There was no way she was calling on her cell.

The hotel phone!

She tossed her cell on the bed and eyed the phone on the nightstand.

Her heart raced. Ronan would kill her if he found out. Resolve filled her. "God, I'd rather die." She reached for the phone.

Chapter Ten

The phone in front of Dylan rang. He had been helping with the tip line for the last half hour. The last call he received was a random woman who only wanted to berate him on how the FBI was failing at their job in finding missing persons. What would this call hold? An actual tip or another rant from an unhappy waste of time?

He lifted the phone from its base. "FBI tip line. This is Special Agent Dylan Harris. Can I have your name?"

The other end was quiet, but the sound of a television echoed in the background.

"Hello?"

"Hi." The voice was tight, but unmistakably female. "I can't give you my name."

"It would help—"

"No. I just …"

"That's all right." Dylan had a sense this woman was taking a risk in calling. "No worries. How can I help?" He clicked a few buttons on the computer in front of him and began tracing the call.

"Help? Oh, no … um." She drew in a breath. "I'm calling regarding the missing girl, Marrissa."

Dylan sat up straighter. "Yes? What can you tell me?"

"I don't know what information you have. I don't know if this will help, but … She was taken by traffickers. Sex traffickers."

Dylan froze. Maybe he *was* wrong. "Traffickers?"

"Yeah."

"Can you give me any more specific information?"

"Well—" A knock sounded loudly on a door. "Just a minute." She spoke away from the phone. "I'm sorry." Barely a whisper.

Click.

"Ma'am?" She was gone.

He dropped the phone back into the base. The tracing software had narrowed it down to a two-block radius. A sketchy hotel sat in the center of the radius. If this was trafficking like the woman claimed, she was likely one of the girls being trafficked. He rubbed his face. She had taken a big risk.

Warren walked up behind him. "Something legit?"

"I honestly don't know." He turned his chair to face Warren. Dylan had made a big deal to Warren earlier that he was sure Lyle was behind Marrissa's kidnapping. Humble pie didn't taste particularly good. He swallowed and told Warren about the call.

"You believe her?"

"She doesn't seem to have a reason to lie. Sounded scared."

"Could she have had a gun to her head?"

"I don't believe so."

"Guess you were wrong. Run with this and see where it leads."

Dylan rubbed his fist into the other palm. "With what? She didn't say any more than it was traffickers. Sounded like she wanted to tell me more but couldn't."

"Go inform the team. Many of you have a connection to the trafficking world. Perhaps this is one of those 'such a time as this' moments. Y'all will figure it out."

Dylan nodded. He knew Aliza's and Gio's stories. But Gio and Warren were the only ones who knew his, and Warren knew he helped rescue someone before he was an agent, not who. Dylan stood and left the call center.

In the elevator he pulled out his phone. He needed to talk to Gio.

After checking in on the Highwaters, Dylan told Gio about the call.

"I was afraid of that. Dylan, *this* is why we are both agents. The reason we do the job. To save these kids."

"The woman I talked to on the phone wasn't a kid. She could easily have been our age. I have to wonder how long she's been forced to endure that world." He leaned back against the wall of the elevator.

"I wish we could save them all." Gio's voice grew distant.

It was Dylan's turn to sound positive. "But we'll find Marrissa."

"Exactly." Resolve filled Gio's voice again. "Thanks for letting me know. I'll help prepare the Highwaters for that possibility. Anything new about Lyle?"

"Not yet. Matt was calling the prison he was recently released from, but I haven't heard more."

"Anything is still possible."

Dylan pushed off the elevator wall and exited into the office hallway. "True. That woman sure sounded believable, but there's no telling. Maybe Lyle is still our guy."

"Like I said." Gio paused. "If you're reporting to the team, put me on speaker or something. The Highwater's priest is in the living room with them, so I'm free for a few."

Dylan entered the office, and they chatted about nothing of consequence. Dylan was careful to avoid the topic of Jacq. Didn't even mention her name, lest Gio ask any questions.

Once in the bullpen, he connected his phone to a speaker so the team could hear one another.

Everyone gathered around Dylan, and he filled them in.

Jacq took a step back and rested against her desk. She was a million miles away as she stared at the floor.

"Jacq?"

She met his eyes. "I know we work trafficking cases. It's part of the job, but every single one always unsettles me."

Did this have to do with the fire?

Aliza walked over to Jacq and matched her posture. "Why?"

"It's the whole reason I became an agent."

Gio's voice came over the phone. "Tell us your story."

"It doesn't end well."

Gio let out a dry snort. "I understand how that goes. You'd be surprise how many of us on our team have personal experiences in this."

Jacq's head jerked to the side and compassion filled her eyes as she looked around the room at their team.

Dylan wanted to pull her aside and tell her his story. But would Scarlet be okay with him telling her?

"When I was in college"—Jacq slid up onto her desk—"I got to know a girl who lived in the next room over. We instantly clicked. I was a sophomore, and she was a freshman."

The year after she had dated Dylan's brother.

"We were fast friends as we had two classes together. We were both in choir and both believers. The following school year we became roommates. Around late October, Morgan—that was her name—started dating a guy who seemed perfect at first. Classic Romeo, spoiling her with gifts. But it gradually turned. He became controlling and manipulative. I didn't learn until much later that around February, he began trafficking her."

Matt put his hands in his pockets. "What do you mean 'until later'?"

"Looking back that's when the change started happening. Her personality shifted. She stopped wanting to go to church with me and other little things. I, of course, knew her boyfriend was to blame, I just didn't know what was going on when they were out all hours of the night. But then in March …" Jacq's voice trailed off.

Dylan fought the urge to go to her. "What happened in March?"

"I begged her to go home with me for spring break, but she couldn't. Her boyfriend wouldn't let her. She stayed with him. When I came back, she was gone. Her stuff was still there, but she didn't come back. The school didn't take it seriously; the police didn't take it seriously. Days later the police finally relented and started searching for her, but we came up with nothing. Weeks of searching and nothing. Couldn't even find her boyfriend. He was long gone."

Aliza nudged her. "But that's not the end of the story?"

Jacq shook her head. "I went to the police academy that summer and got my badge. I kept Morgan's case open. Three years later, right after I joined the FBI, I was working a sting to take down a trafficking ring when I came face to face with one of the pimps. It was Morgan's boyfriend. Nearly got a citation for my reaction."

The mischievous glint in Jacq's eye almost made Dylan laugh, but he suppressed it.

"I caught him. Red-handed too. I was able to question him regarding Morgan's disappearance. He didn't have anything to lose, so he ended up confessing. He had been trafficking her. Then while she was on spring break, he was gambling." Jacq paused. "He lost her in a bet. He bet his 'girlfriend' and the other guy—another pimp—took her. Moved her to D.C., at least that's what the other guy said."

Jacq slid off her desk and took a few steps toward the windows then turned back to the team. "I followed the lead. First one I'd had in years, but it was a dead end. Thirteen years later, and I have no idea what happened to her. She could still be in the game; she could be dead. Heck, she could be out of the life and be fine raising a family somewhere across the country. I have no idea."

Silence fell among the team members until Gio's voice echoed from the speaker. "I'm so sorry. I know I don't know you well yet, Jacq, but I get a sense of your tenacity. If this call we got is accurate, your instincts were right about this case. We will find Marrissa."

Dylan filled his lungs. He didn't want to be Dylan-downer, but they had nothing to go on. Nowhere to look. "Aliza? Has the cyber-crimes unit had any luck identifying Marrissa on the dark web?"

Aliza shook her head. "Nope."

Jacq crossed her arms. "But sometimes they keep a new girl in house, if you will."

"Not to sound crass"—Matt crossed his arms—"but won't they get a higher price for a virgin if they sell her?"

Dylan's gut seized at the thought. "It's true. More than sex traffickers will buy a virgin."

Aliza shook her arms by her sides. "I know this is our job, but can I say I hate talking like this? She's an innocent child. A child! It makes me sick."

Jacq looped her arm through Aliza's. "Right there with you."

Dylan leaned on a single fist on his desk. "Don't think for a second I'm not fighting tossing my cookies over here." Scarlet. He knew what these perverts did to young girls. The veins in his arm grew large.

The ambiance of the room changed as a fire seemed to ignite among the agents. He wasn't the only one who would do whatever it takes to save even one girl from a life of trafficking. *Lord, help us find her before she's touched in anyway.* He'd seen the results. Jacq had just described how abuse changes a girl's personality. Not that healing couldn't happen—he'd seen that too—but it was a long road.

Dylan followed Matt into the warden's office around five thirty, thankful he had been able to sleep while Matt drove to the prison an hour and a half from Knoxville. The warden had invited them to talk to some of the inmates about Lyle, because while they were all inclined to believe the tip-line caller because of their own individual backgrounds, they weren't about to ignore any lead. Plus, there was a chance Lyle had taken Marrissa to traffic her.

"Agents, please sit." The warden took a seat behind his large metal desk, which had three neat stacks of folders across the top of an otherwise bare space. "You said on the phone, Agent Olsen, that this was regarding Lyle Nelson?"

Dylan took one of the chairs facing the warden's desk; Matt sat in the other.

"Yes, sir. Mr. Nelson's biological daughter has been abducted, and we have been unable to contact him."

"You suspect him?" The warden laced his fingers behind his neck.

Matt leaned forward. "We haven't ruled him out, especially since we can't find him. We were wondering if we could speak to some of his fellow inmates, see if anyone knew if he was planning anything."

Dylan matched Matt's posture. "I know it's a long shot, but we're hoping someone will give him up."

"Longest shot possible, but Lyle made plenty of enemies as he cut ties and cleaned up his life, so if they know anything that will get him in trouble, they'll talk." The warden stood. "Follow me. I know exactly who you should talk to. No idea if he'll have anything, but he's the kind of rat who would throw his kid under the bus if he thought it would be to his advantage."

Dylan and Matt followed the warden down a long sterile corridor and into a large, two-story common room lined with cells. About a dozen men sat at the tables bolted into the floor.

The warden strode straight to a table on the far side of the room. "Mario. These gentlemen have a few questions to ask you."

Dylan locked eyes with the convict. Heat flooded to the top of Dylan's head. "Mario Maduro."

Mario crossed his bulging, tattooed arms. "You're Chad Harris's little brother, aren't you?"

Dylan slid onto the round seat across the table from Mario. "How is it that you're in a medium security prison?"

"'Cause your brother's the best dang lawyer a felon could ask for."

Dylan rested his elbows on the table. He couldn't believe this man wasn't in a high-security prison on death row. But here he sat in jeans and a t-shirt looking as smug as ever. "How long did you get?"

"Eight years. Guess when you get caught with your hand in the proverbial cookie jar, you gotta serve something. But your brother worked his magic when it came to the other charges."

Dylan shook his head and worked to reduce his building frustration. "We aren't here to talk about you today, even though I'm sure it's your favorite top—"

"I take it your brother isn't your favorite." The side of Mario's lip curled up.

After removing his arms from the table, Dylan wiped his palms on his pant legs. "Lyle Nelson." He met Mario's eyes. "Talk to me about what you know."

"Lyle? That little piece of sh—"

"I don't care what you thought of him. I want to know if you knew about his daughter."

Mario folded his arms on the table. "He had a kid? I had no idea."

"He never mentioned her?"

Mario shook his head. "I'd tell you if he did."

"Did Lyle owe anyone any money? To the extent that they might take his daughter?"

Mario looked to the side as if to consider this idea. "He owed people plenty … in the past. As far as I know, he squared up most of his debts. Mr. Goody Two-Shoes even cleared his debt with me and became a man of his word."

This didn't seem to be leading anywhere. Had they driven all the way out here for nothing?

Matt pulled out the sketch of their suspect. "Another question. Do you know who this is?"

Mario picked up the sketch and examined it. "Can't say I do. There's something familiar about him, but I can't place it."

Another inmate passed the table but stopped and turned back to look at the picture better. "You know who that looks like?" His Russian accent was thick.

Dylan sat up a little straighter. "That's the question."

The Russian pointed at the image. "Looks like Parilla. Not perfect but reminds me."

"Your Spanish accent sucks, but yeah, it does look like *Parilla*." Mario handed the sketch back to Matt.

Matt took it. "Tell me about Parilla. Got a first name?"

Mario answered, "Pablo. That's not him, but they could be related. Last I heard he was running in Knoxville, but that was six years ago."

"What kind of game was he running?"

"Trafficking little girls. He's the scum that actually deserves those high-security prisons."

Dylan nodded. "And that, Mario, we can agree on."

Chapter Eleven

"Harper!" Jacq let out an exasperated laugh. Her precious little daughter had been driving her a bit crazy for the last two and a half hours. Thankfully, it was bedtime.

Harper, clutching her once-white floppy-eared bunny, grabbed Jacq's leg and jumped on for a ride.

Jacq stuck her toothbrush back in the holder. "Okay fine, one last ride to bed. Mommy's tired, sweetie."

"Book!"

"That's not how you ask. Use your words." One of these days this kid would figure out how much further using precise language could get her.

"More book, peeeease."

"One more." They had been reading and playing since Jacq had picked her up at six. Jacq couldn't help but soak up her time with Harper. "Do you need to go potty again?"

"Nope."

"Okay." She shuffled out of the bathroom into her room. "Why don't you get in my bed tonight, and I'll grab us a couple more books."

Harper jumped up from her perch on Jacq's foot and ran to the bed.

Jacq chuckled and padded through the living room to the little bookcase that held Harper's books. She grabbed a few and went back to the room. "Harper! Don't jump on the bed."

Harper made one last jump and put her feet out in front of

herself, landing on her bottom.

"Oh, girlie. Will you go to sleep tonight? Or did you take too long a nap at Ms. Rachel's today?"

"I not tired."

"I noticed. But mommy is. Can we settle down now?"

"iPad?"

"No, Harper. No screens right now. It's time for bed." Jacq turned off the overhead light before kicking off her slippers and sliding into bed. Harper climbed under the covers and snuggled next to Jacq as she sat against the headboard.

They read a few books and said prayers. Jacq sang "Tis So Sweet to Trust in Jesus," and Harper finally fell asleep curled up in Jacq's arms.

Jacq was exhausted, but she didn't want to put Harper down. She fingered the purple ribbon around Harper's bunny's neck. The bunny had been Morgan's. When Morgan hadn't come home, Jacq had to pack up Morgan's half of the dorm room at the end of the semester. She had won the bunny at a carnival the two of them had gone to right after Jacq and Chad had broken up. Where was Morgan? What had happened to her?

It seemed like everyone Jacq cared for was taken from her.

She glanced to the empty side of the bed. She missed Sean tremendously, but she was beginning to think she might be ready for something new. She was fine by herself; she and Harper did their own thing, and it was wonderful, but she wanted to share their life with someone.

Thoughts of Dylan filled her mind. She was crazy. It had only been two days.

Jesus, I want to honor you with my whole life. Are you doing something here, or am I getting in the way? Of all people for me to start falling for… Dylan? His family doesn't like me. How on earth would that even work?

I wonder how he'd be with Harper… oh Lord, help me to stop this line of thinking.

Jacq laid Harper down in the bed then stretched out beside her. She probably just needed sleep. She squished the pillow under her head, and her thoughts drifted to the case. She didn't want to think about that either. But as she pushed it out of her mind, Dylan's kind, handsome face filled her thoughts. A smile turned up her lips as she slipped into sleep.

Dylan shifted the grocery bag in his arm, locked the front door of his apartment, and tossed his keys on the counter. His phone rang. He groaned. *Does it ever stop?* When Matt had dropped him off a little before eight, he'd quickly realized he had next to no food. He'd scrounged up a meal of random leftovers but knew he had to go to the store. The last thing he wanted to do after such a long two days.

He set the bag on the counter and pulled his phone out of the pocket of his jeans. He looked at the caller ID. His mom. He sighed. It really didn't ever let up.

"Hello." It was better to talk to her than to listen to her message if he let voicemail pick up.

"Hi, hon. How are you doing?" She didn't give him any time to answer. "Did you talk to your brother today? You have got to hear about the case he landed."

"Mom, I haven't heard, but I'd rather not." He unloaded the full bag of groceries onto the counter.

"Why can't you be happy for your brother?"

"It's not that, Mom. I'm happy for him, but sometimes it's better for us if I don't know what cases he's working. Chad understands that. That's why he doesn't call me and tell me these things."

"I don't understand why. You need to talk to your brother."

"Mom, I do. We're gonna hang out this weekend. Already have plans. The reason we don't talk about casework is because it's a conflict of interests. We know it's possible we could end up on opposite sides of the aisle. He knows to give me a heads-up if the FBI is involved with the case he's working, but that's where it ends. We don't talk about work out of respect for each other. He's good at his job. And I'm good at mine."

"I really wish you'd use your law degree."

"I am. The way I always wanted." He turned and put the milk and eggs in the fridge. Why wouldn't his mom listen to his desires? He never wanted to be a lawyer. He wanted to be a cop.

"I don't like you out there chasing bad guys with guns. What if you get hurt?"

He knew, from hours of counseling with his pastor, this was his mother's perverse way of saying she loved him. He wished she'd actually say it for once. "Someone has to catch them, and I love it."

"So you say. Are you coming to church with us next weekend?"

"No, I'm going to my own church."

"I still don't understand how you like that church. I'm not convinced they aren't spouting heresy."

His mom never approved of anything he did. What would she say if she knew he was falling hard and fast for Jacq? "I promise I wouldn't go to a church that wasn't strongly founded in Scripture. There's nothing heretical, just a different style."

"If you say so."

He smiled and shook his head. "I've had a long couple of days and really need to head to bed."

"All right. I called to tell you about your brother, but apparently you don't want to hear it, so I'll call your sister now."

"Mom, Scarlet has an early morning Bible study on Wednesdays. You might want to wait until tomorrow to call her."

"It's only nine o'clock."

"She goes to bed at nine most nights."

"All right. Sleep well."

"You too, Mom."

He hung up and dropped his head back as he let out a long sigh. Why were conversations with his mom so exhausting? He reached over and turned on the radio he kept in the kitchen. The Christian station filled the air with a song that declared, "You are loved!"

Dylan let the Spirit wash the words over his soul. He knew the Lord loved him. Christ wouldn't have died to save his soul if He didn't love him deeply. *Jesus, I know I don't need her approval. I have yours, and that's all that matters, but Lord …* His heart still hurt. Could he ever be healed of a wound that kept on bleeding? Any time he thought he was making strides toward healing from the way his mom had always treated him, she said something that ripped it right open again.

Jacq seemed to understand his relationship with his mom in ways no one else ever had, except Scarlet.

Why was his mind going to Jacq? He'd love to chat with her right now. He had never felt so comfortable talking to anyone else. Melanie hadn't been able to pull out of him the things he had told Jacq in two days, and he had dated Melanie for over six months. Although, he had ruined that. Maybe they hadn't been a good fit, but his lack of trust had made it impossible to get serious. However, something about Jacq …

"God, what are you doing?" he prayed out loud in his empty apartment. "I want to do Your will. You know my desire for a family. But I know You are all I need. Do Your work in my life. And help me be wise about Jacq."

He yawned. Sleep. He needed sleep. There was a lot more work to do tomorrow, starting with figuring out who Pablo Parilla was, and why he looked like their suspect.

Dylan stuffed his duffel bag into the locker and closed it. A good workout was necessary this morning before they dove into the case. He looked down at his watch. Six thirty. Good. He had an hour and a half before he was expected upstairs. He shook out his shoulders, picked up his water bottle, and headed into the FBI's workout room. The fitness center at his apartment building tended to be busy this time of day, and he preferred working out with his fellow agents anyway.

Upon entering, he glanced around the room. His eyes fell on the only other person there, and he nearly tripped over his own feet. The woman ran on the elliptical, her bright red ponytail swinging back and forth across her back. For a moment, he simply stood there, watching her, since her earbuds kept her from hearing him. She was mesmerizing. Her eyes were closed, and her lips moved slightly. She turned one hand up slightly to the ceiling. She was having her own little worship service while she worked out.

His heart danced. Turning his eyes away, he set about his normal routine. He jumped on a treadmill to get his blood flowing. When he looked over toward Jacq again, she was grinning at him in the mirror that lined the wall in front of her. She waved. He waved back. Was he running so fast his heart was racing or was it her? He wasn't sure.

He popped his earbuds in, and Toby Mac filled his ears. Dylan turned his focus onto clearing his mind of all the clutter that plagued him and laying it before the throne of God. A few minutes later, when he finished on the treadmill, he glanced over to where Jacq had been. His heart dropped; she was gone. How had he missed her leaving? He moved toward the weights. She stood there with an amused smirk, curling a pair of dumbbells.

He pulled out his earbuds. "Good morning." He joined her and set his water bottle down.

She removed hers as well. "Mornin'! Did you get some sleep?"

"I did. Head hit the pillow at nine fifteen, and I was out like a light. You?"

"I went to bed at eight with Harper."

It still hadn't fully sunk into his mind that she had a daughter. He smiled. "I'm surprised you're not still sleeping."

"Harper is an early riser. And since this is the only time I can get in a workout, it … works out."

He laughed. "Ha. I see what you did there."

Her lips scrunched into a little smirk; her head rose a little higher and bobbled side to side with pride. How could one woman be so adorable?

"Hey, I'd like to do some free weights. Mind spotting me? I can return the favor." She bit her bottom lip and waited for his reply.

"Sure."

"Is it normally this dead in here? The workout room back in Pittsburgh should have had a revolving door."

"It's not typically too busy, but this is unusual. It's a nice day, so everyone's probably running outside today. Matt's got a bunch of them training for that marathon."

"Not you?"

"I don't run, especially for that length. I don't mind the treadmill to get me started. But twenty-six miles? No, thank you!"

She laughed and adjusted one side of the weights. She walked behind him to the other side and playfully bumped into him. "I can't blame you. I can't stand running on anything but the elliptical."

"Really? I'm surprised after the way you ran after that guy yesterday?"

She shrugged. "I didn't say I *liked* running after him."

"No, but dang, girl. You can run fast."

"For how short I am. You can add that part. It's true."

He laughed. "Are you going to lift these weights now?"

She glared at him.

He winked at her; her already pink cheeks turned a shade darker. She darted to the bench and laid down in a flash. For the next thirty minutes they spotted for each other and then did a few other elements together. They laughed as Dylan teased Jacq that she could never swing undercover work with her bright red hair, and she recounted how Harper got "stuck" at the top of the slide last weekend.

After they finished doing some reps with the dumbbells, Jacq threw a sidekick in Dylan's direction.

He set his weights on the rack and turned toward her. "Hey, watch it, I'll take you to the mat."

"I doubt that." She turned her back toward him and stepped away to put the dumbbells away.

He reached for her waist, but a good look at her back stopped him in his tracks. Her racerback tank top revealed a huge scarred area on her left shoulder blade. Unmistakable burn scars. The fire. No wonder she had jumped at his touch. Without thinking, his hand went toward her shoulder. He wouldn't have touched her, but she turned into his hand.

"Jacq ..." His hand rested on her scar.

She didn't jump. Instead, she smiled and took in a slow breath. "Story time?"

He nodded. "If you want to tell me."

"Of course. If I didn't want to talk about it, I'd cover it up." She stepped closer to him. "Let's sit. I need to stretch my legs anyway."

She sat in the middle of the mat, and he plopped down near her.

"I told you I lost my husband, right?"

He nodded.

"Well, we had gone to bed one night almost four years ago in our old little apartment building. Nothing out of the ordinary, a regular July night. Some punks decided it was a good night to set off some leftover fireworks.

"I had been super tired from a hard case I was working. In fact, it was a little too similar to the one we're working right now. So I didn't wake up, not until Sean was standing over me screaming to wake up. I can still close my eyes and see the flames licking the walls behind him. The heat and the smoke ... that's why I coughed so much the other night. Some days I feel like I still have soot stuck in my lungs."

She switched her legs and took a deep breath. Her face was now serious as she met his eyes. "Sean yanked me out of bed, and we tried to run out of the building." She pressed her lips together. "But the building started collapsing. We had to get to the front door because we didn't have a fire escape. The floor gave out under Sean, but not before he was able to shove me forward. I stumbled to my feet as a beam from the ceiling fell and slammed into my back. I'm still not quite sure what happened after that ... I got out, but I barely remember how. I knew Sean was gone and most of me wanted to die with him, especially as I sat in the hospital in agonizing pain for days. But the Lord is good."

Her smile returned. "He rescued me from that fire. I know it. There was no way I could have stood back up and gotten out of that building without some sort of supernatural force working."

She reached out and took his hand. Warmth rushed up his arm.

"That's why I don't cover it up. It may be an ugly scar, but how could I cover up and hide a testament of God's work in my life? It was in those days of pain and grief that He met me in a fresh and raw way. I wasn't the same woman after that; my confidence in God only increased. So many people didn't understand that. They expected me to yell at Him, to be angry that he took my husband away, but how could I be? God had rescued me. And a little piece of Sean lives on in Harper. I am so thankful for God's faithfulness in carrying me through those impossible days."

He looked down at their hands. Something deep inside him stirred, and it wasn't only his ever-growing feelings for the beautiful woman sitting in front of him. It was a longing for the healing she had experienced. But he had never experienced anything nearly as horrific as she had.

"Dylan, can I say something that I'm not sure where it's coming from? Well, I'm pretty sure it's from the Holy Spirit."

He met her gaze. The intensity in her chocolate-brown eyes comforted him. "Of course."

She pressed her lips together and waited. He could see she was processing, praying God would speak in her words. "Scars aren't always on the surface. Sometimes they are deep inside. Left by things we think we've worked through. Things we expected to have healed, but the scar still pulls and hurts. And sometimes it hurts the most before the greatest healing comes."

Emotion seized his heart. She might as well have hit him between the eyes. "It sounds so simple, yet so painful."

"It is. Definitely not easy to walk through healing. Physically speaking, therapy stretched and pulled, and it hurt to regain complete mobility. And it's the same way with things that aren't physical. It stretches and pulls and even feels like it's bleeding again, but then healing comes, complete healing."

"I think I struggle most with what healing could actually look like. With a physical wound it's easy to say healing happens when… whatever, you know? But this emotional stuff … what's healing look like when the cause of the pain continues to drive a knife into your heart and then twist it ever so slightly?"

"I wish I knew the answer, and I don't know that you're going to like my first thought …"

He took a deep breath. "I'm ready to hear it."

"Forgive. Forgive for the past hurts, and then every single time it happens again. And let it go. It sounds so cliche, and I hate cliches. Goodness knows I've heard enough of them in my day. But I think you have to decide to move past it and not let it control you. I know you can't decide to not let it bother you. It's not that simple, but I think you can choose if it controls you or not."

"You know exactly what I'm talking about, don't you?"

Her lips turned up slightly. "You've said enough in the last few days for me to think you're talking about your mom."

He raised his eyebrows with a nod. "Yeah."

"Seems like God's been working in your heart about it?"

"He has. I've sought counsel from my pastor, but it seems like every few weeks Mom likes to point out everything she doesn't like about my life, normally by pointing out what she likes about Chad's. And then I feel like I'm back at ground zero."

"I'm so sorry. I can only imagine what it's like to be Chad's brother. Being his girlfriend was sufficiently hard. Never quite feel like you're good enough."

"You felt that way?"

"Oh yeah! Especially from your mom." She gave him a knowing look.

"I mean, I know you weren't exactly Mom's favorite, but I didn't realize she actually made you feel that way."

"That decision to go play flag football with you on Thanksgiving apparently was the first shovel full for digging our relational grave."

"You and Chad had barely started dating at that point."

"Yeah, I should have known then that Chad and I wouldn't work. He was actually mad at me for playing with you guys."

"What?"

"Yep. He needed a perfect little housewife, and that was never going to be me. Emma was what he needed. Are they as happy in person as she portrays on social media?"

"They are. It's sick."

She laughed. "I'm glad."

"You have no ill will for them? Wasn't she your friend?"

"Yep, we were close, until she started dating him. They tried hiding it from me, which really was silly. I've always been happy for them. They're a good fit."

"They can't do any wrong in Mom's eyes. I wish she'd understand that this is the job I want to do."

Jacq tilted her head to the side. "Let me ask you this: Do you think God called you to it?"

"I guess so."

"You guess? It's a yes or no answer."

He squirmed. "I really do think He has."

"Then what your mom thinks is irrelevant. Obedience to God trumps her approval."

"Ouch."

"You know I'm right."

He wasn't sure how to respond. Had God truly called him to chase down bad guys?

"Why did you join the FBI?"

"So I could rescue girls from trafficking."

"That's specific. What's the rest of the story?"

He took a deep breath. How would Scarlet feel about him sharing?

Someone entered the gym, and Jacq jerked her hand away.

Dylan chuckled. "Now who's hiding?"

She turned bright red, exactly the reaction he'd been hoping for. She swatted his shoulder. "I want that story, but we probably should actually go to work. And you need a shower before we do."

"Oh, do I?"

"Yep, and"—she fake sniffed herself—"eww, so do I!"

He stood and gave her a hand up. He didn't want to let go of her but made himself. They strolled down the hall, and he watched her disappear into the women's locker room.

He couldn't believe how much of his soul he had bared to her. But it was so natural. Anxiety stirred in his gut. Should he have shared so much? He was overthinking it.

God, settle my spirit. That was a great talk with Jacq. Help her words of encouragement soak into my heart instead of the fear of what she'll think of me. Thank You for her kindness. Thank You that you are at work in my heart. Please heal my heart toward my mom, but also please heal my relationship with her. I don't know how You could, but I trust that You can and will.

Chapter Twelve

Riding up the elevator, Dylan moved in close to Jacq and bumped her with his elbow. She returned the affectionate gesture. She had exited the locker room moments after he had. His mind had bounced all over the place while he was showering, going back and forth about whether he should have let Jacq invade his heart. But right here in this moment, he was glad he had. He felt like he could take on anything. He was ready to get upstairs, learn what the other team had discovered about Pablo Parilla, and rescue Marrissa. He wasn't going to let anything stand in his way, not with this beautiful woman next to him.

He fought the desire to put his arm around her and draw her to his side. They weren't ready for that. He wasn't ready for that. His mom definitely wasn't ready for that.

The elevator doors opened.

Jacq squeezed his elbow and sped down the hallway. Not wanting her to get away, he took two long strides and caught up with her. A soft giggle escaped her lips.

"It was fun working out with you this morning, Agent Sheppard."

Her giggle intensified. "Likewise, *Agent* Harris."

He stepped ahead of her and gave a sweeping bow. "It was my pleasure."

Her giggle gave way to a full laugh. She kept walking, raised her hand, and, placing it on his shoulder, gave him a sturdy shove.

He stumbled backward in faux defeat. "I see how it is." He

caught up with her again and opened the door to the office. "My lady." He swept his arm in front of himself in a grand gesture.

She rolled her eyes and shook her head. But the smile on her face and the rosiness of her cheeks gave her away.

They matched the quietness of the office and parted ways to their own corners. Dylan tossed his backpack on the floor and pulled out his chair. There was no report on his desk like he had expected. Hadn't Lawrence's team followed up on their lead? Or did Matt have the report?

Dylan lifted his head to ask Matt when Warren exited his office, a stern look planted firmly on his face. "Harris, Olsen. My office. Now."

Matt shrugged, and they both moved from behind their desks.

Dylan met Jacq's eyes. She winked at him.

The toe of his shoe caught on the carpet and tripped him. He ducked his head rather than play it up. He had no idea why Warren looked so stern or where the report he expected was.

The guys trekked into Warren's office, and he was leaning back against the front of his desk. Arms crossed. "Close the door."

Dylan's stomach dropped.

Matt shut the door behind them, and neither of them dared to sit. As former military, Matt nearly stood at attention.

Warren tilted his head to the side, and the scar on his cheek twitched. They were in for it. "Am I to believe that you left that prison yesterday with a significant lead, yet you did nothing about it?"

Dylan resisted the urge to look at Matt. What was Warren talking about? "We did leave with a name, but I texted Lawrence as he had offered, and passed on what we knew. He replied with an 'okay,' so as far as I know that lead was pursued overnight."

Matt added, "We both had barely gotten any sleep in the previous thirty-six hours, so we thought it best that we got a good night's sleep so we could be ready for today."

"Lawrence showed me the text but said he didn't get it until this morning. Apparently, his kid had his phone. Texting him wasn't enough. You should have taken care of it."

Dylan felt like he'd been sucker punched. How was he supposed to know Lawrence didn't have his own phone?

Warren continued, "You two need to get out there and find this guy immediately. Figure out who this unsub is and find Marrissa. I expect better from the two of you."

Where was the closest hole he could crawl into? If they were too late, it was on him.

Warren straightened himself. "Go!"

Dylan and Matt left the room without another word. They didn't even look at one another.

Back in their own space, Dylan jerked his chair away from the desk and sat. Why hadn't Lawrence—grrr! After logging into his computer, he pulled up the National Crime Information Center database and entered Pablo Parilla's name.

The search icon spun, mocking him for his incompetence.

Jacq strolled across to him, but he refused to look up at her until she tapped lightly on his desk. "Need coffee?"

"You have a way to insert it intravenously?"

"Cream and sugar?"

"Just cream."

She wandered away. He definitely didn't deserve her.

The stupid database continued to spin. *You have got to be kidding me!* He needed this answer hours ago, not hours from now.

He clicked over to the DMV records. Surely, this guy would come up there. Although the sketch hadn't produced anything, so why would a name?

The DMV database spun as well. "Good grief."

Matt looked over the top of his screen. "Restart your computer."

"Grr." He tried to close out of the search engines, but they were frozen, so he did a hard restart.

Placing his head in his hands, he prayed. What he should have done at first. *God, help. I'm sorry I screwed up again. I can't believe I always miss doing something right. Help Marrissa.*

A coffee cup appeared in front of him. He lifted his gaze to its deliverer. Her smile was intoxicating, and compassion radiated from her eyes. If only she realized how second-rate he was. She would have gotten the job done.

"Your computer's ready for you." She raised her mug to her lips.

He logged on and again pulled up the NCIC. Again, typed in Pablo Parilla's name.

Bingo!

The man, who looked similar yet different enough to not match the sketch, had a rap sheet longer than Dylan's left leg. Mostly petty crimes. Seemed like no one had been able to get anything bigger to stick. But based on what the inmates said, Parilla deserved to be locked away. "Got him."

Jacq came behind his desk and hovered close to look at his screen. The scent of mangos caught him off guard.

"Let's go get him."

Dylan lifted his pointer. "First, let's see if the judge will give us a warrant, so our hands aren't tied while we're there."

"Fine, go be smart about it." She swatted his arm and walked back to her desk.

"I've got his current address." Matt handed a note to Sabrina. "Can you ladies figure out a game plan while we go talk to the judge?"

"Of course." Sabrina took the note.

Dylan stole one more glance at Jacq. Her smile gave him enough umph to move forward. Maybe there was still hope to prove to her he wasn't a complete failure.

Jacq spun a pen in her hand as she stared out the window watching the rain. Once Dylan and Matt left to see the judge, Sabrina, Aliza, and Jacq made a plan for knocking on Pablo's door that included what to do if they found Marrissa or any other girls Pablo might have inside. Or weapons. Or drugs. Now they had to wait for the guys to get back.

Even though he wasn't in the room, her mind kept going to Dylan. She found herself praying for him and his relationship with his mom. It must be weighing heavily on his heart if he would share it with her so quickly. She got the sense he hadn't really talked about it with anyone else. She could be wrong, but something in his voice … as much as he willingly shared, there was still a hesitancy in his tone.

"Knoxville to Jacq!" Sabrina called in a sing-song voice.

Jacq blinked and turned, eyes wide.

"Where are you? Because you aren't focused."

She shook her head.

Sabrina rolled her chair across the aisle and up to Jacq. "Oh, don't play coy with me. You'll learn quickly that doesn't fly in here. Remember we're trained investigators. I've seen the way you and Dylan look at each other. What, pray tell, is happening there?"

Warmth filled Jacq, and she glanced away.

Sabrina clapped. "Ah! Yes, something is going on."

"I don't know. I really don't. We're getting to know each other, that's all."

"Sure, you keep telling yourself that. You came into the office awfully friendly this morning."

Jacq tilted her head. "What are you trying to insinuate?"

"I don't know where you two came from."

"We ran into each other in the gym this morning, and we worked out and talked. That's all."

"Oh." Sabrina's shoulders dropped.

"You sound disappointed."

"I like the idea of you two."

"And maybe we made steps toward something this morning, but sleeping together, if that's what you're trying to imply, won't happen."

"Oh, you're one of those wait-'til-marriage types. I suppose that fits. Dylan's a Christian, so I shouldn't be surprised."

"I'm a Christian too."

"Hmmm. Looks like I'm surrounded by your type now. Between Dylan, Gio, and Aliza ... I definitely don't understand you people."

"No? I'm more than willing to try and help you understand. What don't you understand?"

"Well, especially where we're dealing with cases like this one. Innocent girl is kidnapped, yet Christians claim God is good."

"Well, that's probably the toughest question everyone wrestles with at some point. It's tempting to be like, 'God, if you're so good, why would you let this happen?' I definitely struggled with that when my husband died. But the thing is, we don't live in the perfect world He created. When people started doing things their own way, and sin entered the world, the world started falling apart. And bad stuff came in droves. But that doesn't make God any less God, or any less good. He gave us the freedom to make our own choices, and most people don't make the best ones."

"If you say so." Sabrina sat back in her chair.

Lord, give me wisdom in my words. Help me be Your light to Sabrina.

"But anyway," Sabrina said, clearly done with the God conversation. "Dylan seems really relaxed around you, and I like seeing that. He's a good guy but can't seem to ever settle down with a girl. A few years ago, he was in a serious relationship, but something went horribly wrong. He never really said what happened, but I got the impression it was a nasty split. He needs someone like you in his life."

As much as Jacq wanted to know everything about Dylan, she hated gossip more, and this was starting to feel like it. If Dylan wanted her to know about his ex, he'd tell her. It wasn't Sabrina's place. But Jacq was so bad at cutting people off.

The door opened, and Dylan and Matt appeared. Dylan

winked at her.

"Based on the redness of your cheeks, Dylan walked through the door, didn't he?"

Jacq turned her face downward knowing she was turning redder.

Matt's voice drew her eyes back up. "You ladies have anything new?" He plopped down in his chair.

Jacq shook her head as Dylan picked up the frame with Harper's picture and sat on the corner of her desk. Her heart stopped. What did Dylan think about her having a daughter? He smiled at the picture and then at Jacq. Her heart resumed its regular beating.

"We have a warrant. Y'all have a plan?"

Jacq pushed away. "Indeed, we do. Ready to go knock some heads, I mean, doors?"

Dylan laughed, and she was glad to see he was back to his pre-Warren-talk self.

She stood and slung her backpack over her shoulder. "Then let's do this!"

"Do what?" Gio entered the bullpen. "Whatever it is, I want in."

Matt hopped up. "Gio!" He pulled his teammate into a hug. "Why are you here?"

"Good to see you too. Warren sent relief this morning. I went home and took a nap, and now I'm ready to go get a bad guy. That's what we're doing, right? Please tell me that's what we're doing."

Jacq pointed at Gio. "That's exactly what we're doing."

Dylan, with Matt by his side, strode up the perfectly manicured walk to an oversized house. There was no way this guy had honestly earned it. No one can buy a million-dollar mansion by working odd jobs. No way.

Warren and Aliza went around the southside of the house,

while Jacq and Gio approached from the north. Sabrina was in the van down the street running the op.

Once at the door, Dylan raised his hand and knocked. It barely echoed past the heavy mahogany. This guy was not ashamed to flaunt his wealth.

Matt reached over and rang the doorbell.

No answer came from either attempt. Using the side of his fist, Dylan banged on the door.

The sound of footsteps came through an open window. But the front door didn't open.

"Pablo Parilla. FBI. We'd like to ask you a few questions." Dylan directed his voice toward the open window.

The footsteps quickened. A piece of furniture fell.

Dylan reached for the doorknob. Locked. No way they'd be kicking this door down.

Matt removed his FBI windbreaker and wrapped it around his hand. He punched out the window closest to the lock and cleared the glass.

Dylan reached in and flipped the deadbolt. Matt slipped his jacket back on, and Dylan opened the door. They drew their weapons.

"FBI."

The place looked like the residents had left in a hurry.

A man appeared around the corner with what looked like a hard drive in his hand.

Dylan pointed his gun at him. "Hands up, Pablo."

The man, with expensive-looking clothes and his black hair slicked back, slowly lifted his hands in the air.

Matt inched closer. "Hand over the hard drive."

"That's not what this is."

Matt let out a dry laugh. "I have the same one at home. Hand it over."

"Fine." Pablo tossed the hard drive between the two agents and seized the opportunity to run.

Dylan holstered his gun and darted after him. Pablo rounded the corner into the kitchen. Dylan pursued.

Pablo sprinted toward the back door, but Jacq and Matt appeared behind the glass. Pablo tried to redirect his exit, and Dylan was able to close the gap.

Dylan shoved Pablo into the wall. "Why you running, Pablo? We have a few questions." He grabbed one of Pablo's arms and jerked it behind his back, then caught the other. After pulling his cuffs off his belt, Dylan slapped them onto Pablo's wrists.

Dylan whipped the man around, despite the fact they were the same height. "Now about those questions."

Matt held the hard drive, which he had somehow managed to catch, in Pablo's face. "You're lucky I caught this, although maybe not. Is it damning evidence? Let's find out." Speaking to his mic. "I need a computer, pronto."

Dylan grasped Pablo's arm and pulled him to the couch. "Why don't you have a seat, while we find more evidence to lock you away for a long time?" He pushed Pablo to a sitting position. Matt let the rest of the team into the house.

They all began searching. Sabrina brought a laptop and cords to Matt, and they opened the contents of the hard drive.

Dylan sat on a chair near Pablo. "Why run?"

The man's face was stern and unmoved.

"Real chatty guy, aren't you?"

Pablo kept his eyes forward.

Dylan pulled out his phone and opened it to a picture of the sketch of their suspect. "Do you know this guy? People say he looks like you."

Pablo turned only his eyes toward the image.

Dylan watched for micro-expressions.

Recognition.

"You know who this is."

Pablo finally looked Dylan in the eyes. "I've seen him around. But I don't know him."

"Tell me more, Pablo."

"Nothing more to tell." The man leaned back, giving no indication how uncomfortable he must be with his hands cuffed behind his back.

Silence filled the room save the sound of Matt's clicks and taps on the computer.

"You have got to be kidding me. You disgusting son of a—"

"What is it, Matt?" Dylan joined Matt at the kitchen table halfway across the great room.

"You aren't going to want to see this."

Dylan glanced at the screen. Pornography. Matt scrolled. A lot of pornography. Dylan's stomach churned.

"It's worse than that." With a few clicks, Matt opened a different folder. Children.

Dylan's veins pulsed. He desperately wanted to go over and beat the life out of the man sitting on the couch. Dylan had to walk away from the images.

"Where's Marrissa, Pablo?"

"Who?"

Dylan pulled up her photo on his phone. "This girl. You help us find her and maybe the judge will be lenient. Not that you deserve leniency."

Pablo looked at the phone. "No clue."

Dylan shoved his phone in his pocket. "Listen well, Pablo. You're going away for a very long time."

Dylan and Gio escorted Pablo into the field office and up to the interrogation room. Similar to the interview rooms where they had spoken to Marrissa's friends, but this one also had a two-way mirror. The table in the center of this room had iron bars to cuff a suspect to. So far Pablo had refused to talk. He said nothing about the images found on the hard drive, and he said nothing more about Marrissa, only that he'd never heard of her.

Dylan pressed his hands down on the table. "Talk to us, Pablo. Tell us what you know."

Unflinching, the man's eyes stayed fixed on a spot on the wall behind Dylan.

"Do you even realize how much trouble you are in? Answer me this: was that hard drive yours?"

He didn't even blink.

"Well, we can lock you up for a few days. We'll keep going through your stuff. Pretty sure the judge will throw you in jail for a lot longer, though."

Pablo cleared his throat. "I'd like my lawyer now."

Dylan clenched his fists. He knew this was coming with how little Pablo was saying, but still, he had hoped to avoid it. "I'll call the public defender's office—"

"No. I want *my* lawyer."

"Fine, got his card?"

"Does it look like I can get his card?" Pablo lifted his cuffed hands. "Name's Chad Harris."

Chad? You have got to be kidding me. It was only a matter of time before they sat opposite on a case. But Dylan wasn't just on the opposing side of the aisle, he was the arresting officer.

Jacq. He needed to find her and warn her. She would not want to run into Chad out of the blue.

"We'll call him. Sit tight." If a girl's life wasn't on the line, Dylan would gladly let Pablo sit in the interrogation room for hours before he even called. But they didn't have that kind of luxury at this moment. Dylan spun and exited the little room with Gio right behind him.

Jacq wasn't in the hallway.

Gio grabbed his arm. "I'll call Chad."

Dylan turned to his friend. "Thanks. I'd rather not be the one to do it. In fact, I may have to recuse myself."

"But you were the arresting officer. I'm not sure you'll be able to."

"You were there too."

"And I'll handle as much as I can. I bet Jacq plays a good bad cop. She could take your pl—"

"Not hardly. If you want backup take Aliza. You know she won't let a pedophile off easy."

Gio laughed. "So true. Why not Jacq?"

"Just trust me." Dylan set off to find Jacq.

"I want that story later."

He turned back toward Gio but continued to walk. "And I will. I have to find her and tell her to avoid this area."

Gio's face scrunched up.

Dylan chuckled at his friend's confusion. He popped his head in the office. She wasn't there. When he spun around, he nearly ran into Gio. He gave Dylan a brotherly shove and rolled his eyes. Gio was a man of few words but deep observation. Dylan could almost guarantee he didn't need to be told what was going on in Dylan's mind regarding Jacq. Dylan wanted to care. He wanted to hide his growing feelings, but it was pointless when it came to Gio.

Dylan opened the breakroom door. She wasn't there.

The conference room. Nope.

Where had that woman gone?

Chapter Thirteen

Jacq pushed the button on the vending machine, and the Dr Pepper dropped into the opening. She rarely had a soda pop, but today she'd make an exception. And it was her favorite. It had been Morgan's favorite too. She wondered if Morgan still liked the cherry cola. If she was alive, she probably did.

Jacq twisted the cap off, took a swig, and strolled back toward the elevator. Hopefully, Dylan and Matt were getting something out of Pablo for them to go on. Fifty-four hours into this, and they still had nothing.

Earlier in the day, Jacq had once again looked for any activity in Lyle Nelson's credit cards and online accounts. She found zero activity. Where was that guy? If he didn't take his daughter, why had he dropped off the grid? It didn't make sense. Maybe Dylan was right, and Lyle was involved. Just because she believed it was trafficking didn't eliminate Lyle from being connected.

Lord, we need a lead, a fruitful one. Is Pablo it?

They had searched Pablo's house from top to bottom. From the attic to inside every closet to even the dank crawlspace. And, other than the hard drive, they found nothing to point to trafficking. Sure, there was evidence of women having lived in the house, but Pablo claimed he had a wild party over the weekend and not everyone took all their garments home.

Jacq pressed the up button and waited for the elevator. She took another sip of her soda.

In their plan development earlier in the day, they had looked for other properties connected to Pablo, but nothing had appeared. Even the house Pablo claimed as his permanent address wasn't in his name. In fact, nothing was in his name.

Pimps did this on a regular basis. They would make their girls buy the houses and cars in their names, so nothing pointed back to the pimp himself. She'd seen it plenty of times. If anyone's credit would be ruined, you'd better believe it wasn't going to be the pimp's.

Voices came around the corner behind Jacq, and she turned to see who was coming. A man who looked an awful lot like Dylan—only lighter hair and slightly chubbier—appeared around the corner with an agent from the front desk.

Chad.

No way. She took off to her left and down the closest hallway, almost sloshing Dr Pepper all over her blouse. What on earth was Chad doing here?

She pressed her body against the wall, out of sight. The elevator dinged open. The men commented on it getting there just for them.

Lord, please don't tell me Chad is Pablo's lawyer.

That would be awful. With Dylan being the arresting officer, things could get awkward. And she didn't want to see Dylan's brother. Ever. Sure, she was happy for Chad and Emma. Yes, she had forgiven them for the way they went about their relationship. But it was so uncomfortable.

She leaned her head back against the wall. Could she manage to avoid Chad while he was here? Maybe he wasn't even going up to the third floor. He was probably here for a different case. Surely.

She pushed herself off the wall and shuffled back to the elevator. Yeah, he was going to a different floor. She glanced at the elevator numbers. One of the two was on level four, but the other was on level three. Maybe she should take the stairs.

Yes, take the stairs.

She turned and went down the hallway where she had been hiding. She trudged up the stairs, but her weariness from the busy two days and working out a little too hard this morning was catching up with her.

She opened the door to the third floor. Chad. She had almost forgotten.

He was standing at the other end of the hallway talking to Dylan, whose eyebrows rose when they made eye contact. Chad's back was to her, so she ducked down another hallway.

Only this wasn't a hallway. It was a little alcove that opened to the bathrooms. Women to the left and men to the right.

She didn't know what to do at this point. She had recently used the restroom, and didn't really want to go in there with a pop anyway. Although she would be safe from Chad. Oh, this was stupid.

She should march over there and put her arm around Dylan, maybe plant a kiss on his cheek. No! Wasn't she a grown woman? She hadn't seen Chad since he finished college eons ago. When Morgan had gone missing. He had graduated only a few weeks later. That meant it had been thirteen years.

She stood there, feeling like a fool, drinking her Dr Pepper. A face appeared around the corner.

She jumped.

Dylan came the rest of the way around the corner. "Hiding?"

"You scared me."

He chuckled.

"I'm so glad you're amused. Is Chad really Pablo's lawyer?"

Dylan's expression grew serious. "Do platypuses eat bacon?"

"That doesn't even make sense." She laughed.

"But it had the desired result." He stepped closer.

She swatted at his arm and barely brushed it with her fingertips. But it was enough to send an electrical charge through her fingers and up her arm. Why was she so drawn to this man?

Dylan stepped back and looked down the hallway. "He's gone. It's safe to go to the office now. Assuming you don't want to hang out by the bathrooms all evening."

She narrowed her eyes. "Shut it. I suppose it will have to come out at some point that I'm here … but—"

"I know. Don't I know it." The way he stretched out the words "don't I" was telling.

She couldn't resist reaching out and squeezing his arm. Why was she causing so many problems for herself? She needed to focus.

"Who's going to try to get anything out of stone-faced Pablo with Chad in the room?"

"Not you or me."

Relief filled Jacq. At least that was one thing she didn't have to worry about. She'd focus on the behind-the-scenes investigation.

Gio scribbled notes on his pad of paper at Matt's desk. He planned to be prepared before he went in and interviewed Pablo, especially with Chad there. Chad was known for being a ruthless lawyer, who wasn't afraid to take jabs at the cops working the case. Gio didn't understand how Chad could call himself a believer considering the lowlifes he helped keep out of jail. Especially guys like Pablo. His hard drive had way too many images of women in compromising situations. And not only full-grown women. Girls. Some as young as ten. It made Gio, who was typically able to keep his emotions in check, feel like he could go complete Rambo on the guy.

He tapped Matt's desk with his fist. "Thanks, man."

Matt nodded. "Of course. I'll be in the observation room if you guys need any more data."

Gio turned to Aliza. "You ready for this?" She looked up from her desk with the most serious face he'd ever seen.

"He's going down." She cracked her knuckles.

"You can't lay a finger on him, Blake."

"I won't need to." A mischievous smile crept over her face. "I can already tell I'm going to have to hold *you* back from pummeling him."

"Touché."

They walked toward the door. Dylan and Jacq came in talking

in shushed tones. Without any attempt at being covert, Gio gave Dylan a "you *will* tell me what's going on between the two of you" look.

Confusion flitted across Jacq's face, and Dylan's grin grew.

Without a word, Gio smacked Dylan on the back as they strolled past one another.

He wished life could be simpler. He'd much rather go out to dinner with his friends and hear about their growing affection for one another. Even more, he wished he had someone to go home to, someone he could tell about Dylan and Jacq's attempts to hide their attraction for one another. But neither of those were possible tonight.

Once in the hallway, Aliza said, "I don't get it. I don't understand how men can turn women, and especially children, into objects, into commodities to sell."

"I was thinking this morning about how bad it seems our world has gotten, but then I remembered it's always been that corrupt, since the day Adam and Eve ate the fruit. I mean, how bad must it have been before the flood? And Sodom and Gomorrah? God considered Lot righteous among the inhabitants of the city, and he was willing to hand over his daughters to the men who wanted to rape the visitors from the Lord."

Aliza stopped. "Good point. Makes you wonder how He puts up with us."

"Grace."

"Amen. I know I need more of that every day."

"You and me both."

"Let's go nail that guy to the floor. Maybe he'll have a slip and tell us about all his 'business' dealings."

"I'm praying he will."

They resumed the trek to the interrogation room. Gio knocked on the door and opened it.

Chad sat close to his client, and they spoke in hushed tones. Chad stood and reached out to Gio. "Agent Crespi. Agent Blake."

He shook their hands.

"Mr. Harris." *Care to explain representing this lowlife?* How he wished he could speak his thoughts. "Let's get down to business. Your client was caught with a hard drive in his hand. This drive held over three hundred pornographic images, a third of which were of underage children."

"My client says all of the images were of consenting adults and claims that any supposed children are of age, even if they look young."

"Do you"—Gio looked at Pablo—"have proof of age and consent?"

Pablo leaned toward his cuffed hands and scratched his cheek. "Do you get consent every time you look at a woman?"

"I'll take that as a *no*. What was your purpose in having these images?"

Pablo laughed. "That's the stupidest question I've ever heard from a cop."

"Were you distributing them, either for sale or free?"

Chad laid his hand on the table. "You don't have to answer that."

Gio reclined back in his chair and mimicked Pablo's laissez-faire demeanor. "Where's Marrissa Highwater?"

"Who?"

"You know who I'm talking about."

Aliza slid an eight-by-ten photograph of Marrissa across the table.

"She's pretty."

"She's twelve." Gio swallowed his growing rage. "Where is she? Maybe you didn't have her, but someone does, and I think you know who."

Pablo inched forward. "Look, I'd help if I could. But I can't. I don't know who that loser was that has my face, and I sure as heck don't know who has the girl. So, if we're done here, I'd like to go home."

Someone knocked on the other side of the two-way mirror. "Sit tight. You aren't going anywhere."

Gio went into the hallway.

Matt met him there. "He's *not* going anywhere. We confirmed the identity of one of the children in the pictures. A fourteen-year-old who vanished from her father's home in Kentucky eight months ago."

"Thanks." Gio returned to the interrogation room. "No such luck, Pablo. You're headed to lockup. Possession of underage porn is enough to hold you, hopefully without bail."

He inhaled. *Keep your cool.* He lowered his voice and spoke slowly. "The DA might be willing to work with you if you tell me where Marrissa is. Or even the fourteen-year-old from Kentucky who deserves to go home to her family and not be sexually exploited." He nearly spit the words in Pablo's face.

Pablo slowly shrugged like it might kill him if he gave Gio the tiniest bit of hope. This scumbag didn't have a fingernail's worth of humanity.

Gio'd had enough. He slammed his fist on the table and got in Pablo's face. "Tell us where they are!"

Chad stood and put himself between Gio and Pablo. "He said he doesn't know. Now back away from my client before he presses charges against you."

Gio picked up his notepad and threw it across the room.

"Gio."

He met Aliza's eyes. The sternness there spoke louder than any words ever could.

They were done here. Yet another dead end.

Chapter Fourteen

Jacq rolled over in bed. She rubbed her eyes and looked at the clock. Four forty-seven. It was officially Thursday. The case was bothering her, keeping her from sleeping. Where was Marrissa? Why couldn't they get a break? Where was Lyle? Did he have her? And if so, why? Why would he have taken her, to what end? None of it made sense. Maybe he hadn't taken her, but someone else had and was demanding some sort of ransom from him.

Jacq needed more sleep. However, the case wasn't letting her. They needed to find Marrissa, but they had nothing.

Ring! Jacq jumped. She grabbed her phone off the nightstand. Dylan. Joy filled her, but it quickly vanished. Why was he calling her so early?

She pushed the green button. "Hello."

"Good morning." His voice was soft.

"I think it's too early to call it that." She lay back on her pillow.

"You sound more awake than I expected."

"I can't sleep. This case."

"That's why I called. Jacq, we have a body."

Her heart pounded. "No—"

"It's not Marrissa. It's Lyle."

She sat upright in bed. "What?!"

"Yeah, Warren wants us to go to the scene."

"Okay."

"Want me to pick you up?"

"I have to take Harper to the sitter. Rachel's house is right by the office. Meet you there?"

"That works."

"See you shortly."

Jacq hung up and crawled out of bed. She called Rachel, and then quickly pulled on a pair of jeans and a blouse. After she finished getting herself ready, she scooped Harper up. Within twenty minutes, Jacq had dropped off a still-sleeping Harper and drove into the bureau lot. She parked in the spot next to Dylan's car and grabbed her bag from the passenger's seat.

Dylan appeared.

She climbed out of her burgundy Honda Accord and felt drawn to him. Why did she want so badly to hug him?

"Hey." His hand came to rest on her shoulder after he pushed her door shut.

She looked up and locked eyes with him. Her body froze. "Hey."

"Shall we."

She nodded. "I could drive if you want."

"I'm fine. I like driving."

That didn't surprise her. It was something he could control. She understood that feeling, but she was glad to have him drive. It felt right. "Okay."

Dylan turned and opened the door for her. She immediately noticed two paper coffee cups in the console. When Dylan got in the driver's side, he grabbed the cup closest to her. "I hope it's to your liking."

"Oh, you really are wonderful! Thank you."

He grinned. "Thought you could use some."

"What was that you said yesterday? Do platypuses eat bacon?"

Dylan laughed and pulled out of the parking lot and took them to Interstate 40. They headed west for about thirty minutes before winding their way north on state roads. They rode quietly, sipping their coffee and trying to wake up fully.

When Dylan turned down yet another country road, Jacq

asked, "How far out did they find him?"

"Way out by Lone Mountain State Forest. But that doesn't mean anything to you, does it?"

"Nope."

He chuckled. "We're almost there."

Sure enough, they parked behind the county sheriff's vehicle a few minutes later. The sun was barely turning the horizon pink, but the blue and red lights of the squad cars lit the surroundings along with some large lights that had been set up to illuminate the crime scene. Dylan retrieved FBI jackets from the trunk, and they both shrugged them on and walked toward the scene.

"Agents!" A burly man dressed in a sheriff's uniform approached them.

Dylan shook the man's hand. "Special Agent Dylan Harris. This is Special Agent Jacq Sheppard."

The man shook her hand too. "Sheriff Allen Miller. Thanks for coming out. The ME got here a few minutes ago and is doing a preliminary exam. We were able to get prints off him; that's how we were able determine he's your guy."

"May we see the body?" Dylan asked.

"Of course, this way. Careful of the mud. Yesterday's rains made a mess of the area. Afraid it may have washed away too much of the evidence."

Jacq zipped up her jacket. "How was his body found? This stretch of road seems awfully remote for someone to stumble across."

"For sure. Mr. Jenkins down the street found him when one of his dogs got loose this morning. He apparently chased him down this way. The dog found the body and started barking like crazy."

"Did the dog disturb the body?" Dylan asked.

"No."

"That's good," Jacq said. They carefully made their way down a steep embankment. Jacq was grateful for her choice of jeans and riding boots. They were almost at the bottom where the ME and his team surrounded the body, when Jacq's foot slipped. She instinctively grabbed Dylan's elbow and caught herself from falling. She let out a breath.

"You okay?" Dylan looked down at her.

"I'm good. Glad you were close." He gently put his hand on the small of her back. She regained her footing, and they moved the rest of the way down.

"Jim, the FBI agents are here," Sheriff Miller said. "This is Dr. Jim Williams, medical examiner."

An older man with glasses turned toward them. "Are you taking over the case?"

"No, sir, we're only here for information. We've been looking for Lyle Nelson. That is who we have here?" Dylan pointed past the medical examiner.

"Definitely his fingers, anyway. And since they're attached, I'd say yes, this is Lyle Nelson."

Jacq stifled a chuckle. "What have you learned so far?"

"Cause of death is a gunshot wound to the head. Execution style."

"Here in the woods?" Dylan stepped closer to the body.

"Nope. He definitely rolled from the top of the embankment."

Jacq took a step closer too. That was definitely Lyle Nelson, but he looked in bad shape. "How long has he been dead?"

"Based on what we've been able to assess so far, it would appear he's been dead since sometime between eight and twelve Monday morning, give or take an hour or two. I'll know more when I get him back to the lab."

Jacq's heart dropped. Monday morning? As much as she had doubted Lyle had taken his daughter, she had kind of hoped she was wrong. But if he'd been dead since Monday morning, then he didn't take Marrissa.

At the office late Thursday afternoon, Dylan wandered back to his desk after a quick trip to the bathroom. Jacq still wasn't around. His increasingly grumpy mood longed to be brightened by her infectious smile.

She had disappeared over half an hour ago with her Bible in hand. If they needed her, they could call, but they still didn't have any leads. Aliza and Matt were downstairs combing through surveillance footage again. Only Dylan, Sabrina, and Gio were in their part of the office, going back over everything they had.

He and Jacq hadn't learned anything this morning that would help them find Marrissa. They had pitched in some at the crime scene, but it didn't aid their case. It only squashed a lead. Dylan had even received a call an hour ago from the detective in charge of Lyle's case. Already they had been able to establish that he had been killed within an hour of his disappearance. He was in no way connected to Marrissa's kidnapping.

Dylan sat at his desk with a huff. Sabrina gave him a cross look, which he ignored, but Gio picked up his phone and started texting. A moment later Dylan's phone beeped with a new text message. It was Gio. Dylan shook his head and opened it.

Go find her.

Dylan shot a glare at his friend. Gio sat there with a smug grin.

"Fine." Dylan stood.

"Fine, what?" Sabrina's face scrunched up.

"Don't worry about it. I'll be back in a bit." He walked past her.

Sabrina said, "Find Jacq while you're at it."

He laughed.

"What?" Sabrina said.

"That's where he's going," Gio answered.

Dylan exited the room and ventured down the hallway. He really had no idea where she would be. On his way to the bathroom, he had pecked in the breakroom and hadn't seen her. He turned around and looked back down the hallway. The light was on in the conference room. Perhaps she was in there. A glance through the window told him another team was using the room. He wandered the hallways.

He was about to give up when he reached the last hallway of that floor. No one went down this way. There were a few unused offices, and, other than a light at the end of the hallway, it was dark. But he checked anyway. His heart leaped. She was sitting on the floor against the wall, her Bible open on her lap. He didn't want to startle her, so he cleared his throat.

She looked up. "Hey."

"You all right?" He slowed as he neared her.

"I guess." She patted the floor next to her. "Join me?"

He sat and rested his forearms on his raised knees. "You sure you're okay?"

She leaned her head back. "Processing and praying. I needed a quiet spot."

"You found it."

She gave him a rueful smile.

He waited for her to continue. He already knew her well enough to realize she liked to talk things out, after she had processed them in her head.

"I hate that we haven't been able to find Marrissa. I feel so sick to my stomach over it. I try so hard to not get too emotionally invested in cases, but something about this one has hit me hard."

"It can definitely be difficult to stay emotionally uninvolved."

"Maybe I'm in an emotionally heightened state with the move and new job and everything. Maybe it's because this case is reminding me too much of the one I was working when Sean died."

"In what way?"

"It was a teenage girl; she even looked similar to Marrissa. She was taken from a zoo by a young man she must have thought was flirting with her. She walked out the gates with him on her own, but as soon as they were out, he forced her into a car."

"Crazy similar."

"Yeah."

"Whatever happened?"

"We couldn't find anything. Hardly any leads. Three days in, and that's when the fire happened."

Dylan took a deep breath. His heart hurt for Jacq.

"We didn't find her. But a year later her picture was discovered on the dark web by cybercrimes. She had been trafficked. They rescued her, but she'll never be the same."

Dylan tilted his body a little closer to her. It all made sense. This along with her friend from college, and it was no wonder she strongly suspected human trafficking.

Jacq lowered her head onto his shoulder and sighed. Dylan lifted his arm and wrapped it around her shoulders. She scooted up next to him and rested her head against his chest. He pulled her tight.

He put his chin on her head. She fit perfectly against him. He wished they could sit there forever.

Inside his mind, an alarm sounded and summoned anxiety to attack his heart. What if he screwed this up too? What if he wasn't enough for her? She already had found love and lost it. How could he ever measure up to the husband she had loved so much?

Dylan put his dirty plate in the sink. After work, he'd headed home and ate dinner by himself. Not so unusual, but tonight it felt lonely. He and Jacq had sat in that hallway with each other for over a half hour before they went back to the bullpen and closed up for the day. Despite the thrill of holding her close, his heart was exceptionally heavy.

He hated not knowing where Marrissa was. He hated having nothing to go on. He hated leaving the office and pretending life was normal.

It wasn't normal for Marrissa. And since Jacq had entered his world Monday, his life wasn't either.

He refilled his water glass, padded into the living room, and plopped down on the couch. Grabbing his laptop off the coffee table, he signed into social media, a place he rarely visited. One new friend request: Jacquelyn Irene. Was that Jacq? He didn't know her middle name. The profile was nearly blank, but they had one mutual friend. Emma Harris. It was Jacq.

Once he accepted the request, photos appeared. Mostly of Harper, though her name was never said, just *H*.

He laughed out loud at one of a tiny Harper holding a pacifier crooked in her mouth. It warmed his heart to see Jacq's chronicle of Harper's first three years. As the posts grew older, images of Jacq and a man surfaced. Sean. He was a good-looking guy, who seemed to be quite successful in his career. And the love in his eyes and Jacq's was undeniable.

How could Dylan ever measure up to Sean? It was bad enough he was still living in his brother's wake. But this man had died saving Jacq's life.

He shut his computer and tossed it to the other side of the couch. Resolution grew in him. He needed to step back from Jacq. No one would approve of this relationship. Plus, he could never love her like she deserved.

In Walmart, Daisy turned down the shampoo aisle. She should have come earlier in the day, but one of the girls in the house had had a few rough clients last night and had needed her. So she'd waited until after dinner to shop so the meal wouldn't be late. Because a late dinner made Ronan furious. But now she was rushing through the store before she went to work.

She grabbed a bottle of shampoo and dropped it into the basket on her arm. Next, she needed nail polish.

She turned down a center aisle. A woman with bright-red hair caught her eye. The FBI agent.

Daisy cut down another aisle. Her heart beat faster. She had seen the agent at the mall, and, while she looked like Jacqui, surely it couldn't be her.

Daisy went to the end of the aisle and peeked around the corner.

It *was* her.

A little girl, a replica of her mother, tugged on Jacqui's sleeve.

"Hold on, Harper."

Daisy turned away so Jacqui couldn't see her. Why was she in Knoxville? And why was she FBI?

Was this Daisy's opportunity? For what? She could never get out, but maybe she could help Marrissa. The Feds must be shooting blanks because Ronan didn't seem worried, and he always seemed worried when a new girl was taken. If the Feds were on the right track, he would never have let her go to the store by herself tonight.

But what could she do? She wasn't about to walk up to Jacqui and tell her what she needed to know. And what would she tell her about herself? No. That wouldn't work.

She opened her purse and dug through its contents. She found a piece of paper and a pen.

She glanced around the corner. Jacqui was still there.

The pen didn't work. *God help me help Marrissa.*

She scribbled in the corner and the ink began to flow. She scratched down the information she thought most pertinent.

Jacqui moved down an aisle.

Daisy needed to not lose her. What more should she say?

"We're almost done, Harper."

Daisy was out of time.

Jacqui was inspecting lipstick shades, and her daughter started to wander away. Perfect.

She waved at Harper around the corner of the shelf and beckoned the little girl to come close. Daisy hated to pull a child away from her mother, but what choice did she have?

Harper came close and smiled.

Daisy squatted, as best she could in her short pencil skirt. "Hey, cutie. I need you to do me a favor. Please give this to your mommy and then stay close to her." She rubbed both sides of the paper against her skirt, and, holding it between the length of her fingers in an attempt to not get any new fingerprints on it, she handed the toddler the note.

Chapter Fifteen

Jacq found the right shade of lipstick. Why did companies have to change it all up so often?

She glanced down. Where was Harper? The world froze, and her heart collapsed in on itself.

"Harper!"

Jacq immediately caught sight of her daughter, but a shadow disappeared around the end cap. "Get over here right this instant. I knew I should have put you in a cart."

Harper stomped over. "Hate cart."

Jacq knelt. "We don't say that word. And I know you don't like the cart, but I need you to stay close to me. It's very important."

"But the pretty lady."

"Pretty lady? Who did you see?"

"The pretty lady said to give you this." Harper held up a small, ripped piece of paper.

Jacq scooped Harper up into her arms and darted to the end of the aisle. No one was there. She walked farther but still didn't spot anyone. "Do you see her, Harps?"

"No."

Jacq took the paper from Harper's tiny hand and opened it.

The bubbly handwriting was beautiful but clearly indicated the note was written in haste.

Santiago Alvarez is the guy who took Marrissa
sometimes Al Santiago aka Saul Allen

MEBS
Please save her

The break they needed. "Where is she, Harper? Do you see her?"

"No pretty lady." Harper shook her head. "Sorry, mommy."

"It's all right, baby. I'd like to talk to her. That's all." She held Harper a little tighter. "I think you're going to have to go back to Ms. Rachel's house this evening."

Another little girl needs me tonight.

Dylan rode the elevator to the office. Jacq had texted and said nothing more than come immediately. He had been completely settled into the couch reading the book Aliza's boyfriend, Gabe, had recommended—a welcome distraction from the case and from Jacq's constant plaguing of his mind. But for her, he was eager to put the book down, even if his doubts of a possible relationship had morphed into an ugly monster.

The elevator opened, and he stepped into the hallway. Gio, Aliza, and Matt were down the hall and entering the office. He followed them into the dimly lit room.

Sabrina and Jacq still weren't there.

"Anyone know what this is about?" Dylan propped himself up against the side of Gio's desk.

Aliza sat on the front of hers. "I figured if anyone knew, it'd be you."

Did everyone think something was going on between him and Jacq? "All I got was the same text you all did."

They all nodded.

The door opened behind him, and Sabrina traipsed across the room. "This had better be good. I was deep into binge-watching reruns of *West Wing*." She stopped next to Dylan and crossed her arms.

They all stood there in silence, until Matt finally asked, "So, where's Jacq? She called this party, so why isn't she here yet?"

Gio sat on his desk. "Probably had to drop her daughter off."

Dylan kind of wished she'd bring her daughter. He'd like to meet her.

Matt pulled his chair out and sat. "I called her to ask more, but she didn't give me anything else. I heard a car horn in the background, so I assumed she was already on her way."

The door burst open behind him, and Jacq practically ran into the office and to her desk. "Oh, good, you're all already here. You won't believe what happened. We, Harper and I, were at the store. The crazy kid decides to wander away, she hates riding in the cart. I don't know why she won't—"

"Jacq"—Matt stood and put his hands up in front of her—"we don't care about those details. Why did you call us in? I was about to go to bed."

"Sorry. I'm just so excited." She held up a slip of paper. "I was—I mean, Harper was handed this piece of paper. It has the name and two aliases of the guy who took Marrissa."

Gio and Aliza both catapulted from their desks.

Dylan crossed the room. "Really? What's his name?"

"Santiago Alvarez."

Sabrina came up beside Dylan. "Who gave Harper the note?"

"Harper said she was a 'pretty lady.' I tried to get more information out of her, but she's not even three. She said she had red lips and was wearing a blue or purple dress. But then again, last week she was still mistaking blue for green. So, who knows?"

Matt shoved his hands in his pockets. "Maybe we can check out surveillance. Maybe we'll see this mystery woman handing Harper the note."

Jacq turned to Matt. "Yes! Would you?"

"On it. Which Walmart? And who wants to go with me?"

Sabrina volunteered. And once Jacq told them which store and where in the store they had been at approximately what time, Matt and Sabrina left.

The rest of the team got to work looking for Santiago Alvarez. Dylan searched police records and came up empty.

"No criminal record. Anyone else have any luck?" He wandered over to Jacq's desk. He was worried this lead would be another bust. And he was concerned how Jacq would respond, considering how excited she had been.

"I haven't found anything yet." She tapped away at her keyboard. "There you are. I have a birth certificate for an Al Santiago."

Dylan came around behind her and hovered over her shoulder to see her computer screen.

She clicked on the document. Date of birth: January 20, 1952.

"The guy lied to the girls about his age, but he wasn't that off." Jacq slammed her fist down on her desk.

Dylan put his hand on her shoulder but emotion surged in him. He recoiled it immediately. "Keep looking. Did nothing come up for Santiago Alvarez?"

"No, but perhaps he wasn't born in the states."

"Check immigration records then. If he is related to Pablo, it's possible he was born in Mexico too. I think Pablo gained citizenship at fifteen."

Dylan rested his elbows on the half-wall behind him. He was strangely drawn to and repelled by Jacq. This was ridiculous.

She typed and clicked. "Nothing that fits our approximate age. Plenty of people by that name and his alias."

"Have you tried Saul Allen at all yet?"

"That's next."

The room was quiet save the clacking of keys and the clicking of mouses.

Gio tapped twice on his desk. "I might have something. Pablo has a second cousin by the name Saul Allen."

"I found a driver's license for Santiago Alvarez." Aliza raised her hand. "Twenty-five."

Jacq turned her chair toward Aliza. "If he has a driver's license, why can't I find a birth certificate or a visa or a something for him?"

Aliza shrugged. "Beats me, but I think I figured out why facial recognition didn't pull him up." With a few clicks, Aliza projected her computer up onto the screen near her desk.

The photo on Santiago's driver's license was of a young man with long, curly hair and a scraggly beard.

Dylan snorted a laugh. "No kidding. Is that actually the same guy?"

Aliza nodded. "The eyes don't lie."

Jacq clapped and squeezed her hands together. "We got him!"

Dylan read the address. "Slow your jets, Jacq. Look at a map and check the address. As of three years ago when that license was issued, there was no such address."

Jacq turned back to her computer. She pulled up the map. Nothing. "You have got to be kidding me. Will we ever actually get a break? I'm so tired of this."

"You aren't alone in that sentiment."

Dylan fought the urged to reach out and touch Jacq by going back to his desk. "Gio, what have you found out about Pablo's second cousin?"

"Thank you for not forgetting me over here." Gio sat back in his chair and laced his fingers behind his neck. "Not much other than that the cousin exists. Birth date is the same as Santiago's here."—he pointed at the screen—"but there's nothing past elementary school enrollment records."

"Any pictures?" Aliza asked.

"Not that I've found." Gio sat forward again.

Dylan met Jacq's eyes. "I refuse to let this lead be a bust. Let's find Santiago/Saul, whatever his name is."

Hours ticked by.

Dylan was struggling to stay awake. How was it already midnight? Three hours and still the only thing they had was a name. Matt and Sabrina had returned from Walmart a few minutes after eleven. They had found the mystery "pretty lady" on the surveillance video, but it was too grainy to identify. The manager was working with corporate to get all the feed from the surrounding hours sent to them ASAP.

Gio stood. "I hate to say it, but maybe we need to call it a night and pick it back up in the morning."

"Last time we waited until morning, the person had time to empty his house, taking any girls and evidence of something more out of our grasp."

Gio sat. "Point taken."

Dylan had really messed that one up. Could he ever be enough? Was he destined to live as a screwup for the rest of his life?

God, I don't know if I can keep doing this.

"Dylan." Gio stood again. "Let's go get coffee for everyone."

"Good idea." He joined his friend in a trek to the breakroom.

Dylan pulled out mugs from the cabinet and lined them up.

Gio started the first cup. "Are you beating yourself up for the whole Pablo thing?"

"Why do you have to be so perceptive?"

"Why can't you answer a question with a straight answer?"

Dylan could keep the questions going but chose not to. "Maybe I'm not cut out for field work."

"Hogwash. That has to be the stupidest thing I've ever heard you say."

"You should have heard the one I told Jacq yesterday."

Gio shook his head. "Do you take anything seriously, other than your mishaps?"

"What fun would that be?"

Gio replaced the full mug with the next empty one. "Why did you become an agent?"

"You know the answer to that."

"Because you wanted to save girls, like you saved Scarlet, not because you wanted fame and recognition."

Dylan handed Gio an empty mug. "But I'd at least like to do the job well."

"Why? What happens if your best isn't good enough?"

"This is stupid."

"Answer the question, Dylan."

"Girls could die or be trapped in trafficking."

Gio cleared his throat. "I'd venture to guess you're more concerned about someone else getting the glory for it. Exactly like Chad did that night *you* saved Scarlet."

"Hey, I never cared that they didn't know what happened."

"Didn't you?"

"I promised Scarlet I would never tell Mom, Dad, or Chad what happened."

"But didn't part of you want to scream that you were saving your sister, not scaring off some trespassers?"

"Well—"

"I get it. I really do. But like I've said to you before: whose *well done* are you looking for? What if you'll never be enough? Can you let God use what He's given you?"

"If I can't do my job—"

"Dylan, you are an instrument, God *will* use you. He makes you enough. You will never be enough on your own, and that's okay. He's enough."

"But …" His words fell short. How could he refute that? He knew in his head God was enough. But why didn't that play out in his life?

"Also, are you able to sit back and let others get the glory and not be concerned with being first?"

"We're a team. And I tried to let someone else—"

"Do the legwork, so you could go arrest the perp?"

Dylan's stomach turned over. Why did his friend have to be so spot on?

"I know I'm being harsh, like you've asked me to be in the past." Gio gripped Dylan's shoulder. "Let God use you. He's called you to higher than self-condemnation. We all screw up. But keep praying and doing what you can with God's help. We were never meant to do this on our own."

Dylan knew Gio was right, but how did he get himself to the point of living like he was wholly reliant on God?

God, I want to stop trying to be enough on my own. Help.

Dylan took three of the cups of coffee and doctored them how he, Jacq, and Aliza like them. Gio took the three undoctored cups.

As they walked back to the office, Dylan said, "Thanks for the sucker punch."

Gio laughed. "What are friends for?"

"Who needs enemies?"

They needed a breakthrough in the case. Where was Santiago? Dylan folded his arms on his desk and laid his head down. Three more hours had passed, and all they had done was eliminate every possible lead. Gio and Aliza went to talk to Pablo and see if he'd give up Santiago now that they had a name.

God, we need a bone. We can't do this on our own. We need Your help. If You guided that woman to give Jacq the note, guide us in what to do with the information we now have.

Dylan fought falling asleep, but he was beat. His eyelids were too heavy, and he finally surrendered.

"That's it!"

He jerked his head up at the sound of Jacq's voice.

Matt banged his head on his desk.

"Sorry, didn't mean to wake you guys. But I have something." The smile on Jacq's face indicated that despite little sleep, she was energized by the information she had found.

Dylan rolled his chair over to the front of her desk and craned his neck around to see her screen. "What'd ya find?"

"You know those letters she wrote on the note?"

"'MEBS'? We searched but came up with nothing."

"We weren't looking for the right thing. When I woke up—"

"Woke? When did you sleep?"

"While you were snoring on your desk."

He swallowed. "Snoring?"

Jacq chuckled. "If by snoring I mean sleeping soundly. But, yeah, I caught a few Zs too."

"What time is it?" Dylan looked at his watch. Five-thirty-two. He had slept for over two hours.

"Anyway," Jacq continued, "when I woke up, I was thinking about what the letters could mean. What if they were a business instead of someone's initials?"

"They are?"

"I think so. Mountain Explorers Body Shop. MEBS."

"Never heard of it."

The rest of the team gathered around Jacq's desk.

"It's a good-sized gym on the other side of town. They have a full room of equipment, a short track, rock-climbing wall, and rooms for classes."

Gio stepped up beside Dylan. "Sounds like a cool place. Chance our perp is a regular?"

"I was about to find out. They opened at five."

Sabrina said, "Careful how you phrase your question."

"Of course." Jacq pulled out her cellphone and dialed the number.

"Hi, my friend was telling me about your gym. It sounds like a great place."

She paused.

"Santiago Alvarez." Jacq listened. "He is? Maybe I'll come over now. Do you know how long he normally stays?" A grin seized Jacq's face. "Don't tell him. I want it to be a surprise. Thanks."

Jacq hung up the phone and stood. "He's there. Right now. Let's go!"

They all grabbed their bags. Matt put in a phone call updating the warrant with Santiago's name and aliases, and Aliza called Warren to fill him in.

As they hurried to the door, Matt said, "Apparently the email came in from Walmart while I was asleep. We've got access to all the footage we could need, but it looks like we'll have to find our mystery lady later."

"Good." Dylan opened the door, but Lawrence and one of his agents walked up before the team could exit.

"Where y'all off to this early?" Lawrence asked.

"We found the guy. Going to arrest him. Y'all want to come for backup?"

Lawrence stood in the doorway. "Where's Warren?"

Aliza said, "Meeting us there."

"By all means, let's go." Lawrence turned.

The agent with him, Rob, gave Dylan a fist bump. "How'd you find him?"

Before Dylan could answer, Matt came up beside them. "Everything's in order. Let's get this scumbag."

Dylan thanked God. *Finally! God, please help us take him in peacefully so we can find Marrissa.*

Chapter Sixteen

No one on their team was dressed to enter a gym without raising suspicion. Dylan wished they had thought of that before they left the field office. But since Jacq made the call, she went in first. Dylan gave her a moment, then slipped inside the door. Jacq chatted with the young woman behind the counter.

The employee gave Dylan an uneasy look.

Jacq pulled her badge out and slid it halfway across the counter.

The woman's eyes grew wide.

Dylan turned his attention to the weight room. Four, maybe five, people were using machines, one was at the free weights. Three more people were in the front part of the room on a treadmill, elliptical, and stationary bike. None of them were their suspect.

Where was he?

Aliza, Matt, and Warren had gone around back.

Gio and Sabrina were by the far emergency-only exit.

Lawrence and Rob were ready to come in behind Dylan as soon as he gave them the signal.

Movement by the locker rooms drew Dylan's eye. Santiago disappeared inside. He apparently had been the fifth person on the weight machines.

Dylan knocked on the door behind him and closed the gap between him and Jacq. "He's gone into the locker room. Miss, please go instruct everyone in the front to leave through the far door. We have agents out there waiting to come in."

"An alarm will sound when that door opens."

"Then send people out this door, and one of the agents will open it on my signal." He met Rob's eyes.

Rob gave a curt nod.

"Yes, sir."

The girl ran around the counter and started gathering patrons. Rob and Jacq helped usher them toward the front door.

Dylan placed his hand on the holstered gun on his hip. With his other hand he pointed people toward the door. He checked the classrooms as he passed them. They were empty.

Jacq appeared by his side again. "Everyone's out of the main room. No one has gone up to the track or back climbing wall this morning. Santiago should be the last person in the building."

Santiago exited the locker room with a duffle bag in his hand.

Dylan gave Rob the signal, then drew his weapon.

An alarm sounded.

"Santiago Alvarez?"

Santiago lifted the duffle bag in front of his chest.

"Drop the bag, Santiago. Or should we call you Saul Allen? That's your birth name, right?"

The man stared at him, then looked across the gym. Gio and Sabrina were approaching along the left side of the equipment area. Dylan could sense that Lawrence and Rob were coming up the center as they had planned.

Santiago didn't say a word.

Jacq, gun raised, said, "Why don't you tell us where you took Marrissa?"

He shook his head. Deep beneath the tough exterior, Dylan saw fear. Was he working for someone? Had he been trafficked into trafficking? Dylan had seen it before.

"We can help you, if you come with us and help us find Marrissa."

"That ain't going to happen, man." Santiago finally spoke and fiddled with his bag.

"Put the bag down!"

Santiago shuffled his feet.

Dylan didn't know what was in the bag. "Put the bag down and raise your hands!" They needed to take him in alive.

He messed with the bag again. Dylan inched his finger closer to the trigger.

"Gun." Lawrence's voice echoed through the room.

Dylan didn't see a gun, but Santiago had reached his hand in the bag.

Pkew. Pkew. Pkew. Someone had fired.

Santiago hit the floor.

All of the agents rushed on the body. Dylan kicked the bag away.

Santiago was dead.

Dylan holstered his gun and cursed. "Who fired?"

Lawrence stepped up beside Dylan. "I saw a gun."

"We needed him alive."

"I swear he had a gun."

Santiago had had something, but was it a gun?

Dylan pulled a pair of gloves from his pocket and slid them on. He knelt beside the bag and removed the contents. Sweaty gym clothes. Shoes. Shower kit. A large knife. But no gun. If he was pulling out the knife, it could have looked like a gun, but it wasn't.

Dylan threw the bag against the ground. "We needed him alive. Now we're back to square one at finding Marrissa."

Chapter Seventeen

Jacq shuffled to the car from the gym. Her exhaustion was catching up with her. It had been over an hour since Santiago's body had hit the floor. But since they were done, Warren told them all to leave. He and Lawrence would finish up.

As much as she wished Lawrence hadn't pulled the trigger, she'd been ready to do the same. Santiago was their only lead—the only thread connecting them to Marrissa. Save the mystery woman. Who was she?

Jacq reached the car and was surprised when Dylan went straight around to the other side. She'd almost become accustomed to him opening doors for her. But he was in his own world. The anger at Santiago's death obviously consumed him.

She climbed into the backseat with him. He leaned his head against the headrest. Gio and Aliza climbed in the front seats.

Gio turned to them. "Matt suggested breakfast. You two want food before we all head home?"

Dylan nodded. "I'd like that. Somewhere we can sit somewhat secluded. I know we'll all want to talk about what happened."

Aliza nodded. "I'll call Mama G's and see if her party room is open."

Dylan finally looked at Jacq. "Best French toast this side of the pond." He turned his head back center and closed his eyes.

"Have you had any on the other side?"

His lips curled up. "Nope."

She chuckled.

Once Aliza secured the room at Mama G's diner, the four of them road in silence.

They arrived, and the six tired team members plus Rob headed to the private eating area. Jacq went straight for the closest chair at the long rectangular table in the center of the small room. She preferred to sit near Dylan, but she wasn't sure he wanted to be next to her right now. Nor did she have any desire to be obvious about the emotions welling up in her when she was close to him.

Dylan rounded the table and sat across and down one from her, all while avoiding eye contact. Not that she was trying to make eyes at him. Why was she feeling so stupid about this? She was probably only tired.

They all ordered. Conversation was minimal. After getting by on a few hours of sleep and the adrenaline rush of the encounter, they were spent to the end. Food, then sleep. Then maybe they could find the woman. Or perhaps Santiago's body would give them some clue as to where Marrissa was.

Jacq fiddled with the corner of her napkin and considered her teammates. She had only worked with them for four days, but she already seemed to know them. And more than anything, she trusted them. They had her back, and she had theirs.

A quick glance at the whole group revealed they were exhausted. Sitting at Jacq's right, Gio, who normally came across as the quiet, gentle one in the group, appeared to be a bull about to go on a rampage.

Across from Jacq, Aliza also picked up on it. "Gio. You look like a grenade that's lost its pin."

Gio set his coffee mug down with such force the black liquid sloshed out. "Because I am. I know I'm not the only one mad the perp is dead. We needed answers from him, yet instead he's zipped up in a big, black bag."

Jacq trusted the man with her life but didn't yet know him well enough to be certain if touching his arm would make it better or worse. "I totally agree."

"Lawrence had no reason to shoot him." Gio folded his arms on the table.

Dylan set down the spoon he had been spinning between his fingers. "I don't know. I was moving toward the trigger. I had no way of knowing if he had a gun in that bag."

Gio said, "But you didn't shoot, because you didn't see it."

"As much as I'm livid the perp is dead, I feel it was a justified shooting." Dylan sat back in his chair.

"If you had seen the angle I saw, you would know it wasn't." The veins in Gio's arm were bulging.

"Sabrina?" Dylan looked across the table to Jacq's left.

Sabrina traced the top of her mug with her index finger. "I agree with Gio. From where we were standing, Lawrence's actions were premature."

Jacq played the scene back through her mind, visualizing every second she could.

Sabrina nudged Jacq with her elbow. "You look deep in thought. Care to share with the class?"

"I'm thinking through it again. I think it was justified."

Matt, who was across from Gio, snorted. "Of course, you'd agree with Dylan."

"What's that supposed to mean?" Her words came out sharper than she intended. "I'm perfectly capable of thinking for myself."

Aliza put both hands palm down. "I think we're all a little tired and need to take a step back."

"I was there too." Rob set his mug on the table. "I was standing only a couple of feet from Lawrence, and honestly, I don't know what to think. My finger was on the trigger, but …"

Their food arrived, and instead of cordial conversation, the agents all ate quietly. The tension was palpable.

Dylan got out of his Charger and walked to his apartment building.

He hated how breakfast had been so tense. They were supposed to wind down while they ate, but instead they got more tightly wound. He hated it when a cop's actions had to be called into question. What if he'd been the one to pull the trigger instead of Lawrence? He hated to think about it.

At least Jacq agreed with him. Since she was always right about these things, maybe he finally was too.

He punched the code into his building and went up the stairs to the second floor. He was ready to crash. Thinking straight was a thing of yesterday. If he could only get some sleep.

He rounded the corner. A woman stood in front of his door with her back to him. Could it be ... no way.

She turned. It was.

"Melanie."

"Hey, Dylan. I didn't think you'd be home. I was going to slip a note under your door."

"Getting home after an all-nighter and a rough morning. What are you doing here?" The last person he wanted to deal with this morning was his ex-girlfriend.

Her eyebrows furrowed. "It's good to see you too. I thought maybe you'd be happy to see me."

"Why would I be happy to see you?"

She took a step back.

"I'm sorry." His voice was flat despite his apology. "The case I'm working went sideways, and I want to go to bed. So, please cut to the chase."

"Wow, never known you to be so rude."

If she didn't tell him soon, he was going to be a whole lot ruder. But he knew his curiosity would plague him if he didn't get an answer before he went inside.

"I was wondering if you'd like to go out for dinner. I know it's been years, but ... I'd kind of like to see if we still have a little chemistry."

Melanie ...

Model beautiful. Tall with long, blonde hair. A stark contrast to red-headed, petite Jacq.

A true southern belle. Perfect housewife material. So different from run and arrest Jacq.

Adored by his mother. Fit in wonderfully with the rest of his family. Nothing like Jacq.

Melanie and Jacq were as different as Chad and him.

Melanie reached out and stroked Dylan's arm. "Think about it."

"What do you really want?" He shook his arm free from her touch. "Need a favor from the city council? Need to hobnob with Mrs. Rotary Club? Need a good defense attorney? What is it?"

"Why do you always assume everyone wants something from your family? Do you really think everyone is trying to use you to get to them? Do you really think you have no worth in and of yourself? I thought for sure you'd be beyond this by now, but I see how it is. You still have yet to grow up and be your own man. Forget I ever came here, Dylan. Maybe you really are as worthless as you think."

She shoved past him and stormed down the hall.

At least he could go to bed now.

He tried to make light of it. But her words echoed in his head.

After unlocking the door, he went into his apartment. Tossing his bag on the couch he went straight for his bed and flopped down face first into the queen-size Serta.

He was done. Punched in the gut one too many times this week. What a fool he was to think Jacq would give him a second look! Why would she—someone who wanted nothing to do with his family—consider him?

His phone buzzed in his pocket, alerting him to a text message. Tempted to throw the phone across the room, he looked to see who sent the message first.

Jacq.

Emotion surged within him, making it hard to see what she wrote. He was falling for her, but it could never be.

He opened the message.

Hey. Hope you can get some good sleep. :)

Such a simple text, but it reached deep into his heart.

He replied. *Thanks. You too.*

He started to pray, but sleep overtook him before he could get any words out.

Daisy climbed out of Ronan's Escalade. The afternoon sun was warm on her shoulders. She joined him on the path up to the large house where his buddy lived. She had no idea why they were here today, but she'd learned a long time ago to never ask questions.

Ronan knocked on the door and looked her up and down. "Straighten yourself up." He reached over and adjusted the strap of her dress. "Are you trying to look like a poor skank?"

If he'd let her wear jeans and a t-shirt maybe she wouldn't look like a hooker when she was off the clock.

The door opened and Celeste appeared. "Ronan. Daisy. Bobbi's in his office."

They stepped inside, and Ronan turned to Daisy. "Go help with the girls. Make sure everyone is well and will be ready for work tonight."

"Will do."

He smacked her on the bottom and sauntered to the back of the house.

She carefully hid her disgust for the man she had loved for a short time, but he was nothing more than another pimp who pretended to be her husband but treated her like mere property. She was too privy to the game when she came to him to be completely fooled by his attempted flattery.

"How are you doing, Celeste?" Daisy squeezed Celeste's arm. They started walking to the stairs.

"Tiago's dead."

"What?" Daisy stopped.

"I'm not sure what happened. Bobbi won't talk. All I know is he left for the gym this morning but never came back."

The gym. After giving Jacqui the note, Daisy was worried leaving the letters was a mistake. Had the FBI found him? Then why was he dead?

Daisy rubbed Celeste's back, and the women went up the wide, winding staircase.

Celeste was Bobbi's bottom—the girl who had been with him the longest—and thus cared for the other girls, even Santiago's girls. "You know, Tiago was talking about moving out with Nova and the new girl. Bobbi even said he thought he was almost ready. We could use the space."

Daisy tried not to laugh. This house was plenty big for the seven people who lived here. Well, six now. "Wow, already? I don't think Ronan's ever going to think Ezra will be ready to run his own show."

"Ronan's so controlling."

Daisy let out a dry chuckle. "Tell me about it."

Celeste paused halfway up the stairs. "You did not just—"

"Nope. Forget I said—"

"Of course." Celeste waved her hand in the air.

A girl was never to speak against her man, especially to other girls.

They reached the second floor, and Daisy asked, "How's the new girl?"

"Scared out of her mind. Santiago was treating her like a princess, but she was still resisting him. I'm afraid of what Bobbi will do with her now that Tiago's gone." Celeste didn't need to tell Daisy that Bobbi had a mean streak. Daisy had seen the bruises. Bobbi and Ronan had gone to the same "school" of how to keep girls in pocket.

"Where is she?"

"Locked in the tower." Celeste pointed toward a doorway at the end of the hallway, where a small staircase led to an attic room.

"It must be eighty degrees up there right now."

"Probably. It cools off at night, though. She's fine."

Daisy wished the FBI had been able to find Marrissa.

The women entered a large bedroom and found the other three girls sitting on a king-sized bed.

"Daisy!" Luna jumped up and darted to her.

Daisy drew her into a hug. Luna had recently turned twenty and felt like a sister to Daisy, despite living in a different house. "You okay?"

Luna whispered, "I'm worried about Nova."

Daisy walked to the bed where Nova sat crying. She lowered herself next to the girl who, even though she was twenty-three, looked like a lost child. "Hey." Daisy wrapped Nova in a hug.

"I don't know why I'm crying. I'm not sad he's dead. I'm really not."

"I understand. It doesn't make sense, but he's all you've known for a while."

"What's Bobbi going to do with me?"

"I don't know, but you'll probably work directly for him now. Nothing much will actually change." Daisy lied. Everything had changed for Nova. The possibility remained that Bobbi would sell her instead of taking her under his care. The potential for a worse life lay before Nova if Bobbi sold her. Some of the pimps out there were way worse. Daisy knew that firsthand.

Nova nodded.

"How 'bout I get you a glass of water and a snack. You'll need to regain your strength."

The girl nodded. This wasn't the first time Bobbi had called Ronan over to help, and it wasn't the first time Ronan had brought Daisy along to make sure the girls were staying in pocket.

Daisy went downstairs to the kitchen. Bobbi's and Ronan's voices resonated through the wall between the kitchen and office. The door was mostly closed but not enough to contain their words.

She set about her task of making a tray of food from what she could find in the fridge and pantry. She tried not to eavesdrop, but they were loud.

"Put away the gun, Bobbi. That's not gonna solve anything right now." Ronan was angry. "What I can't figure out is why you guys were so stupid to up and take a local girl."

"You've done it before. Lily—"

"Lily was working for me for months before she moved in. I didn't snatch her from a public place. This has to be the most moronic thing you two have ever done. And it got Santiago killed."

"I don't understand how the cops found him."

"Not just cops, stupid. The FBI. You need to make sure you burn any connections you have to him, so they don't come knocking on your door. They find that girl here, I won't come help you. You'll be on your own."

"They ain't going to find us here. It was probably a fluke they found him."

"Or one of your girls is out of pocket."

"Never."

"You better be sure. Daisy's up there patching up your stupidity. She'll find out if any of them are out of line."

Daisy's chest burned. She was the girl out of pocket, yet she was supposed to question the other girls. What had she done?

Chapter Eighteen

Saturday mid-morning, Jacq shifted Harper on her hip and knocked on Aliza's front door. After taking some time off yesterday, the team had agreed to meet at the office for a few hours today to see if they could identify the mystery woman. Aliza had offered for her cop boyfriend and niece to babysit while the women went to work, and Jacq was grateful to be able to give Rachel a day off.

Aliza opened the front door and invited Jacq and Harper into the family room, where a boy, probably six-years-old with a lightsaber in hand, jumped off the couch in full Jedi mode.

"Ryland!" Aliza turned to Jacq. "That's my nephew. The girls are on their way down."

A handsome, sandy-haired man dressed in flannel turned the corner from the kitchen. "You must be Jacq." He offered his hand. "Welcome to Knoxville."

She shook it. "Thanks. This is Harper."

Harper buried her head against Jacq's shoulder. "It's okay, kiddo. This is Mr. Gabe."

Ryland came over and tugged on Harper's pant leg. "Wanna play Star Wars?"

Without lifting her head, she shook it.

"I have other cool toys we can play with. My baby sister has a lot of toys too. Maybe you'd like those better. She has dolls."

A ten-year-old girl came down the stairs with a toddler on her hip.

Aliza said, "This is Caroline and Mia."

The older girl handed the baby to Gabe and reached for Harper. "I'm Caroline. Wanna go play?"

Harper lifted her head slightly and considered Caroline.

Caroline took a doll Ryland offered and held it up to Harper. "Do you like dolls?"

Harper nodded and squirmed from Jacq's arms.

Jacq laughed. "That's more like it. Sorry, Gabe. I don't know what that's about."

"You two have had a crazy first week. Can't say I blame her." The little one wriggled out of Gabe's arms and toddled over to the other kids. "See, we'll be fine."

Jacq and Aliza said their goodbyes and left for the office. Once in the car, Jacq asked, "How long have you had custody of the kids?"

"Five months."

"That's all? Wow."

"It's been a whirlwind, that's for sure, but I couldn't have done it without Gabe and his family. And Dylan and Gio—those two—rocks in my tempestuous world."

While they rode to the office, Aliza shared her story about how she'd met Gabe and got connected with the FBI in Knoxville.

"That's crazy." Jacq pulled into the field office's parking lot. "No wonder you are all so close. Traumatic experiences will do that."

"For sure. So much so that Gabe and I are starting to talk marriage."

"Yay! That's exciting."

The women giggled and gushed about wedding ideas as they entered the building. But when they walked into the office, the weight of the case planted their feet back on the ground.

"There they are." Matt raised his hand to the pair of women.

"Teenagers are easier to leave than little kids, Matt." Aliza tossed her backpack on her chair.

"Especially when said teenager lives with his mother."

Jacq stopped on her path to her desk and spun toward Matt. "Teenager? How have I worked with you for a week, and you haven't mentioned having a kid?"

Matt shrugged. "Guess teenagers aren't as fun to talk about as three-year-olds."

"Anyone else have any secrets I should know?"

Dylan didn't look up from his desk. That was odd. He normally had a smile for her.

Everyone else shook their heads. Jacq knew better—everyone has secrets—but left it alone.

She set her bag down and turned to the team. "Where are we with our mystery woman?"

Matt lifted his phone in the air. "Ready to go. We've got full access to the store's surveillance. I've sent it to all of you and divided up how we should comb through it."

"Awesome. Let's dig in. We were in the cosmetics section, and there are cameras on every aisle there. We'll have an ID by noon."

One o'clock in the afternoon had rolled around, and Dylan was still searching the footage for Jacq's mystery woman. Oh, they had found Harper and Jacq. And he felt bad for Jacq. She had bit her lip as the whole team watched Harper scurry away from her. What must have felt like an eternity for Jacq was in reality only fifteen seconds. But not one member of the team gave her a hard time. A stupid jab had come to his mind, but thankfully he had squashed it before it reached his lips. He didn't mean it and would never dream of hurting her. That's why he'd kept himself from looking at her for the last three hours.

When Harper was talking to the woman, all they could see was her wrist, nothing more—not a shoe or her hair or anything. They watched all the footage from the surrounding aisles and were fairly sure they identified her. Only one person wore a dress in that part of Walmart on Thursday night. But she didn't go down the brightly lit cosmetic aisles, and when they could spot her on camera, she had her head down, stick-straight black hair falling in her face.

Dylan's eyes were going cross from staring at the screen, hunting for any other points where she showed up on security. There. "I found her again."

Jacq jumped up from her desk and came over to Dylan's. She hovered entirely too close to him.

He swallowed. The scent of mangoes distracted him.

"Where is she?"

Shaking his mind free, he snapped back to it. "Here." He played the clip. "She almost looks up."

"Those sunglasses. There's no way, even if she looked directly at the camera—"

"Which she doesn't—"

"We'll never get a facial match."

Jacq deflated next to him.

How he longed to draw her into a hug.

Another lead that was a complete bust.

Gio spoke up from across the room. "She did pay for the shampoo. Went through self-checkout and paid cash. This girl knows how to hide herself."

"Dylan," Aliza said, "take a screenshot of the best angle you have. I'll try to compile what we've seen of her."

"Sure, but it's not clear." Dylan took the screenshot and sent it to Aliza.

Jacq turned to Gio. "Nothing more from checkout?"

"Nope. She hid her face very well."

Jacq shuffled back to her desk, leaving a wake in Dylan's emotions as she walked away. His interaction with Melanie yesterday had left him questioning everything, and that had led to disturbed sleep. He'd tried reading his Bible. He'd tried to workout. And he'd tried to sleep some more, but he didn't know what to do with himself. He needed to resolve in his heart that Jacq was truly off-limits.

He refocused on searching for the woman again. Of course, they weren't one hundred percent sure this was the woman. What if it had been someone else?

Sabrina pulled out a large whiteboard easel and uncapped a marker. "Okay, let's profile her. What do we know?" Sabrina wrote the obvious things on the board: Black hair. Medium height. Thin.

Matt said, "Her jewelry looks expensive."

"She's dressed like a working girl. Not too many housewives go to Walmart in a tight skirt and heels," Jacq added.

Gio nodded. "Good at hiding. Used to being in the shadows."

Dylan leaned back in his chair. "I wonder if she's the same woman who called the tip line."

Sabrina nodded. "I was thinking the same thing."

Jacq tapped her pen on her desk. "I wonder if she'll risk a third contact?"

"Why?" Dylan locked eyes with Jacq for the first time today. "Why would she risk it? If she's this good at hiding in Walmart—"

"And she's scared," Gio said. "She bolted as soon as she handed Harper that note. She did not want to talk to you."

Dylan nodded. "I think it's really important we keep her help on the DL as long as possible. If the wrong person finds out she's helped the FBI, she could wind up dead."

Jacq shoved the half-eaten slice of pizza on the corner of her desk until it dropped into the trashcan. They were done. Not a single angle left to investigate. Devastated didn't even begin to describe how she felt. Her first case in the new city, and it was a bust. But more than that, Marrissa was still out there. She could be anywhere in the world by now. If Santiago had sold her ... or she could be trapped in a basement somewhere starving to death because her captor wasn't coming back. *Lord, what are we to do?*

Aliza's attempt at a composite hadn't gotten them anywhere. They had the woman's head and nose. That was it. With no eyes or chin, the woman looked like a blob of hair that could be anyone.

She caught Aliza's eye and nodded toward the door.

Aliza nodded in return. They were both ready to go. If only Dylan would look at her. He had been avoiding eye contact most of the day, and it was driving her mad.

Aliza came over to Jacq's desk. "I need to run down to the lab and follow-up on something for Gabe. Meet you in the parking lot?"

"Sure."

Aliza told everyone else goodbye and left.

Jacq took her time gathering her things, hoping Dylan would give some indication he was headed out too, but he was still staring at his screen.

Gio, Matt, and Sabrina said goodbye. Jacq waved, but Dylan barely raised his hand in response.

Jacq left the room without another word.

The others were all entering the elevator when she turned into the hallway. She acted like she was going toward the breakroom and waved nonchalantly to her team as the elevator doors closed.

She didn't go to the breakroom. Instead, she inched down the hall.

Why was she doing this to herself? Why did she want to see him and talk to him so badly? She was being unreasonable, but something tugged in her heart, almost yearned for Dylan. Although, she needed to remember he was Chad's brother. Who knew what Chad had said about her to Dylan? It wasn't like she had had a bad relationship with Chad, but he clearly didn't think very highly of her. Maybe Dylan talked to Chad about her, and Chad told him to stay away? She leaned up against the wall next to the elevator. This was stupid. She'd see him on Monday.

She pushed the button for the elevator. A moment later the doors opened, and she stepped inside. As she pressed the button for the first floor, Dylan appeared down the hall. She stuck her foot in the door to hold it for him. His long-awaited smile appeared.

He stepped in and went to the back of the box and leaned against the wall, setting his bag down on the floor. She took a step closer and shoved her hands in her pockets so she wouldn't draw Dylan into her arms. That was all she wanted to do. Instead, she asked, "Are you okay?"

He shrugged and still didn't make eye contact.

She wanted to grab him and shake him. *Talk to me.* She pulled her right hand out of her pocket and reached out to him and rested it on his arm.

Finally, he looked up at her. His rueful smile drew her closer. "Seriously, are you? What's going on today? Is something going on? Did I do something?"

His sad attempt at a grin vanished. "No. Absolutely not. You've done nothing, I'm … I don't know …"

"You know you can talk to me, right?"

"I do. And I'll be fine, really. I'm just off."

"I think we all are."

"So true. Going to the batting cage tonight. That should help relieve a little stress."

"Sounds like fun."

"Yeah, should be. Going with Chad. It's one of the few things we really enjoy doing together."

The sound of Chad's name seized her heart. "Oh … good."

The doors of the elevator opened. They walked out side by side in silence.

Once outside, Dylan asked, "Any big plans for the rest of this weekend?"

"Nope, nothing more than lots of snuggles with Harper. I'd love you to meet her sometime soon."

"I'd love to meet her too."

Jacq's heart skipped. She couldn't wait to see what they thought of each other.

"Have a good weekend."

"You too, Dylan."

She wanted to hug him, but he didn't move toward her, so she simply strolled to her car to wait for Aliza. Quickly, her longing for

Dylan shifted to excitement to see Harper. It was so hard to leave her every day, but it made the time they did spend together that much more special. Jacq tried hard to keep the weekends and off times focused on Harper. And tonight, she was going to intentionally forget about Dylan as much as her heart would let her and focus on her most precious gift.

Dylan swung the bat. *Crack.* The wood made contact with the ball.

"Nice hit!" Chad said.

The pitching machine loosed the final ball. Dylan hit it as well. He stepped back, and Chad turned off the machine. He sighed. He couldn't get Jacq out of his head. Everything in him wanted to see her. He had been with her all afternoon at work, but it wasn't enough. And he really regretted not drawing her into his arms. They ached to hold her again.

"You all right?" Chad asked.

"Yeah, I'm fine."

"Not believing you. It's a girl, isn't it?"

His lips curled up on one side. At the thought of Jacq, he couldn't help it.

"It is. I knew it. Is it serious?"

"We aren't dating. She recently started working on our team. But I'm not sure anything could ever come from it."

"Why not?"

Dylan took a deep breath. He wasn't about to tell his brother he was quickly falling for his ex-girlfriend. Instead, he shook his head. "I'm not sure I'm her type."

"Oh, come on, Dylan, give yourself a little credit. What woman wouldn't want a strong FBI agent?"

Dylan looked at his brother. The successful one. How could Chad ever understand what was going on in his heart, when he didn't even understand?

"Tell me about her."

Dylan spun the bat in his hands and chuckled to himself. Could he describe Jacq without giving away her identity? "She's kind and passionate. Her love for the Lord is apparent in everything she does and says. She's confident, maybe even a little stubborn. She's been through some tough things but clearly has come out stronger on the other side."

"She sounds amazing. Pretty too?"

"Oh yeah."

"Then what's the problem?"

"It's only been a week."

"So? Sometimes it doesn't take long to know you've met 'the one,' if you will. When you know, you just know. Why do I get the sense you're afraid?"

Dylan shrugged.

"You've got to stop living in fear."

Dylan's stomach caught in his throat. He wanted to balk at his brother for calling him fearful, but he couldn't. Chad was right. He was afraid. Always had been. Afraid he wouldn't live up to others' expectations, afraid no one would notice him in his brother's wake. Being two years younger than the man who did everything right the first time was not easy, especially since Dylan couldn't seem to ever do anything right. Especially after Melanie, he was afraid he'd mess it all up. Again.

"Seriously, if you like the girl, why not go for it?"

"It's more complicated."

"How so? Are you still beating yourself up for what happened with Melanie?"

Dylan let out a dry laugh. "She showed up on my doorstep yesterday."

"What? Why on earth?"

"Claimed she wanted to try us again. I questioned her motives … and …"

"Let it go. She wasn't right for you. And even if you said the same thing that ruined it years ago, you've grown since then. The fact she got along with mom should have been your first indication it wouldn't work with her."

"So you think I'm better off with a girl who doesn't get along with mom?" A spark of hope ignited in his heart.

"For sure. It would be interesting, but I can't imagine the perfect girl for you getting along with mom."

"What kind of girl do you see in my future then?"

"Spunky. Nontraditional. You need someone who loves adventure as much as you do. Someone who's not going to simply sit on the couch and enjoy a cup of tea. Someone who'll give you a run for your money in every area. That would fit you. And mom would *not* approve."

Dylan smiled. Chad was describing Jacq, and he didn't even know it.

"I take it the girl from work fits the bill."

"You have no idea."

"Then go for it."

Dylan felt like he was going to burst with excitement. His brother's encouragement was exactly what he needed. He was tempted to tell Chad it was Jacq, but based on her reaction to Chad being in the same building the other day, he was pretty sure Jacq wasn't ready for Chad to know. But now the big question: text her tonight or wait until tomorrow?

Chapter Nineteen

Jacq shifted Harper on her hip and strolled up the sidewalk to the church. She had tried a few other churches since she'd moved to Knoxville, but none of them had felt like home. They weren't bad, and she was willing to go back to all but one of them.

"Welcome!" A man held the door open.

"Thanks." They entered, and her eyes darted around the large foyer with its modern, craftsman-style architecture. Signs hung from the ceiling and pointed her to the children's area and the sanctuary. It was easy to see where she needed to go despite all the bodies filling the lobby. She glanced around again.

Her eyes landed on a tall, handsome man. Dylan.

He waved at her. Her heart bounced as if on a trampoline. But then it froze. She scanned the area around Dylan. She strode toward him, keeping herself aware of who else was around.

A huge smile took over his face. "No worries," Dylan said when he came within ear shot, "they don't go here. Just me."

She released her breath.

Dylan laughed. "So my family really makes you that uncomfortable."

"No, well, maybe." She gave him a cheesy grin that was all teeth. "I don't look forward to that awkward moment I know will happen if I run into them. 'So good to … see you?' I don't know. I think it'll be weird."

"Probably. But you're not going to run into them here. They all still go to that stuffy little church down the road."

"It's not that bad. I kind of liked it the few times I visited. It's small and cozy. And I love singing hymns."

"Yet you're here? This isn't exactly a traditional church."

"I said I liked it, not that it was my speed. I prefer a place where it's not noticed if I'm gone for a week. I hate all the 'where were you's,' especially if I was working on a case."

"My sentiments exactly. I like that about a larger church. Here it's simply a 'we missed seeing you.'"

"Right! Because you never know if they went to another service."

"Exactly." He touched Harper's shoulder. "This must be Harper."

"Yep."

"Nice to meet you, Miss H."

Harper tucked herself into Jacq's shoulder. "It's okay, Sweetie. This is mommy's friend, Mr. Dylan."

"You want to take her to the children's area?"

"I do."

"I'll take you over there."

"Thanks." She walked along side Dylan toward the area designated for children Harper's age. Dylan stayed with them while she got Harper checked in. As soon as the little girl saw the dolls and other toys, she took off to play. Jacq turned and strolled toward the sanctuary with Dylan.

"That was easier than I expected. With the way she acted toward me, I thought she'd put up a bit of a fight."

"No, she acts shy at first, but she's really quite friendly. And there's nothing gonna keep that girl from playing with baby dolls." She smiled up at Dylan; the one he returned nearly knocked her off her feet.

Once in the sanctuary, Dylan asked, "Where would you like to sit?"

"I prefer close to the front, center."

"Sounds good as long as it's not too close."

They made their way up toward the front and found seats on the aisle with two minutes left on the countdown flashing across the screen.

Dylan seemed different today than he had been yesterday afternoon.

She looked over at him. "Did you have fun at the batting cage last night?"

"I did. Hit some good balls. In fact, I hit more than Chad."

"Nice!"

He laughed, sending her heart soaring. "We had a good conversation too."

"Did you tell him you're working with me?"

"Uh, no."

"No?"

"We did talk about you, though. He just didn't know we were talking about you."

"Oh really? What did you say?"

"That there was an amazing new girl working at the FBI." He raised his eyebrows at her.

She bit her bottom lip, and her cheeks grew warm. She shook her head. The worship leader stepped up to the microphone, and Jacq was able to relax.

"Did you have a good Saturday evening?" Dylan asked as they stood at the worship leader's invitation.

"I did. Harper and I had dinner with Aliza, Gabe, and the kids. Then we went home and watched a princess movie until Harper fell asleep. I read for about five minutes before I was out too."

"Awesome."

They turned their attention to worship. Dylan's voice filled the air next to her. She glanced at him. They weren't even into the chorus yet, and he was already raising his hands. Such a stark difference to his brother who was always so stoic during worship. Jacq closed her eyes and lifted her voice and hands in worship of her Lord.

When the service was over, Dylan turned to Jacq. It had been delightful to sit next to her. They had traded a few quips during the sermon. Something about leaning in close to whisper a stupid joke, then having her cover her mouth to keep from giggling out loud made him fall even harder than he already had.

He let her go ahead of him into the aisle and touched her back. If he wasn't losing his mind, it seemed like she moved slower and might have even pressed back into his hand. Maybe he should tell her what he was feeling. Would that be out of line? Was it too soon? The whole sermon had been about trusting God's timing. *Help me to trust.*

They shuffled out into the lobby. Gio called to them through the crowd of congregants. "Hey Dylan. Jacq, I didn't realize you were checking out our church this weekend."

Jacq tucked a tress of red hair behind her ear. "Didn't realize you guys went here. Aliza and Gabe almost had me convinced to go to their church, but it turns out I visited there a couple of weeks ago."

"Thoughts?" Gio asked.

"It's a nice church too, but this one seems a good fit. Theirs was a bit smaller than I prefer."

Dylan stuck his thumb in his pocket to keep from touching her. "Surprised you didn't meet them if it's so small."

"They weren't there that Sunday, but it turns out I met Gabe's parents."

Gio folded his sermon notes smaller than they already were and held them up. "Nothing like a sermon that hits you between the eyes."

Dylan chuckled. "You could say that."

Jacq raised an eyebrow.

"Gio here's been looking for Miss Right. What's your hope—eight kids?"

Gio shook his head in faux irritation.

Dylan knew he'd hit the mark.

"Probably not eight, but a family, yes. And I have complete faith in God's timing. I'll meet her when God has her ready. I get this sense that something more has to happen for her, whoever she is, before He can bring us together."

"Wow." Jacq squeezed Gio's arm. "I can hear the faith in your voice, and it's encouraging."

Gio nodded. "Thanks. I hope it rubs off on this guy." Gio looked him in the eyes. "Trust God's timing."

Dylan's neck warmed. If only he knew what God was doing.

A few guys Dylan had been in Bible studies with joined them and started chatting.

Jacq tapped his elbow. "I have to get Harper. I'll see you later." She pivoted to Gio and said goodbye.

Before Dylan could say another word, she disappeared into the crowd. He wasn't ready for their time to be over. He was about to go after her, but one of the guys asked him a question, and he lost his opportunity.

They chatted for a few more minutes, but Dylan was barely able to engage. He wanted to see if Jacq would like to grab lunch.

"Go find her." Gio grinned.

"Maybe this isn't God's timing."

"You won't know if you don't ask."

"Point taken. I'll see you tomorrow." Dylan turned toward the kids' ministry wing.

Jacq's heart raced as she unlocked the door to her apartment. Harper raced around her legs, and Dylan stood next to her, arms full of Panera Bread sandwiches and mac and cheese. Dylan had sought her out before she left to ask what they were doing for lunch, but Harper would need a nap soon, so she invited him to her place. He said he'd grab something for them. She couldn't imagine a better Sunday. Also didn't hurt that she enjoyed Dylan's church, and the sermon was exactly what she needed to hear. She diverted her eyes from his intense gaze and pushed the door open.

"Now, I wasn't planning this, so I can't promise the apartment is terribly clean. You're going to see our real life. I'm definitely not your mother." Jacq cringed at the sight before her eyes: Harper's toys scattered everywhere, mail stacked on the counter, and at least two days of dishes in the sink.

He followed her in and set the bags of food on the breakfast bar. Harper ran past her and into the living room. Dylan took her shoulders in his hands. "And for that I am grateful."

She thought she was going to melt into his arms. Their eyes locked; she couldn't move. Her heart pounded in her chest, desire rising.

Thump. Harper started crying.

"Harper!" She ran into the living room where her daughter sat on the ground holding her head. Jacq scooped the little one up. "Let me see it." She moved Harper's hand and revealed a red bump forming.

Dylan came over next to them. "She okay?"

"Must have run into the coffee table. Nothing too bad." Jacq looked down at Harper. "Can we get some ice?"

Harper nodded. Jacq stood with the girl in her arms and went to the kitchen. She retrieved an icepack from the fridge. After a few minutes with the icepack and plenty more kisses, Harper was ready to roll again.

"Let's eat, Harp. Jump up in your chair."

As Jacq pulled plates out of the cupboard, Harper got into her seat with Dylan's assistance. Jacq's heart flooded with joy. Those two were taking to each other quite nicely.

Lord, if something is going to happen with Dylan and me, please help Harper learn to love him too. Jacq stopped halfway to the table. The way that prayer came out implied that *she* was already learning to love him herself. She smiled at him and resumed her way to the table.

Harper ate her mac and cheese quickly and ran off to play while Jacq and Dylan continued to eat.

"She's adorable." Dylan said as he watched Harper.

Jacq followed his gaze to her daughter. "Thanks. I think she's pretty great. Seriously can't imagine life without her. You always hear parents say such stuff, but that's because it's true."

"Awesome."

Jacq took a tentative breath. She wanted to dive a little deeper with Dylan. "You ever imagine yourself with a family?"

His rich brown eyes sparkled. "Always. I very much hope to have a family one day."

Good answer.

"You ever see yourself having more kids?"

"I think so. I adore being a mom, most rewarding thing ever, but it's hard to leave her. Never thought I'd say this, but some days I wish I could stay home with her. But I also love being an FBI agent, so I don't know about not working, but I would like more children."

He smiled, then his brow furrowed.

"What?" she asked.

"I'm not sure how to ask this question, but you were pregnant during the fire, weren't you?"

She sighed. "I was. I didn't know it, though."

"Wow, so Harper never met her dad."

"Nope, Sean never even knew about her. I actually found out in the hospital."

"I can't imagine."

"She's a miracle. The doctors were surprised I didn't lose her with all my body went through, but she's a fighter, even from the very beginning."

"Like her mom."

She looked off to the right and back and nodded. "Yeah."

Harper started fussing.

"Must be naptime."

"Okay, I can leave." Dylan stood.

Jacq reached out and took his arm. "No, no. Don't feel like you need to leave. I mean, if you need to that's fine, but I'd like you to stay."

"I can do that." He sat back down with a huge grin.

Her heart flipped. She padded into the living room. "K, Harper, it's time for a nap."

"No nap." She threw a toy across the room.

"Absolutely no throwing toys. That is unacceptable." Jacq knelt in front of her and lifted Harper to her feet. "Go pick up that toy right now."

Harper stomped across the floor and retrieved the toy, then slammed it into the basket where Jacq pointed.

"Now tell Mr. Dylan night-night."

Harper's expression changed, and she ran over to Dylan and threw her arms around his waist. Jacq melted.

"Nigh' nigh.'" She ran to her bedroom.

Dylan's face glowed. He was equally taken with the little girl.

"I'll be back in a moment." Jacq followed Harper into her room and tucked her in for her nap.

When she came back out, Dylan was in the bathroom, so she leaned her elbow on the back of her grandpa's old wing-backed chair and checked her email on her phone. A moment later, Dylan came up behind her and put his hands on her shoulders. He started massaging her tense muscles. She relaxed into it. Exactly what she needed, and not just the massage. The warmth and comfort of his hands soothed her weary soul.

You don't deserve him.

That's a lie.

It'll never work.

Another lie… Jesus, speak truth in my heart. But could this work? Only you know that. Give us wisdom.

She reached up and placed her hands on Dylan's, stopping him.

"What are we doing?" She dropped her hands and slowly turned, hoping he wouldn't remove his.

He didn't. He took a deep breath and brushed a strand of hair out of her face. Her heart skyrocketed.

Dylan's face was tight and pensive. "I'm not sure."

"Join me on the couch?"

He nodded. She fought the urge to take his hand as they wandered around the chair.

Jacq meandered to the far end of the couch and kicked off her shoes. She tucked her legs under herself and hugged a throw pillow.

"Can I ask you about yesterday?"

He scrunched up his eyebrows and tilted his head. "I guess. What about it?"

"What was going on with you? I don't know if I was imagining it, but it seemed like you were pulling away. If so, why? And what's with the change today?"

"You really don't like beating around the bush, do you?"

"I've learned the hard way that not being honest and asking hard questions leads to wasted time and false hope."

Again, his look questioned her.

She smiled. "Chad. If I had asked the questions on my mind, we would have quickly realized we weren't going to work out. But instead we dated for eight months. Time I could have devoted to school or building relationships with other girls in my dorm, like Morgan."

"Fair enough."

"So what was with your strange behavior?"

Chapter Twenty

Dylan half laughed at Jacq's persistence and shook his head. "Honestly?"

"I wouldn't ask if I didn't want honesty."

"Of course." His heart sank. Being straightforward with his emotions wasn't something that came easy, especially with the woman he liked.

She scooted a little closer.

"I'm not really sure how to explain." His emotions were a jumbled mess.

"You can trust me," she said in a soft whisper.

He leaned his head back. That was exactly it. Did he trust himself to trust her? What if he didn't? He turned a little more to face her. "I have trust issues."

He expected her to make some comment, but she just waited. She was so patient.

"I guess I started letting my fear get the best of me. I'm afraid I'll mess up what we have going on here, whatever that is."

"How so?"

"Well, about three years ago, I was in a fairly serious relationship. At least on the outside it was serious, but… I look back on it now, and I know I never really let Melanie into my heart. But that wasn't the worst. I didn't trust her. It was almost as if I expected her to hurt me. So when I found out she had been talking to an ex-boyfriend, I immediately assumed she had cheated on me. She insisted she didn't, that it was innocent. I didn't believe her. But I made it worse."

Jacq sat there silently, concern, not judgment, on her face.

"I also accused her of only wanting to date me to get connected to my family. To which she completely lost it. It was a nasty break-up."

"Was there any truth to your accusations?"

"Not to the cheating. The family part—I don't know. She never denied it. Even when she stopped by Friday, and I accused her of the same thing all over again."

Jacq's eyebrows rose then scrunched pensively. "So you didn't trust her, but maybe you had good reason."

"Either way, I handled it all wrong. It's happened a few too many times—women have struck up a relationship with me because they think my family has some clout and they want in on it."

"You don't have to worry about that with me. I like you *in spite of* your family."

His heart soared. She liked him. His words were gone.

"Dylan"—Jacq reached forward and place her hand on his forearm—"that's the past. You've already shown you trust me. I can't believe how deep we've gone with each other in barely a week."

Hope raged in his heart. He was falling hard for this redheaded beauty. "I can barely believe it myself." He wrapped his arm around Jacq and drew her closer. She sank in next to him, resting her head on his chest.

"Are we going to get in trouble at work?"

"Nah. Warren married a fellow agent, and they have the best marriage, so he doesn't care as long as we do our jobs."

She snuggled a little tighter against him. Warmth filled his body. Joy. He was actually happy.

He kicked off his shoes and put his heels up on the coffee table. A photo on the end table caught his eye. He grabbed it. The picture showed a college-aged Jacq and another girl with curly, dark brown hair. The woman's skin gave away what was probably a Middle Eastern heritage. "Who's this?"

She raised her head. "Morgan."

"She's beautiful. Looks so happy."

"She was then. We had the best day at the homecoming events. This was a couple of weeks before she started dating the guy who trafficked her."

"I'm sorry."

"I wish life didn't have to be so hard. Bringing up a little girl in the midst of all of this is torturous. I have to keep myself from thinking 'what if' because I'll drive myself crazy."

"It's hard enough having a little sister."

"How is Scarlet?"

Dylan ran his thumb up and down Jacq's arm. "She's good. I never got to tell you why I became an agent."

"That was a sudden shift." She moved to look at his face better.

"Not really. Scarlet is why."

Grief filled Jacq's eyes. "No. What happened?"

"During her freshman year, when I was a senior, an older guy from school started paying a lot of attention to her. It made me uneasy, but I knew she could handle herself. One day in late April I was supposed to give her a ride home, but she was done early, and I ran late.

"I expected to see Scarlet sitting outside waiting by my car. She wasn't there. I felt sick. I had let my baby sister down. I looked frantically all around but couldn't find her anywhere. I started to freak."

Dylan fingered a tress of Jacq's hair. "A few of her friends said they last saw her with that older guy who'd been flirting with her. In the back of my mind, I heard a voice yelling that my mother was going to kill me, but that was drowned out quickly by my heart pounding intensely in my ears." His thundering pulse echoed still today. He had to pause a moment to calm it.

He continued, "At that moment I knew my sister was going to be raped if I didn't find her. I couldn't find her. I didn't find her. Not for a few hours, but it was too late. When she finally came home, she denied that anything happened, but I could tell she wasn't her same happy-go-lucky self."

"Oh, Dylan."

"Eventually she told me the story. She had finished practice early, so the guy—I still can't bear to say his name—had offered her a ride home. He said he needed to stop by a friend's house on the way. She was going to wait in the car, but it was hot, and the guys offered her some lemonade. She went to the backyard with them, refusing to go inside the house.

"Scarlet could take care of herself, but there's only so much a small-framed fifteen-year-old can do against two older boys bent on evil. Plus, they dosed her. She's not sure with what, but she barely remembered what happened afterward. They gang raped my little sister."

Jacq covered her mouth. And she looked as sick as he felt.

"The guys had a plan, and since my dad was starting his political career, running for the school board, they had immense leverage over her. They planned to traffic her. They taunted her. They put her underwear in her locker. Left her cryptic notes. She devolved into depression and anxiety. She desperately tried to keep up the cover for Mom and Dad. But then the guys initiated the next phase of their plan. The trafficking."

Fifteen Years Earlier

Seventeen-year-old Dylan stretched. While working on his homework, he'd fallen asleep at the desk in his room. Only a few more weeks of high school. He picked up the sketch of a tattoo he'd been dreaming about. His mom would kill him. After tucking the paper into the back of his physics book, he slid the text and spiral into his backpack.

Something rattled against the side of the house near Scarlet's room. He should check on her. She was struggling so much since the day she'd gone to that guy's house. Dylan wished she'd talk to him and tell him what happened. He had a pretty good idea, and it made him want to shoot them.

He eased his door open and peeked down the hallway. All clear. He crossed the hall and gently rapped on Scarlet's door. No answer.

He turned the knob as slowly as he could, knowing it could squeak. He didn't want to wake his parents.

Scarlet wasn't in her bed. The window was open, letting the cool night breeze fill the girly room.

"Scarlet?" Nothing.

The rattling came from outside her window. Dylan crossed the room. When he was about three feet from the window, Scarlet's dark hair appeared.

"Scarlet."

Her hand slipped.

He rushed over, caught her arm, and helped her climb in. "What are you doing?"

Her face was streaked with tears, eyes puffy, and nose red.

Dylan drew her into his arms, and they sank to the floor. He let her cry for a long time before he questioned her again.

"Talk to me, Scarlet."

She told him what happened after school a week earlier and over the last few days. "I can't believe I let them—"

"That is not your fault. Why were you out tonight, though?"

She pushed away and grabbed a pillow off her bed. She hugged it. If it had been a living thing, she would have suffocated it. "They called and threatened to tell Dad if I didn't meet them at the road."

"Did they touch you again?"

She looked down at the floor. "Worse."

"What?" Dylan clenched his fists.

"Shh. You'll wake Mom and Dad."

"Scarlet, I can't sit by and let them—"

She put her hand on his arm. "I know. But I don't know what to do."

"You need to go to Dad—"

"No, I can't. It would kill him. And what if they took pictures?"

"What happened tonight?"

She didn't look at him.

"Scarlet?"

"They took me to a party and locked me in a bedroom." She reached in her pocket and pulled out a small wad of cash. "They said this was my cut." She let it fall to the floor.

Bile filled Dylan's mouth. Pizza didn't taste good the second time.

Sobs caused her body to convulse.

He slid closer to her and wrapped his arms around her. His baby sister had been violated, and he hadn't been there to protect her. "How many?"

"Four. Five. I'm not sure."

His whole body shook as fire raged through his veins. Someone had to pay.

After an hour of crying, Scarlet finally fell asleep against his chest. He lifted her into her bed and covered her with her blanket, which, according to her, was periwinkle.

He couldn't let this happen again. But what could he do?

He went to bed pondering a plan.

The next day a reckless idea took shape in his mind. He had stayed up late on a Friday night doing homework so he could go out with his friends on Saturday, but he didn't go. Instead, as soon as his parents went to the hardware store, he sneaked into their bedroom. His dad kept a shotgun under his bed and a pistol in his nightstand.

Dylan chose the shotgun. Dad was less likely to notice it was missing. Dylan hid it under his own bed, then proceeded to clean his room so his mom wouldn't come in and find the gun.

Scarlet spent most of the day in bed. And taking showers. Three of them. If their mom had been home, questions may have been asked.

Friday rolled around again. Chad came home from college, and they had a big dinner to celebrate.

Scarlet and Dylan stayed up watching a movie when everyone else went to bed. But Dylan didn't watch the movie. He watched his sister, sitting on the couch and shaking in fear. When the movie was over, they went upstairs together. They had reached the end of the hallway by their bedroom doors when Scarlet's phone rang.

Tears brimmed in her eyes.

He went into her room with her and closed the door.

She answered. It was them. Meet by the road in ten minutes. She hung up and looked at Dylan. "I can't."

"And you won't. Stay inside. I'll take care of it."

"But—"

"Trust me."

"I do."

He pulled her to him and kissed her forehead. He would do anything to protect her. And right now, going to jail was the better alternative to letting any man touch her again. He had prayed about it all week and was pretty sure God was okay with the deal. Not that Dylan had truly listened for an answer.

"I love you, sis."

"I love you too."

He grabbed the loaded shotgun and climbed out her window.

Their house sat back on a five-acre wooded lot. Dylan wound through the trees toward the road. Adrenaline coursed through his body making it impossible to come up with a plan of attack. Should he shoot them and not ask any questions? Should he make them get out of the car or shoot them while they were still inside?

Scarlet screamed in the distance.

He ran toward her voice. Why had she come outside?

The two boys had cornered Scarlet in a small clearing. The light of the half-moon silhouetted the three figures.

Dylan lifted the gun. "Get away from her now!"

The boys turned around laughing, but as soon as they saw Dylan, they stopped and raised their hands.

"Hey, look, man." One of the guys took a step toward Dylan. Dylan aimed the shotgun at him. "Scarlet, go home."

"Dylan!"

"Don't argue with me. They won't touch you again."

She ran back toward the house.

"Okay, man. We won't touch her again, just let us go."

"And you won't get paid to let anyone else touch her either." Dylan racked the gun. "I'm not sure why I shouldn't shoot you. Make sure you can't harm any other girls."

The other guy let out a nervous laugh. "You aren't going to shoot us."

Dylan aimed at the ground between them and fired a shot.

The boom echoed off the trees and made Dylan's ears ring.

"We swear. We'll leave her alone." They both took off running, but not toward the street.

Dylan knew the shot had awakened his father. Hopefully, Scarlet had made it back inside.

The guys ran onto the driveway. Dylan came out behind them.

His dad, pistol in hand, and Chad, phone to ear, stood on the front porch.

A squad car came down the driveway.

The boys put their hands on their heads. Dylan pointed the shotgun at the ground in front of them.

His dad came forward. "What are you boys up to tonight?"

"Sorry, sir. We shouldn't have been sneaking around."

"I found them coming toward the house." Not a complete lie.

His dad kept his eyes focused on the boys. "Is this true?"

Dylan's heart raced.

"Yes, sir."

The cops came up to Dylan's side. One pointed his gun at Dylan.

His dad lowered the gun. "That's my son."

Dylan handed the shotgun to the officer.

"Were you the one who fired the shot, Dylan?" His dad's eyes were cutting.

"Yes, but at the ground as a warning. My ears are still ringing."

The vein in his dad's forehead pulsed. He wanted to yell but was keeping it in. That was almost scarier. He turned to the boys. "What do you say?"

"It's true, sir. He didn't shoot at us."

Dylan was surprised they didn't throw him to the wolves. But they knew he'd fight back. He'd proved to them that he'd risk it all for his sister.

The officers took the boys under the charge of trespassing but let Dylan go inside with his family.

Once the policemen left, Dylan shuffled up the front walk and into the house. He prepared himself for the yelling.

His dad came up behind him and put a firm hand on his shoulder. "Sit down on the couch. Now." The intensity of his words made Dylan's insides quake.

"Why were you out there? Did you think running after them was a good idea? And stealing my gun? You know you aren't supposed to take that."

Chad sat on the piano bench.

Dylan wanted to pick up the glass coaster in front of him and chuck it at his smug face.

His mom stormed into the room in a flailing fury. "Dylan Andrew Harris, I swear if that wasn't the most stupid thing you've ever done."

He'd never seen his mom like this. She was normally the scary-quiet disciplinarian. Rarely raised her voice and even more rarely spoke with her hands, but she looked like she was swatting a swarm of juiced-up gnats.

"Chad did the right thing and called the police. What were you thinking running after them with a shotgun? What were you going to do? They were nothing more than a couple of hooligans up to a little mischief. I can't believe you would do such a thing. You're lucky you aren't in jail. I'm so disappointed in you, Dylan."

The dagger of her words drove deep into him, ripping apart the last bit of strength he had left. He'd done the right thing. Hadn't his parents taught him to stand up for his sister? Well, he had. But Chad was the hero because Dylan refused to break the promise of silence he'd made to his sister.

The yelling continued, but Dylan's still-ringing ears filtered it out. In his heart, a new mission for life began to stir. What if he became a cop and legally chased down scoundrels like those two guys who hurt girls? He'd heard that trafficking was a thing, but now it had slapped him in the face. If it was here in Knoxville, how bad was it? This wasn't Las Vegas or Atlantic City or a third-world country. This was a suburban high school in the Bible belt.

God, what do you want me to do?

After about twenty minutes, Scarlet came down the stairs. "What's going on?" She made it look like she'd been sleeping, but Dylan saw through the facade. She'd been crying.

Their mom, putting in as many jabs at Dylan as possible, told Scarlet her version of what happened.

After everyone else decided to go to bed, Dylan and Scarlet sat on the couch beside one another. Scarlet slipped her hand around Dylan's elbow. "Thank you."

"We should probably tell the truth." He patted her hand with his.

"Probably."

But they didn't.

Present Day

Jacq's heart broke for Scarlet and Dylan. But her heart also swelled with love for him. He was a true man, someone who would stand up for others, regardless of how much it put him in harm's way. He was a warrior.

Dylan's arm was still wrapped around her shoulder. She took his hand and wove her fingers between his. "Whatever happened to the boys?"

He rubbed a thumb along the side of her hand, and a satisfied look crossed his face. "After I graduated from the Academy, I worked in Richmond. We ran a sting to catch a bunch of pimps, johns, and girls. Those two guys were among the pimps. It was deeply gratifying to slap cuffs on both of them. They are still in jail doing some pretty hard time on trafficking, false imprisonment, and drug charges. They may not be in for hurting Scarlet, but they are locked away, and for that, I'm grateful."

"You never told your parents? Didn't they think Scarlet's behavior was strange? There's no way she was able to hide that much trauma."

"Somehow she managed. She started seeing a counselor in college and has since worked through much of it."

"But have you?"

His eyes narrowed.

"I see it in your expression. Your mom was harsh, even considering she didn't know the whole situation. But she doesn't understand why you became an agent."

"It doesn't matter. Regardless of what I do, I'll never be enough. I'll never measure up to Chad in her eyes."

"So what?" She let go of his hand and sat up to face him. His hand fell to her lower back, and she leaned her knees against him. "So what if you aren't what she wants you to be? Are you doing what God has called you to do? Obedience to Him is way more important than her opinion. I think even she'd agree with that."

"But am I doing what God has called me to do?"

"Only you can answer that."

He shifted slightly and stared at his lap. "I think so. I've never felt closer to the Lord than when I'm on the job"—he met her gaze—"and especially when working cases where we free people from slavery. I'm most myself and alive then."

"That's what I thought."

Withdrawing his arm from around her, he sat up and leaned his elbows on his knees. "I want nothing more than to please the Lord."

She put her hand on his back. "And you do."

"Can I ever be sure? All I know is that I've disappointed everyone in my life."

"What's that verse in Philippians? 'For it is God who works in you, giving you the desire and the power to do what pleases Him.'"

He turned his face toward her and smiled. "You *are* good for me."

She couldn't contain a giggle that inched its way up from her soul. "You're pretty good for me too."

He raised his eyebrows. "How so?"

"You're making my heart do things I didn't know it would ever be able to do again."

He reached up and brushed a strand of hair away from her face.

Desire grew inside her, but her stomach growled before she could react. "Maybe we should have a snack?"

"How are you possibly hungry after all you ate for lunch?"

She shrugged. She wasn't sure what words could describe his expression, but it made her giggle again.

Sunday afternoon, Daisy looked out the passenger-side window of Ronan's Escalade as he drove yet again to Bobbi's, dragging her along with him. She hated that he was pulling her into more than her job, but since Rose had disappeared, she was the bottom girl in his house now. She was expected to do more recruiting and help with the "business."

She wanted to ask a bunch of questions but knew it was better if she kept her mouth shut.

They passed a church with a tall white steeple. A pang in her heart nearly knocked the breath right out of her. She wished she could have gone to church this morning. She hadn't wanted that in thirteen years. But the sight of the brick building stirred something in her soul.

"Are you even listening to me?" Ronan smacked her thigh.

"I'm sorry." A list of excuses crossed her mind, but any would be worse than simply not listening.

"I said"—his irritation drew out the word—"when we get there, you are to do hair and makeup for the new girl."

"Okay." Her heart sank. What did they have planned for Marrissa?

They arrived at Bobbi's house, and Daisy went straight upstairs.

Celeste met her there. "Hey, Daisy. Thanks for coming. You're so good at these things. You have a way of making the girls feel special and getting them to relax. This girl is a pistol."

They walked down the hall toward the tower. "Do you know Bobbi's plan?"

"Auction. He's hoping to get a lofty price, seeing as how she's a virgin."

Daisy's stomach twisted. *What can I do?* She wasn't sure if she prayed the question or not. "So today is a photo shoot."

"Yep. She goes up tomorrow at six p.m." Celeste unlocked the door to the attic and let Daisy lead the way up the stairs.

At the top, a young girl with long blonde hair sat on a mattress tucked close to the slanted ceiling. She hugged her knees, eyes wide in fear.

Daisy knew her job, but something had changed when she saw this girl grabbed at the mall, and then spotted Jacqui with the FBI. It now felt wrong. Maybe it was the way they took her. Rather than a promiscuous teen getting involved with the wrong guy, this was an innocent child. It was one thing for Daisy, at thirty-two, to be in the game, but this girl was just that, a girl.

Celeste stepped up beside Daisy and pointed to the teen. "This is Halley."

"That's not my name." Her voice shook despite her obstinacy.

Celeste shook her head. "It is now." She turned back to Daisy. "Bobbi says like Halley's Comet, she's going to come and go."

Daisy nodded. "I'll take it from here. I should have her ready in about an hour or so."

"Excellent. Feel free to use my bathroom. Everything you should need is in the linen closet." Celeste turned and left.

Halley glowered up at Daisy.

"I'm not going to hurt you. My name is Daisy. I'm apparently an expert at hair and makeup. We're going to make you look like a model, which won't be hard. You're gorgeous, girl."

Halley's expression softened into confusion.

Daisy knelt in front of her, reached out, and took her hands. "Trust me, okay? Haven't you always wanted a makeover? I mean, really, what girl hasn't?"

Halley almost smiled.

"It'll be fun. And you get to leave the attic. But stick close to me as we go downstairs. Bobbi doesn't take well to girls wandering where they aren't supposed to be." Daisy stood and tugged on Halley's hands to join her. "Has Bobbi come up here since Santiago brought you home?"

She nodded.

Daisy lowered her voice and wrapped her arm around Halley's shoulders. "Did he hurt you?"

Halley shrugged.

Daisy rubbed the girl's arm. "You'll be okay." Why was it so natural to lie? Of course she wouldn't be okay. So Bobbi didn't rape her, but as soon as she was sold in the auction, someone would.

Daisy guided Halley down to Celeste's bathroom. Once there, she had Halley step into a warm shower and wash up. She probably hadn't had one since the first day here.

The uneasy feeling in Daisy's gut grew. Halley was so young she didn't even need to shave. *God, I don't know what to do, but I don't want to let this girl be sold.*

While Halley showered, Celeste dropped off some new underclothes and several outfits for Halley to choose from.

Daisy pulled out her phone and a Bluetooth speaker and turned on some music. "How's this? Or do you prefer something different?" Daisy stuck her head into the shower.

Halley tried to hide. "I like country."

"Then country it is." Daisy switched to a country station and waited for the girl to finish.

Once she was out and wrapped in a towel, Daisy had her sit on a stool in front of a large mirror and began to brush her hair.

"What other things do you like, Halley?"

"My name isn't Halley. It's Marrissa."

Daisy stopped mid-stroke and met the girl's eyes in the mirror. "I know. The guys give us nicknames to—" She was lost for words. The truth was they wanted every ounce of control over the girls, but she would get a massive beating if she stepped that far out of pocket. "To make us feel special."

"It doesn't feel special."

"I know, but it'll be okay. Halley is a pretty name, and maybe you'll get to keep it for a while."

"Your name isn't really Daisy, is it?"

"Has been for the last three years. Was Angel for years before that."

Marrissa grabbed Daisy's arm. "But what's your real name?" She turned and met her eyes face to face rather than in the mirror.

She hadn't heard or even thought about her name in years.

"Morgan."

Chapter Twenty-One

Dylan thought his heart was going to float away. Jacq was exactly what he needed in his life. They sat at the kitchen table scraping their ice cream bowls clean. Despite the soul-baring that had happened, they were both positively giddy.

He licked his spoon and set it back in his bowl. "Finished?"

Jacq nodded.

He took both their bowls to the sink and ran water in them. Jacq came up beside him. The magnetic energy refused to let them be more than a few feet apart. Shutting off the water, he turned toward her and leaned a hip against the counter.

She reached out and touched his arm below his tattoo. His skin tingled at the sensation. She pulled up his sleeve and inspected the shield and sword.

He turned so she could see it more easily, leaning his back against the counter.

Tracing the words with her forefinger, she let her eyes meet his. "Make sure you remember what these words say. God is your strength, whether you're facing down a trafficker or your mother." Her eyes sparkled.

He ran his hand over her shoulder and pulled her to his side. "Yes, ma'am."

She giggled. One arm wrapped around his back, and the other rested on his chest.

The scent of mangoes floated up to him. Intoxicating.

But it wasn't just the scent of her. The eyes. The deep brown drew him in. He was going to melt under their gaze. Her lips. Full and inviting.

He ran the tips of his fingers along her hairline and into her hair, drawing her closer still.

"What are we doing, Dylan?" The way his name rolled off her tongue. She truly cared about him. The teasing in her voice gave it away.

"What do they say about fools?"

"Oh, they'd be the ones to rush into this like we are."

"Are you okay with that?"

"I'm up for a little foolhardiness with you." She ran her fingers along the center of his chest.

He could barely breathe. Keeping his eyes locked with hers, he lowered his head while gently drawing her closer with the hand pressed against her lower back.

Their faces were only inches away from one another.

He wanted to kiss her, but were they ready for that? Was she? Was he?

He rubbed her cheek with his thumb. But his brother filled his mind.

"What's wrong?" She pulled back ever so slightly.

The thought must have shown on his face. "You kissed my brother?"

"I did. Does it matter?"

"No."

She moved her body in front of his but stayed close.

He wrapped his arms around her and pulled her against him. "I don't care. I care about you. And what is happening here between us is more important than whatever happened between you and him."

Her grin grew wide. "Good. Because he's ancient history to me." She traced his jawline. "I like the scruffy look on you."

He hadn't shaved since Thursday, and now he was glad. "We'll see if you say that in a minute."

She giggled.

It was his new favorite sound. He leaned down and nuzzled his cheek against hers. Her giggling grew, and a chuckle worked its way out of his chest.

She slid her arms around his neck, then inched her face back until their foreheads were touching.

The desire to kiss her had reached eleven. He couldn't contain it, but still he hesitated.

"Are you going to kiss me today?" Her voice was barely a whisper.

"Maybe."

She drew in a sharp breath. Anticipation.

He moved his face closer, but still didn't touch her lips with his.

"You sure about this, Jacq?" He redirected his eyes from her lips to her eyes. They were wide with desire.

He moved in, meeting his lips to hers. They were soft, even a little cold still from the ice cream. He pressed in. Vanilla intermingled with chocolate syrup.

She held him tighter. They really couldn't get any closer, but he tightened his embrace as well.

Her lips moved in response to his. And he didn't want to pull away. But they must breathe.

They released one another and took quick, deep breaths. However, that magnet that refused to be denied pulled them back together. And they kissed again. This time deeper and slower. Passion growing and intensifying.

He moved his hands to her hips and gently pushed her away. He needed a break. Not that he wanted it.

Their eyes locked. His soul felt full of things he wanted to say, but the words weren't there. Instead, he drew her against his chest and wrapped his arms around her.

She slid her arms around his waist and laid her head on him.

"I'm crazy for you, Jacq." He rested his chin on her hair.

She didn't say anything, so he lifted his head. He brushed her hair away from her face. Two small tears escaped her eyes, which were squeezed shut.

He wiped them with his thumb. Did he do something wrong?

She raised her head. A smile danced on her lips. It grew until her teeth showed. "I can't even come up with the words."

"Who needs words?"

"Not me." She cupped his face in her hands, rose on her toes, and kissed his lips tenderly, before pulling back and out of his arms.

He couldn't move but rested his palms on the counter behind him and watched her.

She retrieved a pair of glasses from a cabinet and filled them with ice water from the fridge. She offered him one.

After chugging it, she opened the freezer and stared for a moment. She closed it and turned. "I don't want to be presumptuous. I mean, I don't know if you had plans for today. I bet this wasn't it."

He wanted to burst out laughing. "True, kissing you was not on my agenda today."

The redness in her cheeks nearly matched her hair. "But if you'd like, you could stay for dinner and maybe a movie. I've really been wanting to watch *The Princess Bride* again." She bit her lip and finally made eye contact.

"I'd love to stay for dinner."

"I can't cook like your mom."

"How many times do I have to tell you, that's okay."

She raised her hands and shoulders. "Probably a lot."

He laughed, reached across the small kitchen, and drew her into his arms again.

The sound of tiny feet padding on the floor echoed behind him. He loosened one arm from around Jacq and turned toward Harper.

"Hey, Harps." Jacq pulled away from their hug and opened her arms to the toddler.

Harper ran to her mom, who picked her up.

Dylan reached over and tickled her. "Did you sleep well, little one?"

She snickered and pulled away from his hand. "Good nap."

"Mr. Dylan is going to stay for dinner tonight."

Harper clapped her hands. "Yay. Play with me?"

"Sure, kiddo!" He reached out to the little girl, and she jumped from her mom's arms to him. His heart soared.

Dylan knelt in front of Harper. "Thanks for letting me hang out with you and your mom today."

The two-year-old gave him a cheesy grin. "I like movie."

"I like the man-in-black. Who was your favorite character? Buttercup?"

Harper shook her head. "Fuzzy."

"Fezzik, the giant?"

She nodded.

"He is pretty cool." Dylan gave Harper a hug. "Good night, kiddo. I'll see you later." She ran off to her room, and Dylan stood and turned to Jacq. "Thanks for such a great day. I'm falling hard for that little girl, and her mom too."

Jacq swatted his arm, then stepped into her daughter's room. "Harper, I'm going to step into the hallway. I'll be right back. Get in bed, and I'll come tuck you in soon."

"Okay, Momma."

Dylan walked out of the apartment with Jacq's hand in his.

She double-checked the door was unlocked and then pulled it closed. "I don't suppose we have to hide from Harper, but I'd rather not have that conversation with her yet."

He laughed and drew her into his arms. They kissed, and he let his lips linger on hers.

Once they pulled out of the kiss, Dylan drew her hand to his lips. "I will see you tomorrow. Working out in the morning?"

"I think so. You?"

"Definitely."

"Well, then, I'll see you at the gym."

He stole another kiss. "Good night." He pivoted and strolled down the hall. Right before he turned to go out the door, he glanced over his shoulder and waved.

Jacq waved back before disappearing into her apartment.

He exited the building and pulled his phone from his pocket. It was getting a little late to call Scarlet, and he couldn't wait until he got home. He had to tell her now.

"Hello." She sounded tired.

"It's only eight o'clock, are you seriously tired already?"

"Shut up. I was on worship team this morning."

"And you went running before you had to be at church at six thirty." He knew his sister.

"Maybe. I only did two miles."

"You're crazy."

"I know. What's going on? You sound like you have news." Her voice was a little more chipper.

"I do."

"Spit it out."

He let the silence hang for a moment. "I met someone."

Squeals filled the other end of the line.

He pulled the phone away from his ear and laughed.

"Tell me about her." He could imagine her sitting forward in anticipation.

"You've actually already met her."

"What? I've met no girl worthy of Dylan Harris."

Heart soaring, he stepped off the curb into the parking lot. "Thanks, sis. You won't believe me if I tell you."

"I definitely won't if you don't tell me!"

He stopped to talk instead of turning down the aisle where he'd parked. "Do you remember Jacq? Or I guess you knew her as Jacqui."

"Jacq? Jacqui … as in Chad's ex-girlfriend?"

"Yeah."

"No way! How on earth?"

"We're working together."

"At the FBI?"

"No, at my other job."

"Shut it. Okay, obviously the FBI, but an agent?"

"Yep."

"You didn't tell me about her last week."

"She started on Monday. We're working on a tough case together and really hit it off. She has a daughter."

"A kid? Oh, Dylan, you'll make a great dad."

"Whoa, don't marry us off yet. We're barely starting to figure it all out right now. But we hung out all day today after we ran into each other at church."

"Wow! Did you tell Chad yet? Didn't you two hit balls last night?"

"We did, and no, I didn't tell him. We talked about her abstractly, and he said he thought she was perfect for me."

"Ha! That's hilarious. It'll be interesting for sure. I remember how much Mom didn't like her. How's that going to work?"

"You know what? I don't care."

Scarlet started clapping on the other end. "Then Jacq sounds perfect for you! That's huge for you to say. You've always cared about what Mom thought, even when you said you didn't. But I heard honesty in your voice just now. Yay! I'm so excited."

Dylan laughed. "Me too. Me too." He turned down the aisle as Scarlet started to tell him about her week.

A figure caught his eye—someone was hunched over his windshield. "Hey, who's there?"

"What is it, Dylan?"

"I've got to go." He hung up on Scarlet and, shoving his phone in his pocket, ran toward the car.

The figure disappeared. But a folded piece of paper fluttered under his windshield wiper. He grabbed it and spun around. Where did that person go?

Chapter Twenty-Two

Around the corner of an SUV, a shadow caught Dylan's eye. "Wait!"

The figure froze.

"What is this?" He held up the paper.

"A clue that will hopefully be more fruitful than the last."

Dylan could now tell he was speaking to a woman. Dressed in a short, tight skirt and high heels, she was covered with a large, hooded sweatshirt and had the hood pulled up over her head and low over her eyes. He couldn't see her face at all.

"Come talk to me—"

"No."

"We need as much information as possible. Is this about Marrissa?"

"Yes. I have to go."

"Is she still alive?"

"Yes, but if you don't do something immediately, she'll be gone for good."

Dylan took a cautious step forward. "Who are you?"

"No one of consequence."

"Are you the person that gave us the other two clues?"

"The call and note in Walmart?"

"Those are the ones. Guess I have my answer. What's your name?"

"I've stayed anonymous for a reason."

He inched closer. "But what can I call you?"

"A dead girl if the wrong person finds out I've stepped so far out of pocket. Trust me. The info's good, but I can't get any more involved."

"We can help you."

"Just help Marrissa."

She moved around the vehicle. He had more questions before she disappeared again.

"Please, wait. Will you be there too?"

She spoke over her shoulder but didn't stop. "No, I won't. Just save her."

He let her go. He was tempted to follow her but knew it wasn't worth the fight. She was right. They needed to help Marrissa before they did anything else.

He unfolded the paper in his hand and read the note.

> *Marrissa is going to be sold at a dark web auction tomorrow (Monday) at six pm.*
> *She's at 1862 West Juniper Ave in Knoxville.*
> *The other four girls will be home by seven Monday morning. Rescue them too.*

His stomach pitted out. Sold. But they had an address. He ran back to Jacq's apartment.

Bang. Bang. Bang.

Jacq jumped. "Stay in bed, Harper. It's time to go to sleep." She covered her daughter and kissed her forehead. "Love you."

"I yuyou too!"

"Sweet dreams." Jacq closed the bedroom door.

Whoever was at the front knocked again.

She rushed over to peer through the peephole. "Dylan!" She unlocked the deadbolt and yanked the door open. "Couldn't stay away, huh?"

He half-laughed and held up a slip of paper. "I could kiss you all night, but we have a break in our case."

"What?" She took the paper from Dylan's hand. She wandered into the kitchen, unfolding the note as she went.

Dylan closed the door behind him. "I'll call Warren and text the team."

"Wait." She spun back toward him. "Where did this come from?"

He told her about the woman by his car.

"That's crazy. I wonder why she decided to come forward." Something strange stirred in her soul. She wished she could identify it—she wasn't even sure if it was a feeling, a thought, a longing.

"Who knows, but let's get on it."

"Absolutely."

Over the next twenty minutes they contacted the team with a plan to meet at the office around nine.

Jacq rubbed the back of her neck. "I'm not sure I'm up for a third all-nighter in one week."

Dylan walked around the table to where she sat and placed his hands on her shoulders. He gently massaged them, rubbing his thumbs into the tight muscles. "Couldn't agree more. But maybe we'll figure out what we need to do by midnight, go home, sleep, and save the girls in the morning."

"I like your positive attitude, but nothing has been that simple with this case."

"True." He leaned down and kissed her cheek.

How on earth were they going to keep it professional at the office? She didn't want to be far from him at all. Why did she feel like a goofy teenager all over again? After she lifted herself from the chair, she slid her arms around his waist. "I guess we should get going."

"You aren't acting like it."

She laughed and tried to give him a faux-innocent look. "I called Rachel while you were on the phone with Warren. She's expecting Harper."

"How can I help?"

"Do you mind scooping her out of bed? She's a sound sleeper and probably won't notice."

"Can do." He cupped the side of her face and kissed her lips. "Had to sneak one more in."

"You're getting no argument out of me. But let's go."

Dylan went and got Harper, and Jacq grabbed Harper's bag and bunny.

Dylan slung his backpack over his shoulder and rounded Jacq's car to accompany her to the FBI field office. He had ridden with Jacq and was surprised how quick a task it had been to drop off Harper. The little one hadn't woken at all. Dylan questioned whether she'd be confused when she woke up, but Jacq wasn't worried. He guessed after a week like the past one, the girl had quickly learned where she'd wake up was anyone's guess.

The temptation to take Jacq's hand as they entered the building was strong, but he resisted. When they reached the elevator, he depressed the button and waited. Sometimes these elevators took way longer than reasonable, especially when agents needed to pursue a strong lead.

He reached over and rubbed Jacq's neck. She leaned into it.

Someone cleared their throat behind them.

Dylan dropped his hand and spun around.

Gio and Aliza stood there. A smile toyed with Aliza's lips, and Gio looked like he was about to laugh. Instead, he said, "I thought we had info about Marrissa, not—"

"We do." Dylan wasn't in the mood for teasing from his friend.

The elevator doors opened, and the four agents stepped on.

Gio's face grew serious. "Since it's the four of us, let's pray while we're on our way up."

Despite Gio being the quiet one, Dylan could always count on him to point them back to the Lord, especially in the tough moments.

Jacq's eyebrows rose. "I love working with other believers."

Gio pushed the third-floor button. Then he said, "Father God, let this be the fruitful lead we all hope it is. Direct us to Marrissa and keep her safe. Give us wisdom and guidance. Protect us all from harm. Work out everything according to Your will and plan. We implore You for Your help in finding and rescuing Marrissa and any other girls that may be trapped in this life. Go before us and behind us. And surround Marrissa with Your wings of protection."

The elevator dinged, announcing their arrival on the third floor. "In Your name we pray—"

"Amen," they all said in unison before exiting the elevator.

Dylan placed his hand on Jacq's back to tell her to go first. They all entered the office, and once Matt and Sabrina arrived, Dylan took charge.

"Warren said not to wait for him, since he's still on his way back from his trip to his kid's college." Dylan held up the note. "I feel like we've been at this exact crossroad before, but I hope this one is different. The same woman who gave Jacq the note at Walmart gave me this note tonight." He filled them in about the encounter with the mystery woman.

Matt held out an evidence bag. "I'll take the note to the lab and see if we can pull any fingerprints, other than yours—"

"And Jacq's." He took a picture of the note with his phone and slid it into the bag.

"You'd think you two would know better."

"We were excited."

"Oh, I get it. I'll see what I can do." Matt left for the lab.

Dylan typed the address into Google maps. It was valid, and the map pointed them to a large house in a well-to-do neighborhood on the southwest side of Knoxville. Circular drive and four-car garage. They would need to find out more, starting with who lived there.

With such a broad window of time, they should be able to save the whole house of girls. By seven tomorrow morning, they'd have a warrant and a plan to rescue the five girls who had been trafficked for who knew how long.

At one o'clock in the morning, Jacq and Dylan walked up to the judge's house. Dylan's jaw was rigid, and his fists clenched. She elbowed him. "You okay?"

"I don't have a good feeling about this. If I had realized Judge Hanover was the judge on call, I think I would have waited until morning."

"You know this can't wait until morning."

"Of course, but this isn't going to be easy. Hanover doesn't like the FBI or me."

"You? What's his problem with you?"

Dylan laughed. "My brother, actually. I would normally like this guy for how hard he goes on Chad in the courtroom, except every time I come to him for a warrant, he's sure to point out that I'm Chad's brother and then proceeds to list out all of Chad's weaknesses and assume they apply to me as well, especially since I'm FBI to top it off."

"Oh, dear."

"Exactly." Dylan knocked on the ornate mahogany door of the judge's house.

Now Jacq was nervous too. What if they couldn't get the warrant? Surely the judge would see the necessity of it so they could save Marrissa and the other girls in that house. But what if he didn't? She focused all her energy into her hand and tapped her thumb against her thigh.

The door creaked open. "Seriously, you? Why must you wake me in the middle of the night? It'd better be good." Judge Hanover opened the door and swept his arm in obligatory welcome. "You know, your brother made an innocent witness look like a fool in court the other day. She was an idiot, but it didn't serve his case any to make her look *that* foolish. Your brother reeks of arrogance."

Jacq swallowed the brutally honest words forming in her mouth.

"Follow me." The judge led them around the corner and into a large home office. Towering bookshelves flanked a fireplace with two riveted leather sofas facing one another. The judge leaned up against the front of his large desk and crossed his arms. "So, get on with it already."

Dylan introduced Jacq and explained the whole situation with Marrissa's kidnapping, his encounter with the mystery woman and how she had helped in the past, and the note she gave him earlier that evening.

"Did she sign an affidavit?" the judge asked.

"No, sir. She wishes to remain anonymous."

The judge shook his head. "You expect me to take the word of a nameless prostitute who won't even show her face, so you and your careless agents can ransack the house of a well-to-do couple down the street from me?"

Jacq's ears grew warm. How could this judge not understand how important it was for their informant to stay anonymous? Traffickers were often an extremely violent set of men. Jacq had no doubt the woman would die or worse if they found out she had spoken up.

But what if this judge was dirty? Would she be safe? It was hard enough for women to leave that life, but especially if they felt they had nowhere to go.

"You don't have enough for a warrant. You don't even have the title information yet. No idea what you're going into. Stake the place out if you need to, but you aren't getting my permission to bust into a house on little more than a whore's word." The judge pushed himself off his desk. "Now, if you don't mind, I'd like to get some sleep."

Dylan didn't move. "Sir, listen. We need to save this girl."

"Then find me more substantial evidence that warrants the disruption of someone's home and life."

Jacq squeezed Dylan's elbow, and he moved toward the door.

They left the judge's house. By the time they climbed into Jacq's car, Dylan was fuming.

Jacq took his hand in hers. "Look at me."

He obeyed.

She raised his hand to her lips. "We'll find her, warrant or not. A stakeout is our best bet."

He nodded.

Matt and Sabrina were already parked down the street from the house. Dylan and Jacq would take over at six and be there in time for the girls to start getting home. But without a warrant it was going to take an act of God to save Marrissa.

Chapter Twenty-Three

Dylan took a bite of his caffeinated protein bar. Even though they had only been in place for half an hour, he already needed a boost, and stakeouts were no time for coffee. After getting about four hours of sleep each, he and Jacq now sat in his Charger one house down and across the street from the address the woman had given him, armed with a camera with telephoto lens and a pair of high-powered binoculars.

"I don't like this." Jacq lowered the binoculars. "I don't have a marvelous view. The house is set so far back we can't see anything more than the front door."

"Any closer and they'll spot us for sure. Matt said their location in the opposite direction wasn't any better."

"I know." She grunted.

Dylan noticed headlights coming up in the rearview mirror. "Vehicle coming up behind us."

She turned to look back between the seats, bringing her body closer to his.

His heart did a little hop. She was amazing, but he needed to focus on Marrissa right now.

The car pulled into the driveway of the suspect house.

"What do you see?" Dylan grabbed the camera, but Jacq already had the binoculars up.

"The car went into the garage. I see a woman getting out. Dressed like a working girl but young. Maybe twenty."

Dylan zoomed in with the camera and caught a shot of the girl before the garage door closed. Any evidence that might suggest trafficking could persuade the judge to change his mind. One scantily clad young adult wasn't going to cut it. She could be the homeowner's daughter getting home after a late night of partying.

He set the camera on the center console and glanced over at Jacq.

She'd only lowered the binoculars part way, and her eyes were fixed in a far-off place.

He rubbed her back. "You okay?"

"Yeah, my heart is doing some weird things lately when I think about these girls stuck in this life. How many of them don't even realize they're being trafficked? How many of them could get out, would get out, if they had a place to go? I know from talking to a few girls over the years that so often they don't think they can go home after being in the game. They think there's no way their family would take them back. It breaks my heart."

"I can't even imagine. I know what it feels like to have your family not approve, but my situation seems silly in comparison."

She gripped his upper arm. "Just because it's a different level doesn't mean it's not valid."

"I know. I was praying as I fell asleep this morning and thought maybe God will use it somehow."

"That's what He does. I've always been a firm believer that God uses the wounds in our lives not only to draw us closer to Him, but also to further His kingdom."

"How did you get so wise?"

"Traversed enough trials of my own. And for some reason I don't think I've seen the end of those trials."

"What makes you say that?"

Another car came down the road. This one pulled into the circular driveway but stopped in front of the house instead of going around to the garage. Dylan raised the camera and took a few photos. "Did you see the plates?"

"Nope."

The front of the car was now facing them, and Tennessee doesn't require front plates. Dylan continued taking pictures. A woman got out of the car.

"Dylan, she's even younger."

"Underage?"

"I don't think so, but barely. She's really skinny too."

Dylan zoomed in as far as he could and snapped a few more. Still could be another daughter getting home from a night out. This wasn't enough.

Gio sat at the computer station in the cyber-crimes office and rubbed his face. He could have used more sleep, and staring at a screen full of provocatively dressed women and children—both boys and girls—wasn't doing anything to keep his frustration down. People being sold for sex. It disgusted him. He wanted to punch the screen, but that wouldn't save them. He couldn't save them. What he could do, though, was keep looking for Marrissa. He could go in the chat rooms and try to pick up some chatter about a virgin for sale in Knoxville.

Two separate images floated in his mind's eye as he took in what he was seeing and reading. First, his younger brother's face. He was why Gio did this job and stomached these images. Gio would do anything to avenge his kid brother. And the second seemed unrelated, but still, every time they worked a trafficking case, the face of a woman he had once dreamed about danced in his mind. Who she was or what it had to do with this, he didn't know, but if she was a real person, he prayed God would help her.

"Gio!" Aliza called from the other side of the desk.

He looked around the computer at her. "What's up?"

"Come here."

He jumped up and darted around to her.

Aliza was pale in the dim lights of the warm room full of computers. She pointed at the screen. "Is that … ?"

"Marrissa." He had no doubt the girl in front of him was the one they were looking for.

"She's already for sale, Gio. The informant had the time wrong, or they changed it. And the numbers are going high fast."

Gio's stomach twisted in on itself. "Foster!"

An agent across the room looked up.

Gio waved him over. Agent Foster was arguably the best hacker employed by the FBI. "Work your magic and find out where this sale is originating."

Foster cracked his fingers. "On it."

Aliza leaped out of the seat and gave it to Foster.

Gio pulled out his phone. "I'll let Dylan and Jacq know."

Jacq dropped her head back against the headrest, not wanting to believe what Gio was saying over Dylan's phone. If Marrissa was already for sale, did they have time to get her? Was she still even in the house? Had they moved her to another location where the buyer could pick her up? Would she be shipped across the country? *Jesus, help us save her.*

Dylan wrapped up the call with Gio. "What do we do?"

Jacq's blood pulsed. She focused all her nervous energy to her right hand and rapped the side of her thigh. She needed to clear her mind. What could they do? "We need to get in there."

"We have no probable cause."

"I know. We could fake car trouble?"

"But this isn't a through road. It'd be too suspect."

"Let's keep watching and try to think of some way in," she said. "We need proof she's in there." She raised the binoculars to her eyes again and examined every room she could see. All of them were covered. Blinds and curtains, not a single ray of light shone through.

Silence fell for the next ten minutes. They watched and waited.

She didn't take her eyes off the house. "I didn't forget about your question."

"Which question?"

"Though apparently you did." She shook her head and glanced at him. "About why I think those trials aren't over."

"Oh yeah." His voice was soft. "That's kind of a scary thought, isn't it?"

"Indeed. But God's already walked me through so much. As I pray and seek Him, I get the impression the flames of trial are going to get hotter. The deeper we go into *this* case, the stronger the sense I have that I'm going to have to step in even deeper."

"I can tell you one thing: you won't have to walk through them alone. To stick with the analogy, I'll go into the flames with you, if that's where God calls us."

"Feeling confident to follow God's calling over your mom's preference now?"

"Definitely. A certain redhead has helped me see that following God is more important than others' opinions. Also helps that I find myself happier with her than my family ever made me."

Jacq gave him a gentle smile and looked back at the house. "I'm glad I can help."

A third vehicle approached the house. This time it was a large, white SUV. It pulled around the drive toward the garage.

Jacq kept the binoculars trained on the vehicle, waiting to identify who got out. *Please don't close the garage yet.*

Two people exited the SUV, another young woman and a man, who was probably in his upper-thirties. His build matched that of the second man at the mall, but that wasn't enough.

The garage closed, hiding the pair. Jacq lowered the binoculars. "Please tell me one thirty-year-old man in the same house with three twenty-something women is suspect enough for Judge Hanover."

"Who knows. But without a sign of Marrissa—"

"I know." She ran her hands into her hair.

The sun was finally starting to break along the horizon, but it seemed as though Jacq's hope was going to set with the moon. "That's three girls home. Only one left."

"If we had a reason to go in without a warrant—"

"We need that probable cause."

She reached over and took his hand in hers. "God, give us an in. Keep our eyes sharp, so we can spot a way to legally enter the premise and find Marrissa. And if she's not in there, show the team where she is. Help her not be sold before we can find her."

Gio leaned over Foster's shoulder.

"I could work a lot better if you weren't breathing on my neck, Agent Crespi."

Gio stood. "Sorry, man. I just—"

"I get it. We'll find her." Foster kept tapping away at the keyboard.

Gio didn't have a clue what Foster was doing. It went way beyond Gio's skills.

Foster slammed his fist against the table. "Blast. They've got this well-hidden. These guys know how to mask their auction."

Gio watched as the bid for Marrissa climbed. More pictures had been added to the posting, enticing the bidders to keep fighting for her.

"No, no, no, no, no!" Foster typed away.

"What?"

"Someone outbid everyone and the bidding has stopped. I'm trying to capture all the info. I don't want them to close this down before I have everything I need." Foster frantically typed and clicked. Gio had never seen someone's hands fly on a keyboard like Foster's.

Large red letters filled the comments. SOLD.

Gio's legs shook beneath him. They were going to lose Marrissa. To get so close but have her slip through their fingers.

The auction disappeared from the screen, but Foster didn't stop typing.

Gio leaned forward on the desk and let his head drop down. The humming of the computers and the tapping of Foster's fingers on the keyboard numbed Gio's mind. What if they couldn't catch whoever sold Marrissa?

"Gotcha!"

Gio jerked his head toward Foster. "What?"

"I think I got our buyer. Hold on." Foster craned his neck closer to the screen and typed. "Yes. Come on, please tell me you're a fool."

Gio waited. Could it be possible they could get the buyer? He met Aliza's eyes. Her thumbnail was firmly planted between her teeth.

She raised her eyebrows in expectation.

"Yes!" Foster smacked the table. "I got him." He typed a little more and pulled up a mugshot of a Gary Grabowski.

"Please tell me you saved all that somehow, so we can actually put him away for buying a human being."

Foster grinned at Gio. "You better believe it." He typed a little more. "There. Sent you this guy's file."

Gio slapped Foster on the back. "Good work."

Chapter Twenty-Four

Dylan was fighting discouragement. Jacq's prayer helped, but they stood before a seemingly impenetrable wall with their hands tied. His phone rang again. "Harris."

"Hey. We don't have a location of the seller, but we've got the buyer's identity." Gio's excitement bled through the phone.

"I'm putting you on speaker. Tell us more. What do you mean 'buyer'?" Dylan's heart slammed against his ribs.

Gio filled them in. "I'm sending you his file. Aliza and I will pursue him on this end but keep your eyes peeled for Marrissa. Foster's trying to track down the conversation regarding the exchange, but it doesn't look promising."

"Thanks, Gio." Dylan hung up with Gio and pulled out his laptop. He logged on and opened the file Gio had sent.

The photo of a man, nearly as large as Fezzik the giant, appeared. Gary Grabowski was a creepy thug, but nothing more than a dozen misdemeanors for solicitation of a prostitute, drug possession, assault, and other relatively small crimes from years ago. Dylan stared at the picture and memorized the man's face. If he showed up, they would get him.

Quiet fell between Dylan and Jacq, and they continued to watch the house, waiting.

The minutes seemed to inch past. One painful minute after another.

Marrissa had been sold. He didn't want to imagine what would happen to her if she slipped away from them now. Human trafficking was more rampant in America than most people would care to acknowledge. But what many people didn't realize was how disturbing it truly was. More often than not, these women, girls, and boys, were sold as sex slaves, but he'd also seen times when girls, especially virgins, were sold for ritualistic satanic sacrifices.

Given the buyer's history, the former was more likely the case in this instance, but that meant Marrissa faced a slow death. One where her soul would be ripped away from her every night as multiple men had their way with her, as drugs were forced into her body—Dylan couldn't stomach the idea. Every time he thought about any young woman being forced into that life, he pictured Scarlet.

The only sound in the car was the ticking of his wristwatch. How many minutes did they have? Would they miss their opportunity?

Jacq's voice broke into his thoughts. "Looks like our fourth girl is arriving home."

A black SUV with dark-tinted windows drove past them and pulled into the driveway. Dylan glanced back at the file on Gary Grabowski. Registered vehicles included a black Lincoln Navigator. Same as what was in the driveway. "What was the license plate?"

"Started with eight-five."

"That's our buyer."

"No way."

Dylan's heart started racing. This was it. Do something now or Marrissa would be lost. He lifted the camera and took a few shots of the man who matched Gary Grabowski's description getting out of the SUV and walking to the front door. It opened, and the man they had seen go into the garage earlier appeared. The two shook hands and went inside. The door closed behind them.

"Please tell me that's probable cause." Jacq lowered her binoculars.

Dylan snorted. He called Gio. "The buyer is here. We're going to need backup and a warrant for his arrest."

"Warren just left for the judge's house. Warrant should be available ASAP. Aliza and I are headed your way. I'll call local LEOs."

"We're going in for a closer look."

"Don't do anything stupid."

"Will only do what it takes to save the kid."

"That's what I'm afraid of. See you soon."

They hung up, and Dylan and Jacq checked their sidearms. Dylan set his phone to vibrate only.

"What's our plan?" Jacq gripped his arm.

"Observation. But if we see an opportunity to get the girls out, I think we should take it."

"Agreed. Backup is on its way, right?"

Dylan nodded. They were less than ten minutes from the office. He reached over and cupped Jacq's head and pressed his lips to hers.

She ran her hand along the side of his face. "For good luck?"

"If I believed in such a thing."

She let out a tense giggle. "Let's do this."

They decided to forgo the FBI windbreakers so as not to give themselves away prematurely, and they casually strolled down the road hand-in-hand.

The neighborhood was filled with million-dollar houses. If Dylan didn't know better, he'd think no riffraff lived here. Why was selling flesh such a lucrative business?

The sun was coming up quickly now, giving them less cover. They wandered past the house and down a neighbor's driveway, which gave them a view of the backyard.

The two men came out of the back of the house and meandered out onto the expansive deck.

Dylan drew Jacq to him in a ruse of affection. But he could see past her and watch the men.

"What's going on?"

"Pretend to be flirting; the men came outside."

"Do I have to pretend?"

He met her eyes and chuckled, but quickly looked back.

"They're going down by the pool. This may be our opportunity."

She raised herself up on her toes and kissed his cheek. "Then let's go rescue some girls."

Careful to not draw attention to themselves, they walked as slowly as they could manage back down the driveway until they were out of sight, at which point they jogged toward the front door.

Dylan grabbed Jacq's arm as they closed in, and he checked the house for cameras. Nothing. Surveillance was a double-edged sword for people like this. Cameras would give them security from cops and let them keep track of the girls, but it also gave opportunity for hackers or law enforcement to have evidence against them.

Dylan motioned for Jacq. He reached for the doorknob. Could this guy be so excited about selling a girl that he would carelessly leave the door unlocked?

No such luck. Dylan knocked lightly, not wanting to alarm the men outback, but hoping one of the girls was downstairs and willing to let them in.

No answer.

He knocked again, slightly harder.

The door inched open. The youngest girl they saw earlier appeared. "Hello?"

Jacq stepped forward. "We know your pimp is out back. I'm FBI Special Agent Jacq Sheppard. We're here to help you."

"We don't need any help. We're fine."

"You didn't deny that man is your pimp."

Her eyes grew wide, and she closed the door.

But Jacq's foot was in the way. "Nope. Not going to get away that easy. I promise we're here to help. Is Marrissa here?"

Her eyes flashed with recognition. "There's no one by that name here."

"Where is she?" Dylan kept his voice as gentle and soft as he could while the adrenaline pounded in his ears.

Jacq pushed the door open.

"I think she's still upstairs." The girl's voice was barely audible.

"Who's here? Luna, don't let anybody in." Another voice approached from the back of the house.

Luna turned, and Jacq and Dylan were able to enter the two-story foyer.

The voice belonged to the older of the three girls, but she was still young—maybe mid-twenties. "Who are you people? Get out of our house."

Dylan steadied his breathing. They may need to take a different approach with this one. *God, give me the words.* "We're looking for Marrissa. Where is she?"

"Why would I tell you that?" Her eyes darted to the stairs and then back to Dylan.

"So she is upstairs."

"Stella, they're here to get us out."

"You're a fool if you think you can leave the life that easily. Look at Daisy and Celeste. If there was an out, don't you think one of them would have taken it years ago?"

Jacq moved toward Stella. "But we can help you. At the very least, help us get Marrissa out."

"And have Bobbi dump my body in the river?" Stella turned to leave.

Jacq grabbed her arm. "Don't make me cuff you. I want to *help* you."

Luna came closer to Dylan. "I want you to help me, even if Stella doesn't."

Jacq and Stella stared one another down, Stella's arm firmly in Jacq's grasp.

Another girl came around the corner and looked like she was about to scream. Luna raised her hands. "Nova, they're here to get us out."

Nova rushed over to Dylan. "Really?"

"Yes. Are those guys armed?"

Luna and Nova nodded, but Stella answered, "Bobbi always has a gun, not that he has a permit for it." Stella seemed to relax in Jacq's hold, but Jacq didn't let go.

"More help is on the way, but we need to find Marrissa."

Jacq pulled on Stella's arm. "Please, come with us." The girl's expression softened, and Jacq drew her into her arms.

"Let's get you girls safely away from the house." Dylan reached his arm out to Stella.

Jacq nudged Stella toward him. "I'll go look for Marrissa."

Dylan nodded.

Stella stopped. "But what about our things?"

Dylan gently laid a hand on her shoulder. "We can get it later." He wanted to shake her—things didn't matter, but he knew from talking to multiple women who had been in this life that the pull of material things was often an addiction that made it difficult to leave the game.

He ushered them out but looked over his shoulder at Jacq. "Be careful."

She nodded and ran up the stairs with her hand resting on her firearm.

Dylan escorted the girls outside. "Stay close and quiet. Let's head toward that black car over there."

They all scurried over the lawn and across the road.

Once they were on the other side of his car, he pulled out his phone and called Gio. "We've got three girls out, but Jacq's still looking for Marrissa in the house."

"We're close—"

Aliza broke in. "Gabe is on-duty and should be there before we are."

"Good. Hurry."

Jacq cleared one giant room after another but wasn't finding Marrissa. Every closet, every bathroom, yet no sign of the girl. *God, where is she?*

Jacq came out of the last bedroom. She saw only one more door, but it looked like a closet. When she tried it, though, she found it locked, and it wasn't a simple push or twist lock from the other side. It needed a key.

Stretching up on her toes she felt along the edge of the doorframe. No key. She searched around. Nothing.

What do I do?

She pulled her knife out of her pocket, but it was too thick to slip between the doorjamb and the door.

She knocked. "Marrissa? Are you in there?"

"Hello? Who is that?" A shaky voice came from behind the door, but it seemed far away rather than on the other side.

"FBI Special Agent Jacq Sheppard. Do you know where he keeps the key? Assuming you can't get the door open from that side."

Footsteps echoed down what sounded like wooden steps. The doorknob jiggled. "I can't." The voice started crying.

"Marrissa. We're going to get you out of there. I need to find a key or something. The door opens out so I can't kick it in. Can you try to kick it? Kick close to the doorknob."

One kick. Two. Three. The door wasn't budging.

"Can you kick it harder?"

"I can't." A sob erupted. "I'm too weak."

Jacq could hear it in her voice. "It's okay, Marrissa. We'll get you out. I'm going to go find a key. Just give me a minute. I'll be right back."

"O-o-okay."

Jacq ran into the bathroom and searched for bobby pins. None. Surely these girls wore their hair up. She didn't have time for a deep search. She abandoned the bathroom and ran down the stairs to the kitchen. Carefully, she glanced out the window over the sink. The two men were still talking out back by the pool. But she didn't know how long they would stay there.

Hopefully backup would arrive and they could get both of those men in cuffs before there was an altercation.

Jacq looked through the drawers but found nothing that would allow her to pick the lock.

Next to the kitchen, Jacq noticed an office. She went in. Maybe the pimp kept the key in the desk. Seemed too obvious, but it was the most practical place to look. She pushed aside piles of papers on the desktop, rifled through all the drawers, but didn't find a single key. She turned and searched along the bookcase with glass shelves that lined the wall behind the desk. The shelves mostly held trinkets from around the world that all had a celestial theme. The girls' names: Stella, Luna, Nova. The man had a clear motif going.

She lifted a model of the solar system. A key. She grabbed it.

A click sounded behind her. She spun. The door to the patio had opened, and there stood the pimp of the house.

She reached for her gun.

"Don't even think about it." He pointed his weapon at her.

She raised her hands slowly. She had to think and react carefully.

She took a step to her right, putting her in a clearer line to the pimp. "Bobbi, is it?"

"That's what they call me." He stalked toward her.

She didn't like staring down the barrel of a 1911. "Nice gun. Don't suppose you could show me your permit for that?"

"Oh, a wise a—"

"What can I say? It's standard training at the FBI academy."

"So, you're a fed, huh?" He came closer. Almost close enough.

"If by fed you mean federal agent, then yes."

He finally stepped close enough. Jacq leaned to the side and grabbed the top of the gun with her left hand as fast as she could. She slammed her right hand into his wrist as hard as she could.

His wrist twisted, and he lost his grip on the gun. Jacq ripped it from his hands and took a hard step away.

But he didn't relent. He rushed at her and slammed her back into the glass bookcase. The shelves collapsed. Glass shattered.

She raised the gun toward him, but he grabbed her wrist and

slammed it back against the wooden beam that supported the shelves. Her other arm was trapped behind her against a broken shelf.

"Bobbi!" The other man's voice sounded.

Bobbi reached in his pocket and threw a keychain at the other man. "Get the girl and get out. Be careful. With one fed here, there are bound to be more close by."

Jacq fought against Bobbi, but he was strong.

He grabbed Jacq's hair and yanked her head back. "Now, tell me what you're doing here."

"I thought that was obvious."

"Awfully impertinent for a woman who's about to die." He slammed her hand against the wood again.

Her reflexes forced her to lose her grip on the gun.

He pulled her away from the shelves, freeing her right arm.

She grabbed her gun.

But he saw it. He released her hand and smashed his fist into the left side of her head.

Stars filled her vision, and she lost her balance.

Chapter Twenty-Five

Dylan grabbed a blanket out of his trunk and wrapped it around Nova. What was taking Jacq so long? He needed to get in there and help her. What if the guys came back in the house?

A squad car pulled up beside Dylan. Gabe jumped out.

"Hey! We got these ladies out of there. But Jacq's still inside looking for Marrissa."

"Go. I got them."

Pkew. A gunshot.

"Jesus, no!" Dylan ran across the lawn and yanked the front door open.

"Jacq!" No response.

He turned to run up the stairs, but the sound of a struggle redirected his course.

A door was open next to the kitchen. He crossed the foyer and pulled his Glock from its holster.

Through the door he saw Jacq and Bobbi in a full-on MMA fight. He needed to save her.

A scream filled the air above him.

He took a step back and looked up. At the end of the hall, Gary Grabowski pulled Marrissa from what looked like a closet.

Jacq. He caught her eye.

"Save Marrissa!"

He was torn more than any other time in his life. What was he supposed to do? Save the girl or the woman he loved? Either way he lost.

His insides shattered, paralyzing him.

Jesus, help!

He turned and bounded up the stairs three at a time. He met the massive Gary, with Marrissa slung over his shoulder, halfway across the hallway that was open to the living room and foyer below.

Gary tossed Marrissa to the floor and raised his fists.

Dylan raised his gun. "FBI. Put your hands up."

"They already are. Fight me like a man."

Dylan steadied his gun in his hands and secured his stance, not ready to give up his weapon as simply as Westley had against Fezzik.

Jacq screamed.

A burly fist slammed into Dylan's face.

But Dylan didn't lose his footing. He fired.

Point blank. To the chest. Gary didn't move.

Dylan fired again.

Gary stumbled backward and into the railing. It gave way under his mass, and the giant plummeted to the floor below.

Dylan holstered his gun and turned to Marrissa, who was cowering against the wall. He knelt next to her. "I'm Special Agent Dylan Harris."

She flung her arms around his neck.

He scooped her up and held her close. He had to get her out of here. He had to get to Jacq. He had to save the woman he loved.

A door slammed.

"Jacq!"

No response.

Dylan carried Marrissa downstairs. Three uniformed officers breeched the front door. Dylan stepped aside and let them pass, and carried Marrissa outside.

Gio appeared at Dylan's side. "Where's Jacq?"

"She hasn't come out with Bobbi in cuffs yet?" He set Marrissa on the ground.

She patted his arm. "Go help her."

Gio put his arm around Marrissa. "Go!"

A crashing sound came from the garage, and the white SUV careened down the driveway and turned onto the road, barely missing Dylan's car.

Gabe yelled, "I got it!" He jumped in his squad car and raced after the SUV. Two other squad cars sped past the house.

Dylan pivoted on his heels and bolted back into the house. "Jacq!"

He ran into the office. The place looked like a war zone. But Jacq wasn't there. He darted around the room. Not behind the desk.

He jutted his head out the backdoor. "Jacq!" Not outside.

Returning inside, he looked down the hall and opened the door to the garage. "Jacq!" Not in the garage.

His pulse pounded.

He ran back into the house and into the master suite. Not there either.

He collapsed to his knees on the marble of the foyer. He'd lost her.

Where was she? Bobbi must have taken her.

He couldn't breathe. The first time in his entire life he'd actually found someone who—But he'd saved the girl. The thing Jacq had wanted him to do. But at what cost?

I'm trusting You, God. I trusted You. Get her out of this. Please let her still be alive.

Chapter Twenty-Six

A few squad cars and FBI along with an ambulance arrived around Gio. More squad cars had joined Gabe in his pursuit of the suspect, and agents swarmed the house. He put a blanket across Marrissa's shoulders and helped her to the EMTs.

She was alive. They had saved her.

Sabrina came up beside him and said hi to Marrissa.

Aliza was talking with the other three girls and helping them feel confident about getting out of there.

Dylan had gone inside two minutes ago, but Gio hadn't heard anything yet. He grew uneasy. Although with no "agent down" call, maybe they had joined the search.

He tapped Sabrina's arm. "I'm going in." He ran toward the house.

He shoved the front door open.

Dylan, head drooped low, knelt on the ground of a massive two-story foyer.

"Dylan." Gio rushed over to him and dropped to his knees beside Dylan.

Dylan raised his head. "I can't find her. She's gone."

"Gone?"

"He took her." Dylan grabbed Gio's shoulder. "Call Gabe."

Gio pulled his phone off his belt and dialed the police dispatch. Gio identified himself. "Connect me with Officer Gabe Jacobs. He's in pursuit of a suspect."

A few seconds later Gabe's voice came across the line. "Jacobs."

"It's Gio. You still on his tail?"

"No, he evaded me a few blocks ago. I've got air support coming in but—"

"He's got Jacq. Find him."

Gio heard a thump, like Gabe hit his steering wheel.

"I'll find him. I'll find her."

"Please." Gio hung up the phone and turned back to his friend. Dylan was pale, but determination filled his eyes.

They stood, and Dylan pushed past Gio. "I'll find her."

"I know you will. And I'm with you."

Dylan turned back around. "No. I'll have the rest of the bureau and LEOs. You need to get Marrissa's family."

Gio pulled Dylan into a hug. "Godspeed."

Dylan slapped the side of his arm and bolted out of the house.

Gio stood inside a moment longer and lifted a prayer up for Dylan and Jacq. *God, we need Your help. Keep Jacq safe, and help Dylan find her.*

Dylan ran to his car and pulled out his laptop. Surely they had something about this Bobbi, something that would point him in the right direction. Where would Bobbi go? Where would he take Jacq?

The girls. Maybe they would know.

They were all huddled near the back of an ambulance where the EMTs were taking care of Marrissa.

He tucked the laptop under his arm and raced over to them. "Hey girls. I need your help. Where would Bobbi go?"

Stella answered, "He might go to Ronan's house."

"Who's Ronan?"

"One of his buddies. Another pimp."

Nova shook her head. "I'm not sure he would. Ronan would kill him if he brought the cops over."

"Bobbi took my—the other agent, Jacq."

Stella hugged herself. "Then he definitely didn't go to Ronan's. He'll call Ronan, but not go to his place. Maybe he went to the shop."

"Shop?"

"A little warehouse space where we make stuff we sell on the internet."

"What's the address?"

"I don't know the address, but I can tell you how to get there."

Dylan opened his laptop and typed the directions Stella gave him. "Thank you. Please tell Agent Blake anything else you think of that might help."

Stella nodded and turned to Aliza.

Aliza squeezed Dylan's arm. "Find her. I'll call immediately if there's anything else."

He strode toward his car, fighting to keep himself together, clenching and unclenching his fist the entire way. If that lowlife touched Jacq, he—what would he do? He didn't want to think about it. The exact same feelings he'd had when faced with Scarlet's assailants filled him again. He was ready to do whatever was necessary.

Dylan got in his car and slammed the door. He turned the engine on and was about to pull away when Warren sprinted over. Dylan lowered the window.

"What are you doing?"

"I'm going after Jacq."

Warren smacked the top of the car. "Go get her. We're on your six. Don't do anything stupid."

Dylan nodded, cranked the wheel hard, and peeled away from the curb.

Jacq shifted on the hard ground as she came to. How long had she been out? The last thing she remembered was Dylan running up the stairs to save Marrissa. Bobbi had knocked her upside the head with her gun. How had she failed so miserably at maintaining control of the situation?

She opened her eyes. She was no longer in the house. The pain in her head was excruciating, making it nearly impossible to focus on what was in front of her.

After a few deep breaths, she could finally identify her surroundings. On two opposite sides, metal frame shelves towered up toward the twenty-foot ceiling. The bottom four shelves held boxes, lots of them. Stacks of unused mailing boxes. Others that were labeled *fabric*.

A voice caught her attention. It was Bobbi, and it sounded like he was on the other side of the shelves. "I don't know what to do, man."

Another voice came across what must be a speaker phone. "Run, you idiot."

"Where do I go?"

"What am I, your mother? You screwed up, Bobbi. You're on your own."

"Ronan, I—"

The phone beeped, indicating the call was over.

A string of profanity spewed from Bobbi's mouth.

Jacq pushed on the concrete floor and raised herself to a sitting position. The cut on her right arm from the glass shelf was still bleeding. The blood trickled down her arm and dripped onto the floor. Her left hand ached from gripping Bobbi's gun when she took it out of his hands. Fortunately, Bobbi hadn't tied her up, so maybe she could make a run for it. Find a phone and call for backup.

Her whole body resisted the movement, and, once upright, she was incredibly dizzy. She grabbed the edge of the shelf.

Bobbi dialed another number. "Scar. Hey. Bobbi here. I hope Celeste has been good to you."

"You know she's my favorite. Why are you calling me?" The voice sounded familiar, but Jacq couldn't place it.

"I'm in a bit of a bind."

"I'd say you are. Every branch of law enforcement in Tennessee is after you right now. Is it true you took an agent?"

Jacq rubbed her head. Who could the man on the phoneline be?

"I didn't know what to do. I was going to use her as a hostage to get out but didn't have to. What do I do with her now?"

"Get rid of her and run. Where are you now?"

"At the girls' shop."

"Burn it. Your girls stepped out of line, teach 'em a lesson. Just leave the agent inside, and burn the whole place down to the ground. Then run. And whatever you do, don't take your car. They're looking for it."

"Yes, sir."

"And don't ever call me again." *Beep.*

Jacq steadied herself. She needed to get out before Bobbi came back around that corner.

Chapter Twenty-Seven

Gio strode up the sidewalk in front of the Highwaters' house and rang the doorbell.

A moment later, Mrs. Highwater opened the door. "Gio. How are you?" Her face was thinner than it had been a week ago, and her eyes were sunk deep and shadowed by dark circles.

"I'm well. May I come in? Is Mr. Highwater around?" His excitement had to be obvious on his face, but she barely looked at him.

She shuffled away. "Yes. He's getting ready to go back to work. He doesn't want to, but what are we to do?" Mrs. Highwater twisted the ring on her finger.

Gio followed her to the living room.

Mr. Highwater came around the corner. "Do you have news about Marrissa?"

Mrs. Highwater met Gio's gaze. Her lips parted in anticipation of his answer.

Gio couldn't contain the joy any longer. "We found her. She's alive and safe."

Mrs. Highwater screamed. "My baby, she's okay?"

"Yes, ma'am. And asking for you."

The woman collapsed into her husband's arms. They both cried tears of relief and joy.

Mr. Highwater looked up at Gio. "Well, where is she?"

"On her way to the hospital. I'm here to take you there."

Dylan made another turn. He must have misunderstood something Stella had said because he couldn't find the little warehouse space she had described, and now he was driving in circles. Plus, there was no sign of Bobbi's SUV.

In fact, there was no sign of anything that resembled a warehouse.

He slammed his fist against the steering wheel. Why was he driving around in a rundown neighborhood?

He needed to back up and figure out where he'd gone wrong with Stella's directions, assuming it was his fault. Which it probably was.

Stop it. Berating himself wouldn't get Jacq back.

He called Gabe. "Any sign of them?"

"Sorry, Dylan. Nothing."

"Okay, keep looking."

"You know I will."

Dylan hung up and pulled over to the side of the road. He picked up his laptop off the passenger's seat—the seat Jacq had been sitting in only an hour ago.

He swallowed and opened his map app. Following the directions Stella had given him, he realized he wasn't where he was supposed to be. A wrong turn had lost him ten minutes. Why hadn't he taken the thirty seconds to find the address with the GPS?

Dylan slammed the laptop shut and dropped it back in the passenger's seat. Jerking the car into drive, he pulled a one-eighty and drove in the right direction.

Jacq had to fight to stay on her feet as she made her way down the aisle of shelving. Only twenty feet to go. Each step and each breath increased her dizziness.

Stay with it, Jacq. God, I need You now like never before.

Bobbi's SUV was parked inside the warehouse. She glanced around it and spotted the door.

She peered around the shelves.

Bobbi appeared in front of her. "What the—"

He swung his fist, but her reflexes were too slow. She took the blow to the face and stumbled backward.

I need strength. She pleaded with heaven. She needed an angel—or the cavalry. Where was backup? Hadn't someone followed them here?

She steadied herself and lunged at Bobbi.

Her fist met his cheek, but he grabbed her arms and spun her into his grasp. Both of his arms encircled her.

She tried to stomp on his feet, but she was too slow.

"You're a feisty one." He shoved her to the floor.

She slid into the corner of a shelf.

"Do you know what I do to feisty girls?" He towered over her. "They get taught a lesson about where women belong." He slapped her across the face.

Her head jerked to the side, and her cheek stung. She scrambled across the floor.

But he came after her, jumped on top of her, and pinned her legs against the ground. He hurled punches on her, but not at her head. His fist slammed into her ribs repeatedly.

She couldn't catch her breath. This was it. She was going to die. She would never kiss her baby again. Or Dylan.

A rib cracked. She shrieked. The pain radiated through her entire torso.

Bobbi stood and grabbed her hair. He dragged her back down the aisle of boxes. "I found these"—he pulled a pair of cuffs out of his back pocket—"hanging from your belt." He laughed maniacally.

She tried to crawl away, but Bobbi stepped on her ankle. The unworn tread of his boots dug into her skin.

She pulled her leg, but his stance was too firm.

He yanked her hands behind her back and cuffed them around one of the metal beams that created the shelving unit.

She fought against the cuffs, but he had secured them too tightly. *God, help me get out of here. I need to get out for Harper.*

He ambled to his SUV, lifted the back, and removed a gas can.

"You keep a gas can in your car?" Her chest burned from trying to speak.

"I swear, woman, you need to learn to keep to your own business."

"Seems like it *is* my business right now."

He laughed. "I guess you're right. We have to be ready to run any time, extra gas means you get farther when you run. But now it's going to serve a different purpose." He poured the gasoline across the boxes along the shelves opposite of Jacq.

Breathing was hard enough, but as realization that Bobbi was following the advice of the man he called Scar sunk in, the terror made breathing impossible.

He worked down the shelves on the same side as Jacq but ran out right before he got to her. "Man!" He tossed the canister against the wall. "Guess you'll die slowly today."

"I'd rather wait until tomorrow."

He stopped and stared at her.

If she hadn't been scared out of her mind, she'd laugh at the shock on his face.

He shook his head and pulled a lighter out of his pocket. He stalked straight toward her. "Any last words."

"Yeah, let me out of here."

Bobbi leaned his head back and laughed. His laughter abruptly stopped, and he glared down at Jacq. He raised his fist and punched her again.

The world faded around her. She tried to stay conscious, but it was one too many blows.

Chapter Twenty-Eight

Dylan made the last turn and the set of warehouses appeared. He was finally in the right place. Hopefully, he wasn't too late. He called Matt and relayed his location.

Matt said, "We'll be there in a jiffy."

"I'll let you know if they're here."

They hung up, and Dylan stopped the car shy of the end of the building Stella said held their little warehouse unit. Dylan jumped out of the car, pulled his gun from its holster, and crept around the side of the building. Stella indicated their unit was three down from this end with a ramp leading up to the loading dock's garage door. If they were inside, the loading dock or steel door next to it was the only way out since the building didn't have a back door.

Dylan inched around the corner and passed the first unit, torn between running and a stealthy approach.

He chose something in-between. Moving as quickly yet quietly as possible, he skirted the first and second sets of stairs, approaching the third. Jacq might be behind the solid brown door, but he didn't know. Too many unknowns.

His heart pounded.

He planned to go up the stairs and try the doorknob, even though he doubted it was unlocked. But first he examined the garage door on the opposite side of the stairs. Didn't look like there was a lock. But if he pulled that up, the noise would surely alert Bobbi and any cronies he had in there with him. That wasn't the best choice. Door first.

He raised his gun to the door and skirted the handrail that flanked the stairs.

Boom! A small explosion came from inside the building. Dylan took a step back. What had exploded?

Boom! Boom! Boom!

Dylan ducked low to the ground.

The door flew open. Bobbi ran down the stairs toward Dylan, colliding with him before he could react.

"What the—" Bobbi shoved him away.

"FBI. Put your hands—"

Bobbi kicked Dylan's arm, redirecting the gun away from himself, then came at him. Dylan swung his arm back toward Bobbi. The hand holding the gun smacked into the side of Bobbi's head.

Bobbi caught Dylan's arm and twisted it behind his back, stretching it beyond its normal range.

Dylan's shoulder screamed in pain. He couldn't get his finger on the trigger.

He jabbed his elbow back toward Bobbi's gut. He missed.

Bobbi punched him in the side. One, two, three times in rapid succession.

Dylan's insides burned.

He swung his left arm high over Bobbi's head, twisting enough to free his right arm from Bobbi's grasp. Dylan's arm slammed down onto Bobbi's shoulder.

Dylan spun around the rest of the way, but Bobbi was just as quick and blocked Dylan's gun hand.

Dylan punched Bobbi with his left fist. Bobbi dodged it and swung in return.

Heat from the building behind Dylan licked at his back. Jacq!

Bobbi threw another punch that landed on Dylan's cheekbone. Pain radiated through his face.

Again, Dylan attempted to raise his gun at Bobbi, but he grabbed Dylan's arm and the gun.

He was in danger of losing control of his firearm.

Dylan yanked back. But with Bobbi pulling on his arm, Dylan struggled to get his thumb on the magazine release. He got it and dropped the magazine out of his Glock. But there was still one in the chamber. Enough to kill either one of them.

Chapter Twenty-Nine

Heat permeated the air around Jacq as she regained consciousness. Sweat dripped down her aching forehead.

Boom! An aerosol can exploded and whizzed past her head. She ducked.

The sudden motion made her dizziness return.

God, I can't die. Please.

Smoke strangled her. She coughed. Pain shot through her chest cavity.

She shifted her body to the ground and lay as close to the floor as she could.

But the heat from the flames felt like it was going to melt her to the floor.

"Jesus, please help." She fought the feelings of hopelessness that attacked her. "God, you are able. Save me from the fire again."

Tears formed in her eyes but evaporated before they could stream out.

Was this really the end?

Pkew. Another little explosion. No. That was a gunshot.

"Dylan!"

Had he come to save her? Was he out there? Was he hurt?

"Jesus, help!"

The fire crackled loudly around her. Would anyone hear her?

"Dylan!" She gasped for air.

The gunshot wound in Dylan's thigh burned, but at least the gun was empty now. He continued to wrestle with Bobbi. Each of them fighting to get the upper hand.

"Dylan!" A faint voice floated out among the crackle of the fire in the building.

Jacq!

New determination swelled in Dylan. He smashed the pistol against the side of Bobbi's head again.

Bobbi stumbled back, and Dylan swung his wounded leg against Bobbi's and drove him to the ground.

Dylan threw the man onto his front, dropped the knee of his good leg on his back, grabbed his cuffs, and yanked Bobbi's arm back.

A squad car pulled up beside him, and Gabe jumped out.

Dylan got up. Pain seized his thigh, but he ignored it. He yanked Bobbi up and shoved him toward Gabe.

"He's all yours. Jacq's inside." Dylan turned and ran to the building.

"Dylan, wait!"

Dylan ignored Gabe's pleading and went inside.

The heat assaulted him. He raised his hands in front of his face and stepped back. The fire was intense and growing. The flames were encroaching on the SUV parked inside the bay. He needed to get Jacq out of there before the gas tank caught fire.

The smoke was getting thick. He crouched and trudged deeper into the warehouse.

"Jacq!" He coughed.

He needed her to call back, but the smoke would be too much for her sensitive lungs. Why fire? The mental assault that must be on her mind.

"Jacqui!"

"Dylan." Her voice was faint, but it was enough to give him

direction.

Two pillars of fire rose on either side of an aisle. She must be between them.

The heat was intense and almost made him forget about the pain in his thigh, until he took another step. He'd rather die in here than lose Jacq, so he stepped forward again and rushed in between the pillars of fire.

He came closer to the back of the building. The fire was less intense, but the smoke was so thick he couldn't see anything.

"Jacq, where are you?"

"I'm right here." She coughed. It sounded even more pained than he had expected.

He dropped to the ground and felt for her. When he found her leg, he moved his hand up to the rest of her.

"I'm"—she coughed—"cuffed to the"—she coughed again—"shelf."

He dug in his pocket for his keys and fumbled for the right one.

The smoke now burned his eyes and lungs. And it was so hot. Sweat soaked through his shirt.

He dropped his keys but scooped them off the floor. He leaned his body over her as he fumbled with the keys again and tried to shield her body from the heat as best he could.

Boom! Another small explosion.

"What on earth?"

"Aerosol cans." A coughing spasm seized Jacq's lungs.

"Don't talk. I'll get you out."

He felt for the cuffs and the tiny keyhole. He inserted the key and twisted. The cuffs popped open.

Dylan scooped Jacq into his arms, but they didn't linger. The heat and smoke were growing by the moment. If they didn't get out of there now, they wouldn't.

"Can you crawl?"

"Yeah." Jacq's lungs sounded tight.

Dylan removed his outer shirt and ripped it into four. They

wrapped it around their hands and pulled their shirts over their noses. "Stay close."

They crawled along the ground, careful to avoid burning debris around them. Once free of the towers of flames, they stood and hobbled around the now-burning SUV.

Someone had opened the garage door, and the firefighters were running toward the building.

Something popped behind him. Dylan pushed Jacq forward down the ramp toward a firefighter.

The car exploded behind him. He ducked, but the flames engulfed his back.

Chapter Thirty

Jacq stumbled forward from the force of Dylan's shove and the explosion. She fell into a firefighter's arms. Pushing off him, she spun around.

Dylan's back was on fire.

"Dylan!" The screech her voice made was unrecognizable. She lunged forward toward him, but the fireman grabbed her arms and pulled her away from the building.

Another firefighter grabbed Dylan and put out the flames.

The fireman holding her finally let go, and she ran to Dylan. She grabbed his hand. "Are you okay?" Her lungs seized up, and a coughing fit took over.

Dylan squeezed her hand. "The question is, are you?"

One of the firefighters pointed to an ambulance. "Let's get you *both* to the hospital."

Jacq leaned heavily on the firefighter's arm until they met the EMT halfway to the ambulance.

The EMT took her arm. "I'm Holly, and this is my partner, Max. Let's see how you two are. We've got another ambulance en route."

"I'm fine." She coughed. "Can we ride together?"

"You are not fine, but maybe." Holly helped Jacq into the back of the ambulance. "First, put this on." She handed Jacq an oxygen mask.

Jacq raised it to her face. The oxygen filled her lungs. Sweet relief.

"You too, mister." Holly grabbed another one and handed it to Max, who helped Dylan sit on the gurney next to Jacq.

Jacq slipped her hand into Dylan's. The thigh of his jeans was saturated in blood. She pulled the mask away from her face. "Dylan! Your leg."

"You should see the other guy." His voice was muffled through the mask.

"You mean the guy sitting in the back of the squad car?"

He dropped her hand and nudged the mask back to her face.

Holly took Jacq's vitals, and Max took Dylan's. Max said, "We need to get them to the hospital, ASAP."

Holly nodded.

"Dylan! Jacq!" Matt ran to the back of the ambulance, Sabrina right behind him. "Are y'all okay?"

Dylan gave him a thumbs-up, but the pain was deeply etched in his face.

Jacq pulled away her mask again. "If by 'okay' you mean not dead."

Holly grabbed Jacq's hand with the mask. "Leave this on. You're going to be in worse shape if you don't get more oxygen in your blood." She took elastic bands and stretched them over Jacq's head, bumping the spot where Bobbi had hit her with the side of the gun.

She winced.

"I'm so sorry." Holly gingerly felt Jacq's head. "Nasty bump. You're headed to the MRI machine."

Jacq took a deep breath of oxygen, but pain in her side seized her lungs. Once she got the spasm to settle, she said, "And x-ray. Fairly sure I have a broken rib."

Holly lifted Jacq's shirt. "I'd say so. You're all kinds of black 'n blue."

Dylan groaned next to her. Max was examining Dylan's burnt back.

Matt shut one of the ambulance doors. "Get them out of here." He looked at Dylan and Jacq. "We'll see you guys there."

Jacq nodded. Even if they were in bad shape, at least they were alive. *Thank you, Jesus!*

Daisy padded down the stairs in her robe and slippers. She caught a glimpse of herself in the mirror that hung above a little table in the foyer. Without all her makeup and hair done up she actually looked more like her real self—Morgan. That's who she wanted to be. She didn't want to be Daisy any longer.

A yawn crept out of her weary body. The clock in the entryway read eleven. She'd barely slept for an hour. But the doorbell was ringing, and Ronan always expected her to answer it. She glanced through the peephole.

"Celeste!" She opened the door. "What are you doing here?"

Celeste all but ran into the house. "Nice to see you too." There was no humor in her eyes.

"What's wrong?"

"Where's Bobbi?"

"I don't know. What do you mean? Isn't he at home?"

Or did the FBI come? If so, why aren't you with them?

"No!" Celeste became frantic. "He isn't there. The cops are. The house is filled with people. I tried going home, but there were cop cars all over. And the coroner's van. Daisy, I'm freaking out. Where's my Bobbi?"

Morgan drew Celeste into her arms. "I don't know, babe." She ushered Celeste deeper into the house. "Have you eaten anything?"

"No."

"Let's get you something." They wandered into the kitchen.

Morgan directed Celeste to a stool at the large kitchen island and opened the fridge. A strange feeling overcame Morgan. She almost felt guilty that Celeste's home had been invaded, but at the same time, she felt proud. She slid a yogurt over to Celeste and got her a spoon.

Celeste took the spoon and used it to talk with. "I don't understand. How on earth did the cops find out where he had her? Why did he even bring that little—"

"Because he's a moron." Ronan walked into the kitchen.

Morgan stood a little taller. Ronan hated it when she slouched.

Celeste turned to Ronan and opened her mouth to ask a question but shut it quickly.

Ronan put his hand on her back. "Go ahead, ask your question."

Something panged in Morgan's heart. She hated Ronan's control over her life, but she was still jealous.

"What happened? Where's Bobbi?"

"Good chance he's dead. If not, the cops have him, or he's long gone. He screwed up. As did one of you girls. That's the only thing I can figure." Ronan ran his fingers along Celeste's collarbone. "He was even stupid enough to take one of the feds with him. But she should be good and dead by now."

Morgan's stomach dropped. She gripped the counter in front of her and carefully maintained her composure. Which agent was dead? Surely it wasn't Jacqui. She'd never forgive herself.

Ronan continued, "But the problem is that someone is playing out of pocket, and how do I know that wasn't you"—Ronan moved his hand up Celeste's throat—"Celeste?" He gripped her throat and lifted her off the stool.

Terror filled Celeste's eyes.

Every cell in Morgan's body wanted to run around the island and start wailing on Ronan. But she couldn't move. She didn't dare.

Celeste shook her head as much as she could, and he released her. "Ronan, I promise it wasn't me. I would never. You know that."

"You're right, I do. Bobbi never had anything negative to say about you. You can stay here with us." Ronan raked his hand into Celeste's hair. "Maybe you can show Daisy here what it actually means to be bottom."

"Yes, sir." She leaned into Ronan's touch.

Morgan thought she was going to hurl. Now she wasn't sure who she wanted to hit more.

Ronan kissed Celeste's forehead. "You can sleep in my room today and take tonight off. Let Daisy know if you need anything." Ronan looked over at Daisy. "You need to get some sleep. You look awful."

"Will do." She mustered all she could to give him the sweetest smile possible.

"Good." He turned and left the room.

Celeste met Morgan's gaze with wide eyes. "I'm sorry, Daze. I didn't mean to come in here and—"

Morgan waved her hand through the air. "Don't worry about it." But her heart wanted to scream. "Need anything before I get some sleep?"

"Nah, I'll find things myself. I know the rules."

Morgan nodded and slipped out of the kitchen, ambling up the back staircase. Once in her room, she slung her robe across the end of the bed and curled up under the sheets.

God, why does it hurt so much when Ronan looks at her like that? I'm used to sharing him with Lily. I hate this life. But thank You that the feds were able to act on my tip. Help the agent Bobbi had. Help her to not be dead. Jacqui. What if she had been the agent? *Please let Jacqui be alive.*

She shook her head against the pillow. Was she really praying? Was she really starting to long to get out of the game? Yes, she was. For the first time in years, the idea stirred in her head. But it was foolish. This was all she knew. At least Ronan kept a roof over her head, food in her belly, and expensive clothes on her body. She'd never be able to get a "normal" job. This was where she was. And where she would stay.

Chapter Thirty-One

Dylan shifted. Lying on his stomach in a hospital bed was awkward, not to mention he was simply uncomfortable. The area around the burn hurt more than the center, but the painkillers helped. By putting out the fire on his back so quickly, the firefighter had helped keep the burns from becoming too extensive. But he wasn't going to be back in the field for at least a few weeks.

Dylan groaned. He wanted to lie on his back, but that wasn't going to happen anytime soon. Good thing he was usually a stomach sleeper.

More than anything, though, he wanted to see Jacq. Where was she? When they arrived at the hospital, they had been taken in different directions, and he hadn't seen her since. He was sure she had a concussion, but he didn't know how bad it was. Had they admitted her too?

What if something more was wrong?

"Don't worry about anything." The Scripture resounded in his head. "Instead, pray about everything. Tell God what you need, and thank him for all he has done."

Thank You, Jesus, for saving us from the fire. Thank You that we were able to save Marrissa and those girls. Please be with Jacq. Help her to be okay. Bring healing to both of us.

The door to his hospital room opened, but his back was to it. Seeing his visitor required too much effort, so he waited for them to reveal themselves.

"Hey!" the voice of an angel spoke.

He lifted himself enough to turn his head away from the wall, but the pain soared. He ignored it. "Jacq." The stitches in his leg pulled. "Ow!"

"Careful." She was sitting in a wheelchair pushed by his nurse, Yolanda.

Yolanda said, "Your roommate has arrived, Agent Harris. Figured it would be good to get her settled in here while we wait for her MRI results."

Jacq stood and came to Dylan.

Yolanda reached out to stop her. "Slow down, girl!"

Jacq swayed, leaning heavily on the IV pole with oxygen tank she dragged with her. Dylan reached out too, and their hands met. Their eyes connected. Gratitude and love surged in his heart. She let go of his hand and cupped the side of his face. The little oxygen cannula in her nose was adorable. She stepped closer, leaned down, and planted a kiss on his forehead. His heart soared. How he wished he could simply turn over and take her in his arms.

"How are you feeling?" She leaned her forehead against his.

"Okay, I guess. Pain meds are helping, but I can't get comfortable. And I already had my first visit from physical therapy." He looked past Jacq to Yolanda, who was parking the wheelchair against the wall. "Is there any way I could sit up?"

"I'm not sure about sitting, but we sure can prop you up so it's easier to visit." Yolanda rounded his bed. "The key is you have to stay leaning forward to aid in keeping your dressings in place."

"Not a problem. I just want to see this lady a little better."

A tiny giggle escaped Jacq's lips. "I bet your leg will be more comfortable without the pressure of lying on it."

"I'm not going to deny that."

With more effort on his part than he'd expected, Yolanda raised the head of the bed and stuffed a zillion pillows under his chest, abdomen, and leg, putting him almost all the way on his side, but not quite.

"That's a little better. But I'm guessing comfortable won't be in my vocabulary for a while."

Yolanda pulled another chair over for Jacq.

Jacq sat close. "I'd imagine not. How bad are the burns?" She looked over his shoulder at his dressing.

"They said second degree, but some parts are worse than others." He reached for her hand.

She took it. "Is it going to need grafting?"

"Probably not."

"Good! Grafting is no fun. Looks like we'll have matching scars." Her smile caused butterflies to do cannonballs in his stomach.

He smiled back. "Jacq, I love you."

Her already red cheeks turned a shade darker. "I love you too."

"I know."

"So how are you going to explain this to your family? Maybe something like, 'Hey, I saved Jacq Sheppard from a burning building.'"

"I could. They wouldn't know it was you. After all, they know you as Jacqui Schurmann." He rubbed her knuckles with his thumb. "But seriously, I don't tend to talk about work, so I won't say much about it. My mom doesn't like knowing what the risks of my job really are, so I don't tell her."

"She's going to want to know more about a giant burn on your back." She squeezed his hand.

"Yeah, I suppose. You think you'll be ready to see them soon?"

Her eyes widened.

He laughed. "You do know that if what we have here gets serious, seeing them will be inevitable?"

"I do. But I definitely don't want them seeing me like this. Plus, I want to be sure about us."

"Well, I'm pretty certain, and I'm not embarrassed about what's going on between us, so you tell me when you're ready." He reached up and stroked her hair away from the bandage on her forehead. "You aren't the same Jacq who dated my brother. You've changed and grown in ways I'm sure they won't appreciate, but I love who you've become. And I was pretty keen on you back then."

"You hardly knew me." She playfully slapped his arm.

"Oh, but I had two good eyes."

She looked at the floor. "You aren't the only one."

"What's *that* supposed to mean?"

She met his gaze. "I had two good eyes back then too."

"While you were dating my brother?"

"Yeah. But hey, you were the one checking out your brother's girlfriend."

"I was a high school boy; can you blame me?"

Jacq laughed. "No, I guess not. You think it'll be okay that we're …"

"We're what?"

"I don't know. What do you call what we are?"

"Dating?"

"How can we be dating? You haven't taken me out on a date yet."

He gave her an irritated look in mock annoyance at her obsession with vernacular precision.

She laughed.

He shook his head. "Whatever you want to call it, I'd like to think of you as my girlfriend. You okay with that title?"

"Absolutely. But you didn't answer my question about whether it's okay." She tilted her head and gave him a pointed look. "What's your family going to say?"

"It's fine. Emma will think it's great."

"But Chad? Your mom?"

"What should he care? He broke up with you and married your friend. I'm pretty sure he doesn't get to have an opinion on this. And Mom…"

"She's never liked me, Dylan."

"I know. You two are so different."

"I'll never be the prim and proper southern woman she wants

me to be."

"Nor do I want you to be. I'm not falling in love with a southern belle. I'm falling in love with a kick-butt FBI agent."

"Oh, your mom's going to *love* that."

"Well, I'm not her precious Chad, so we might be okay." He winked at her.

She laughed.

A knock echoed on the door, and it opened before either of them could answer. Aliza appeared. "Hey, you two."

Dylan lifted his hand in a wave. "You'll pardon me if I don't get up."

"Duh." Aliza's expression turned serious. "I'm really glad you two are okay."

The door opened again, and Yolanda entered. "Hey, guys, sorry to interrupt, but Agent Harris, your parents and brother are here to see you. Would you like me to let them in?"

Jacq's eyes grew wide once more.

Dylan suppressed a chuckle. "Wait just a minute, please."

"Not a problem. Let me know when you're ready."

"Thanks."

The nurse disappeared.

His heart raced. He had said he was ready for them to know about her, but presented with the opportunity, he had second thoughts. "Jacq, there's no time like the present." He rubbed his thumb along the back of her hand.

"Maybe, but … no." She shook her head. "Not here. Plus, Rachel is bringing Harper over. Maybe I can go see her downstairs."

He squeezed her hand. "They'll let you?"

Aliza stepped forward. "I'll take her." She pulled her badge out of her jacket pocket. "This thing holds a little leverage around here." She grabbed the wheelchair. "Shall we?"

Jacq nodded and grasped her IV pole.

"Excellent. Then hurry back."

"I will."

He slid his hand behind her neck, under her hair, and drew her in for a kiss. Their lips met, and his heart finished its preflight checklist. He deepened the kiss until he had to release her to catch his breath.

She giggled and walked over to Aliza, who was pretending not to pay attention to them.

"Take care of her, Aliza," Dylan said.

"Of course." Aliza turned the wheelchair, and the two ladies left.

Dylan tried to tether his heart to the ground, but it didn't want to stay down.

Father God, thank You so much for Jacq and protecting us today. Help me now with my family.

Jacq closed her eyes and let Aliza push her out of Dylan's hospital room. That kiss! The concussion wasn't helping, but that kiss had made her lightheaded.

"You okay?" Yolanda came up to her. "You look a little woozy."

She rubbed her forehead. "A kiss and a concussion are not a good combo."

The nurse chuckled. "I'd say not. I got your MRI result, and it's what we expected—nothing too concerning. But we're definitely keeping you here overnight for observation."

"Thank you."

"Not a problem at all. But where are you off to? You need to rest."

"Aliza is taking me down to the lobby to see my daughter. I'll be back when Dylan's family is gone."

"He's ready to see his family?"

"He is."

"Pardon my nosiness, but why aren't you sticking around? Thought you two—"

Jacq snorted. "Complicated story, but the short version is that I dated his brother back in the day, and we haven't told them about us yet."

"Ah. That makes complete sense. I'll be sure not to say anything to give y'all away."

"Thanks."

The nurse turned and went back toward the waiting room.

Lord, I'm not ready to face Dylan's mom and brother right now, not with the way my head is killing me. "Aliza? Do you mind getting to the elevator faster than light speed?"

"I don't mind helping you avoid them, but I'm not going to go so fast it makes you dizzy."

"Ah, you're no fun."

"Oh, I can be fun, but I don't want to deal with Dylan's wrath if anything befalls you."

"All right, I guess I can't argue with that." Jacq wished she could run to the elevator to be sure to avoid Chad and Mrs. Harris, but she was still too shaky. She'd trust Aliza to help.

They passed the waiting room area, and she heard his family talking behind her.

Aliza pressed the elevator button.

Jacq breathed a little easier when the doors opened, and Aliza rolled her in. *Thank you!*

She pushed the button on the inside of the elevator, and, once the door shut, relaxed further.

Aliza moved where she could see Jacq. "Okay, I can't handle it any longer. You and Dylan?" Her eyebrows were high, and her smile wide.

"Guess we didn't try to hide it from you at all."

Aliza laughed. "No, you didn't, but I can't say I'm surprised after how you two have been all week. I'm so excited for y'all."

The elevator doors opened, and Aliza rolled Jacq out to the lobby.

"Mommy!" Harper's voice sang out above the bustle.

Jacq opened her arms, and Harper came running toward her. The two-year-old stopped shy and looked at the wheelchair.

"I'm okay, a little dizzy and don't want to fall over. Come here."

Harper climbed up on her lap, and Jacq held her tightly until she started squirming.

"Did you have a good day today?"

Harper nodded, then reached up and touched her bandage. "Mommy got an owie?"

"I did. My head hurts pretty bad."

"I kiss it and make it feel better." Harper's little hands took Jacq's head and pulled it to her lips. She planted the loudest, most slobbery kiss in history on Jacq's forehead. "Mommy all better?"

"That definitely helped, kiddo."

Dylan tried to shift in his bed. This position was more comfortable than lying flat on his stomach, but he needed one more pillow under his chest. The door opened as he tried to reach an extra pillow on the chair next to the bed. But reaching was a bad idea. His back pulled. He let out a deep groan.

"Dylan!" His mom ran across the room and grabbed the pillow for him. She drew his head into a hug, carefully avoiding his bandages.

He wrapped his arm around her. "Hey, Mom."

"I'm so glad you're okay. When your boss called—" Her hand rested on his upper left arm, right on his tattoo, as if she didn't even care it was there.

"I'm all right."

Matt strolled in. "All right? You're a hero." He scanned the room. "Where's J—um … Sheppard? Thought she was in here."

Dylan shook his head. "Nope." He was grateful Matt kept from saying Jacq's name.

"Have you seen her? Is she okay?" Matt asked.

"I have. She's got a nasty concussion and a cracked rib, but she'll be all right."

"Hero?" his mom questioned. His brother, sister-in-law, and father all stood there with faces ready to hear the story.

Matt obliged. "Oh, most definitely. Not only did he and Sheppard save four girls from sex trafficking, but Dylan here cuffed the bad guy, then ran into a burning warehouse to save his partner."

"Really?" Chad said.

"Is this true?" his mom said, her hand still gripping his arm.

"It is."

Matt continued, "Oh, and I forgot to add he got shot before he ran back in. Then a car blew up as he was trying to get away from the fire."

"Oh, Dylan!" There was a look on his mom's face he'd never seen before.

"Mom, I'm fine."

"But shot?"

"It only grazed my leg."

Dylan met Matt's eyes. Matt was pressing his lips together. Probably to keep himself from mentioning the fact Dylan had been shot with his own gun, but that would not help his mother's apparent anxiety. Mom had always been worried he'd get shot; it was part of why she hated him being an agent.

Matt said, "I'm going to find Sheppard."

"She went down to the lobby with Aliza."

Matt nodded and left the room.

Dylan looked back at his dad, then at his mom. He stuffed the pillow Mom had handed him under his chest.

"Shouldn't you lie back?"

"Mom, I can't." He turned slightly and looked over his shoulder. "Second-degree burns."

"Oh, of course. I'm so glad you're okay. I was sick all the way over here." She brushed a strand of his hair away from his forehead. "I know I don't say this enough, but I love you. And the thought of losing you …" She waved a hand at her face as tears formed in her eyes.

His heart lifted. He took his mom's hand and squeezed it. "I love you too, Mom."

It meant the world to hear his mom say she loved him. But would she accept his love for a girl she didn't get along with?

It was good to have his family surrounding him, but he longed to have Jacq by his side too.

"Guess we aren't going to be hitting balls at the batting cage anytime soon, huh?" Chad crossed his arms.

"Probably not. But give me a month. I'll be fine, and I'll still out-hit you."

"Depends on how distracted you are. This partner you saved … Is that the girl you were telling me about?"

His mom tilted her head. "Girl? As in a woman you're interested in?"

Dylan couldn't fight the smile that took over his face.

Chad laughed. "I'll take that as a *yes*."

"What girl?" his mom demanded.

Chad stepped forward. "You won't like her, Mom."

Dylan suppressed the enormous laugh that wanted to escape. "I'll be the judge of that."

Dylan squeezed his mom's hand. "She's an FBI agent."

"Well, that is one thing against her, I suppose. I don't understand why any woman would want to do a man's job like that."

Dylan took a deep breath and let it out slowly. "Mom, having a woman on the job made a huge difference in helping those girls feel safe when we rescued them today. It's important to have female FBI agents."

"I suppose. Why else don't you think I'll like her?" She let go of his hand.

"Let's just say I know what kind of girls you like, and she's not that."

She crossed her arms. "We'll see."

His dad smiled. "When do we get to meet her?"

"I'm not sure. But not today."

Jacq squeezed Rachel in a tight hug before letting go. "Thank you so much for bringing her and for keeping her tonight."

Rachel held her at arm's length. "You are most welcome. Whatever I can do to help, let me know."

Jacq nodded before drawing Harper into her arms. "You're going to sleep at Ms. Rachel's again tonight, understand?"

Harper nodded. "Mommy get better?"

"Yep. I'm going to get better tonight, and then I'll come get you tomorrow, and we'll go home and watch a movie."

"Yay! I yuv you, Mommy."

"I love you too, Harper. Be a good listener." She kissed the toddler's forehead and gave her a hug.

Harper skipped to the door holding Rachel's hand and turned around before exiting and waved.

Jacq waved in return. She sighed. She missed her baby girl already and couldn't wait to be home with her. But a strange feeling overcame her. She also missed Dylan and wanted, almost needed, to be by his side right now. He had saved her life, risking his own. Tears welled up in her eyes and her nose tingled. Her heart felt like it was going to burst. How did she have so much love inside her to give? Where had it come from?

When she'd lost Sean, she wondered if she could ever love again, but then she had Harper, and all the emotions she had felt for Sean funneled into loving Harper. But now, without her feelings for Harper diminishing an iota, she found her heart bursting with love for Dylan.

She rubbed her forehead. Her head still throbbed and probably would for days.

"Too much?" Aliza had been chatting with officers who had

come in with a patient while she waited for Jacq.

"No. But I'm hoping it's time for more painkillers soon."

"Didn't you take some like an hour ago?"

"Probably."

"We should get you to bed."

"You know I don't want to go back in there until Dylan's family is gone."

Matt jogged toward them. "There you are. How are you feeling?"

Jacq shrugged, but the movement pulled on her rib. She winced. "I've been better."

He stuck his hands in his pockets. "I'd imagine. Would you feel up to seeing Marrissa? She was asking about you."

"I think I can manage. I can't go back to my room yet anyway."

Aliza grabbed the handles of the wheelchair. "Then let's go."

The three of them took the elevator one floor up from Dylan and Jacq's. Matt led them to the right room and knocked on the door. Gio answered.

"Hey, guys. You doing all right, Jacq?"

"Well enough."

Aliza rolled her into the room. The beautiful young blonde they had spent the whole week looking for sat in the hospital bed looking vulnerable and scared. That fear could take a long time to subside. Jacq felt the same way about fire right now.

"Hi, Marrissa. I'm Agent Sheppard, but you can call me Jacq. I was the one banging on that door.."

"I'm glad you're okay. That Bobbi guy—" Her body released a shudder.

Jacq nodded. No words were needed. Jacq stood and, dragging her IV pole, walked over to Marrissa's bedside.

The girl reached out her arms, and Jacq accepted the hug.

"I'm so glad you're safe, Marrissa." She pulled out of the hug and looked in the girl's eyes. "If there's anything you need, please let me know."

Marrissa gave her a weak "okay."

Jacq sat back in her wheelchair and got to know Marrissa a little better, connecting what she knew about the girl with the girl herself.

After nearly an hour of visiting, Jacq waved goodbye to Marrissa. However, as Gio pushed her wheelchair out of the girl's room, fear churned in Jacq's stomach. What if Dylan's family was still there? But she was tired and needed to lay down. Gio hadn't given her any choice.

"You do know Dylan's family will be more stressful than visiting with Marrissa."

Gio rested a hand on her shoulder. "I know, but I have every intention of going in there first and kicking them out, for both your sakes."

"You're a good friend, Gio."

"So I've been told."

They entered the elevator and took it down one floor. When the elevator door opened on their floor, voices echoed in the hallway in front of them. Chad.

She froze. *Don't look. Don't look at me.*

Gio waited to push her out.

The voices disappeared into the second elevator.

She stuck her foot out and nudged the closing doors open.

"Sounds like they're gone." Gio pushed the wheelchair out of the elevator and down the hall. "See, that wasn't so bad. I didn't even have to kick them out."

"Praise the Lord."

Gio knocked on the door and pushed it open. "Can we come in? I have a very tired patient here."

"Please!" Dylan sounded happy.

She bit her lower lip as Gio rolled her into the room. Dylan was lying on his stomach, and Yolanda was checking his burns. Emotions flooded her being—gratitude and love mixed with fear and a bit of anger. They stopped her from moving forward.

Dylan beckoned her over with his hand. She willed herself to stand and go to him.

"You okay?" he asked.

She nodded, but when she glanced at his burn her stomach churned.

The nurse's hands paused. "You don't have to look; burns are kinda gross."

"I know. I had third degree all across my back three and a half years ago."

"Oh, dear. That's rough. I'm almost done here. Then you two need to get some rest. I'll be in every couple of hours to check on both of you. But I'm only a call button away, so don't hesitate to ask for anything. And I mean that—absolutely anything."

"Thanks," they said in unison.

"And Jacq, you are to get in bed ASAP."

"Yes, ma'am."

Yolanda gave her a thumbs up and left the room.

Gio had parked the wheelchair against the wall and brought a chair over to Jacq. "Do either of you need anything from me?"

Jacq shook her head.

Dylan said, "Can you swing by my apartment and grab me a pair of basketball shorts, so I don't have to wear this stupid hospital gown?"

"Absolutely."

Dylan gave Gio a short list of other things, and Gio left.

Dylan took Jacq's hand. "Harper's okay?"

Her heart warmed. "She is. I'm so grateful to have found Rachel. I'm not sure what I'd do without her."

"No doubt. And I take it Matt found you since Gio brought you back instead of Aliza."

"He did and took me to see Marrissa. Can I just say? We really have a marvelous team."

"We do, and you make it that much better."
"Thanks. How was seeing your family?"
"Good. They know I like my partner now."
"Oh, do they?"
"Don't worry, I didn't tell them it's you. Though they want to meet you."
She leaned her head back and laughed. "At least they think they do."
"Hey, don't be so hard on yourself."
"Oh, I'm not meaning to be. It's reality, darling."
He smiled at her term of endearment but shook his head.
Her eyes watered as they locked eyes again. "Thank you for saving me."
He let go of her hand and cupped the side of her face. "You don't have to thank me. I couldn't stand the idea of life without you. I was so scared, I didn't think twice about running in. I love you."
She wiped her tears. "I love you too." She leaned over and kissed his head. "I should get in bed."
"Get some sleep. I'll be right here."
"I know. And I'm here for you." Jacq lay down facing Dylan.
His eyelids grew heavy, and he fell asleep as she stared at him.
Thank you, Jesus, for Dylan, for our safety, for Marrissa's safety. In a matter of minutes, Jacq was asleep too.

Chapter Thirty-Two

The doorbell rang Tuesday afternoon two weeks after the fire had scorched his back. Dylan stood from the couch and stretched. Bad idea. The skin on his back was healing, but it was still tight.

"Coming." He limped to the door. Much of the last two weeks had been spent with Jacq by his side. During those days of her and Harper coming over to take care of him, they had grown even closer. Now, more than ever, he was sure she was the woman he wanted to spend the rest of his life with.

He opened the door and revealed the redheaded love of his life. "Hey, you!"

"Hey." She touched his jawline. "I'm glad you haven't shaved yet. I kind of like the bearded look."

"Maybe I'll keep it—"

"Except we have to go back to work." She rose on her toes and met his lips.

He relished the tenderness of her kiss and wrapped his arm around her waist, drawing her closer.

She ran her fingers into his hair and deepened the kiss. When she stepped back, she wheezed.

He gently rubbed her back. "Didn't mean to take your breath away."

She giggled and coughed. "One of these days my lungs will return to normal. This happened the first time too."

He closed the door behind her.

She bit her lip. "Are you sure you're up to going with me today?

You know you'll have to put a shirt on."

"If you insist."

"Oh I don't mind, but it's probably not appropriate."

He raised his palms to the ceiling. "I guess. But seriously, I do want to go. I'd really like to see if they know anything about our mystery woman." They were going to visit with the three other women they had saved from Bobbi's "business."

Jacq followed him into the kitchen and leaned against the counter. "I'm a little afraid to find out who she is."

"Why?"

"I don't want anything to happen to her. What if we discover who she is, but her pimp does too? I wish she'd come to us."

"I thought for a minute maybe she'd reveal herself when we talked by the cars, but she was really scared."

"Can't say I blame her." Jacq wiggled her nose like she was trying not to cry.

"You okay?"

She shook her head. "I don't know. I feel unsettled about the whole situation still. I know we rescued Marrissa and the three we're going to see today, but it's as if God is stirring something in my heart. I just don't know what."

He took the sides of her face and tilted it up toward his. "We'll pray about it. He'll show us the way, and whatever He says, we'll do it."

A smile curled her lips. "I love you."

"Duh."

She smacked his bare abs. The chill of her fingers tightened his muscles.

"Those fingers! Isn't it like seventy-five degrees outside?"

She laughed. "If you had a shirt on—"

"Whatever." He leaned down and kissed her cheek before turning to get ready to leave.

Thirty minutes later, Dylan shifted uncomfortably as Jacq pulled up in front of a house that was part of a rehabilitation program to help women escape trafficking and learn how to function in society in a way they weren't used to. On the way over, Jacq had chatted with him about plans for Harper's birthday party on Saturday. Jacq was anxious about it.

"It'll be great, Jacq. Don't worry."

She opened the car door. "If you say so." She got out.

He climbed out and came up next to her as she took the sidewalk leading to the house. "Is there anything I can do to help?"

"Could you pick up the cake from the grocery store on your way over Saturday?"

"That I can do."

They took the two steps to the front door and knocked. Luna, whose name was actually Lexi, opened the door. "Jacq! Dylan!"

Jacq drew Lexi into a hug. "How are you doing?"

"I'm good. I've never slept as much as I have in the last two weeks." Lexi invited them in, and the three of them went to the living room.

Nova and Stella—whose real names were Natalie and Sydney—came in from the kitchen and gave Jacq hugs.

"It's so good to see you. You look marvelous."

Sydney nodded. "Feeling pretty great too, finally."

They all sat and talked about how the girls were settling into the transition house and starting the process of looking for jobs and continuing their education. The young women, especially Lexi and Natalie, were excited about the freedom in front of them, but Sydney didn't give off the same vibe.

Dylan leaned forward. "What about you, Sydney? What do you look forward to most about your new life?"

She shrugged. "It's all too much. I've been in the game for ten years. I don't know anything else. I mean, I've dreamed of getting out, but I never really, truly imagined it would happen or what it would be like." She smiled. "You know, I always wanted to be a mom." She put her hand on her belly and looked up at them. "I recently found out I'm pregnant. Guess that's why it's extra-overwhelming."

"Congratulations." Jacq reached over and squeezed her hand. "That's wonderful. A child is a gift."

"Even when you have to go about it on your own? I have no idea who the dad is, nor do I want to."

"Even then." Jacq told them her story about Harper and losing Sean. "I know it's not the same circumstance, but I also know God is all you need."

"Now you sound like Daisy." Lexi laughed. "I never understood how that girl could talk about God while she lived that life."

Dylan tilted his head. "Who's Daisy?"

"One of Ronan's girls."

Dylan nodded, remembering that Ronan was the other pimp they thought maybe Bobbi had reached out to. "I was wondering. From the tip we received, we were under the impression there would be one more girl in the house."

The girls all agreed, but Sydney answered. "Celeste—don't know her real name. She was Bobbi's bottom. He'd already started fuming that she was late. But as soon as y'all showed up I'm sure she hightailed it out of there. She's been in the life a long time—"

"Not as long as Daisy."

"Yet Daisy is just now bottom."

"That's because she got bounced around. Celeste has been with Bobbi since she started."

"And Daisy doesn't stay in pocket as well as Celeste."

All three girls laughed.

Dylan wished he could understand their life a little better. Maybe then he'd know how to help other girls get out. "Can I continue to be nosy?"

Natalie giggled. "Sure."

"The tip we received was from a woman who wanted to remain anonymous, but we'd really like to know who she is and see if there is any way we can help her. Any chance this Daisy is our informant?"

Sydney shook her head. "I wouldn't count on it. Ronan would kill her if she stepped out like that—"

Natalie cut in. "Most likely strangle her to death."

Lexi nodded. "For sure. But I guess it's possible."

Dylan rubbed his thigh still tight from the dissolving stitches. "Anyone else you think it could be?"

They all three shook their heads. Sydney's face grew serious. "You guys can't say her name around though. Ronan is even meaner than Bobbi—"

"Bobbi was a pushover compared to Ronan." Lexi shuddered.

Jacq touched her head where she'd been pistol-whipped. "And Bobbi was no sissy."

Lexi nodded.

Dylan rested his elbows on his thighs. "I give you my word, we won't mention her name. If you ever run into her, tell her we want to help."

They continued chatting, and the girls took them on a tour of the house. Dylan and Jacq then talked to the girls' advocate for a little bit before leaving.

When they got back in the car, Jacq didn't start it right away. She simply sat there staring at her hands.

"What is it, babe?"

She smiled and met his eyes. "I like that. Babe." Then she took a deep breath. "I want to help more."

"How?"

"I don't know yet."

"Let me know when you do."

"I will." She finally turned the car on and drove away from the house.

Dylan reached across the car and rubbed the back of her neck. This was only the beginning, and he couldn't wait to see what God had in store for him and Jacq.

Saturday Evening

"Happy birthday, dear Harper. Happy birthday to you!"

Dylan smiled at the now three-year-old redhead who sat at the end of the table with a large pink cake in front of her. He adored the little girl and her mom. He rested his hand on the small of Jacq's back

She told Harper to make a wish and blow out the candle.

Harper leaned onto the table and let out a huge poof of nothing. The flame didn't even flicker. Dylan stifled a chuckle and looked around at the rest of the party attenders—Rachel and her family, Aliza and the kids, Gabe, and Jacq's mom, who had flown down from Pittsburgh for the weekend.

"Try again, Harper," Jacq encouraged.

Harper took another deep breath and let it out. This time the three little flames surrendered and went out.

Dylan put his hands together and clapped with everyone. The grin on Harper's face could light up the entire world.

He stepped back to give Jacq a little space to grab the cake.

"Let me take this to the counter and cut it."

"Yay!" Harper squealed and rapidly clapped her hands.

Dylan helped Jacq pass out slices of cake. Once everyone else had a slice, he took a piece for himself and watched Jacq interact with her mom, Rachel, and Aliza while he ate.

It had been almost three weeks since he had run into that burning building to save Jacq. They were both healing nicely and headed back to work on Monday. His life had changed completely in the last four weeks since Jacq had been assigned to his team. His breath caught in his lungs. Without a shadow of a doubt, she was a perfect fit for him. But how would she fit with his family? He adored Jacq's mom, and she seemed to like him too. He was bummed for them that she didn't live closer. Jacq could use having family nearby, but at least she had Rachel, who was a complete blessing for Jacq and Harper.

Once the little party was over, and the other guests had left, Jacq's mom took Harper into her room to read some stories before bed. Jacq and Dylan settled on the couch. He needed to talk to her, but he wasn't quite sure what she would say in response.

"How are your burns feeling today?" Jacq snuggled close to him.

"Not bad. A little itchy, and the skin's pulling but seems to be getting a little better every day."

"Good." She lay her head on his shoulder.

The silence lingered for a moment, but he needed to ask and get it over with. "Jacq?" His voice shook more than he intended.

"Yes?" She sat up a bit and turned toward him, resting her knee on his leg.

"I … want to talk to you … I guess." He struggled with the words. "I have a question." He finally blurted it out.

Her eyes narrowed. "Okay. What is it?"

He swallowed the lump in his throat. "Do you think you're ready to have dinner with my family? My mom's invited us over on Friday evening."

Any hint of a smile vanished, and her eyes grew wide. Her mouth parted as if to say something, but nothing came out.

"Is it too soon?"

"No, it really isn't too soon. If your family wasn't …"

"My family."

"Yeah. Well, then I would expect to meet them at about this point. I love you, and it seems appropriate, but…"

"It's my family."

She scrunched her face and nodded.

He didn't want to push, but at the same time he wanted to get it over with and move forward with whatever their response would be. "Jacq, I don't want to push you if you're not ready. I get it. I honestly can't believe I'm actually asking. I told Scarlett only four weeks ago I didn't think I could ever invite a girl home. But wouldn't it be better to do it sooner rather than later?"

Her shoulders dropped. "Yes."

He bit his lip.

"Okay."

He sat up a little straighter. "Really? Dinner on Friday?"

"Yes. It's time. Should we get a sitter?"

"Totally up to you."

"Maybe getting a sitter would be best this time. They can meet Harper another day."

"It'll be good." He nodded trying to convince himself. "I love you, and I don't want to hide that from my family. Let them react how they will. I pray they'll accept you and see what a great fit we are, but if they don't, we'll figure it out."

Jacq reached up and ran her fingers through his hair. "We will. One step at a time. I promise to be conscientious of your mother's expectations."

"You be you. I love *you*, Jacq. Not some Jacq trying to act like my mom would like."

She smiled. "All right. Conscientious, but not manipulated."

"Perfect. I love you."

"I love you too." She leaned forward and kissed him.

"Mommy, Dylan, Mommy, Dylan." Harper came running from her room and jumped onto their laps. "Goo' nigh'!" She wrapped her little arms around his neck and planted a kiss on his cheek. His heart soared. He loved the idea that one day he could be this little girl's daddy. He drew Jacq and Harper closer. "Good night, Harper! Sweet dreams, little girl."

Harper pulled back from the hug and gave him a cross look. "I big girl."

He tried not to laugh. "Yes, you are."

Jacq's laughter floated through the air like music. He was more content than he could have ever imagined.

Stay in Touch with Liz Bradford

Be sure to sign up for Liz's newsletter. By signing up you will have a short story delivered to your inbox. You'll also be able to stay up to date on release dates and sales!

Sign Up for Liz's mailing list by going to: http://eepurl.com/dGuIjr

You can also find Liz at:

www.pinterest.com/lizbradfordwrites
https://www.goodreads.com/author/show/18532678.Liz_Bradford

Author's Note

As the Knoxville FBI series has come alive in my mind, the issue of human trafficking has become near and dear to my heart. It's real. It's tough. It needs to be talked about.

I've been tempted to feel as though I'm trivializing this sensitive issue as I write fiction about it, but I would never want to make light of the real pain that people experience at the hand of the evil one. But what better way to shed light on this dark world than to write stories. Jesus Himself used stories to bring His light, and I believe that He will use stories like this one to do the same today.

This story is fiction, and I don't claim to be an expert about anything I wrote about, but I do know that trafficking takes many different forms. Most victims are not snatched by a stranger, like Marrissa was. Some, like Morgan, are lured in by a boyfriend that promises the world. Others are trafficked right out of their own homes, like Scarlet. Some are trafficked by family members. Whatever form it takes, there is hope for those who have found themselves trapped in this life.

In my research, I listened to numerous stories of women who survived the game, escaped, and are now sharing their stories with the world. One of my favorite pieces of research was Rebecca Bender's memoir, *In Pursuit of Love* (published by Zondervan and available for purchase from Amazon, Christian Books, and other major book distributors). That seems strange to say, but it is amazing to see how Jesus transforms the life of a real person and rescues her from the dark world. You can find out more about Rebecca's mission to educate and equip leaders and organizations to make lasting change at **rebeccabender.org**.

If you or someone you know is a victim of human trafficking, please call the National Human Trafficking Hotline at 1-888-373-7888 or visit their website at **humantraffickinghotline.com**.

More by Liz Bradford

Knoxville FBI

The next installment of the Knoxville FBI series will be the prequel novella to the series, *Revenge Ignited*—Aliza and Gabe's story. It was previously release in *Mistletoe and Murder: A Christmas Suspense Collection* that was available during the 2020 Christmas season. Expect to see this available for purchase as an ebook and paperback in October 2021.

Under Fire – Book Two – Coming early 2022
Smoky Escape – Book Three – Release to be determined
Out of the Ashes – Book Four – Release to be determined

The Detectives of Hazel Hill

Prequel – Book Four available at
www.amazon.com/author/lizbradford

Not Alone – Book One
A Frightful Noel – Christmas Novella – Prequel
Pursued – Book Two
On Your Knees – Book Three
A Shot at Redemption – Book Four
<Title to be announced soon!> – Book Five – Coming August
<Title to be determined> – Book Six – Release to be determined

Coming later in 2021 – Book Five
(Title to be Announced)

Another man has been executed, just like Tom. What secrets will be revealed by the light of the truth?

Police Captain Keith Baker loves leading the detectives' squad in Hazel Hill, but he's beginning to wonder if it is a good fit for him. Would crime be less rampant in the city if someone else led these detectives? When Keith is offered the position as Chief of Police, his lack of confidence leaves him suspicions of the mayor's intents. After all, Keith and his detectives couldn't solve the murder of his friend, Tom Davis. However, Tom's case comes alive again when another body turns up in the same location. Could they finally solve Tom's murder?

Amy Davis is still trying to heal from the tragic loss of her husband over a year ago. She's leaning into God, but the pain has left her feeling numb until Keith stirs up feelings she never expected to feel again. When her family starts receiving strange threats, she turns to Keith for help. Can he protect her from the secrets that surround her husband's murder?

Acknowledgments

First and foremost, I must thank my Lord and Savior, Jesus! Thank You for the gift of story and allowing me to pen words. I hope and pray that You will use them to touch hearts and draw readers closer to You!

Thank you, Ken for being so supportive as I pursue my dreams and make the voices in my head earn their keep.

Thank you to my daughters for doing your school work ~~without complaint~~ eventually and helping me by ~~not fighting~~ not killing each other while I'm working.

Thank you, Mom for always being just a text or phone call away when I get stuck on a medical issue, a word, or whatnot.

Thank you, Teresa for helping me make my story make sense and my characters likeable!

Thank you, Sharyn for making my words sparkle (and say what I mean)!

Thank you, Kari for your deft formatting skills!

Thank you, Alyssa for yet another amazingly beautiful cover!

Thank you, ACFW-Louisville Chapter for welcoming me with open arms and making me feel at home immediately.

Thank you to my new dear friend Crystal Caudill for your help with my blurb and just hanging out writing together.

Thank you, Cliff Bars, for your coffee collection that sustained me in writing this book. The chocolate mocha is my favorite.

About The Author

Liz didn't always know she a writer, but she was. Before she even knew it, God was plotting out this path for her. From her earliest days, stories were a natural part of her imagination. In high school, she toyed around with writing, but it was nothing more than a secret hobby. But one day, when her middle daughter was a little over a year old, a story idea crept in her mind and wouldn't leave her alone. So, she started writing. She would stay up late after everyone else was in bed and frantically write the words that brought her characters to life.

That first novel lives buried deep in her hard drive, and maybe one day it will see the light of day, but that would take a LOT of editing. About the time she couldn't figure out where that first book would end, another idea persisted in her mind. That was Becca and Jared's story, book one in The Detectives of Hazel Hill series. Before she knew it, what started as a single novel turned into a trilogy… but wait, there's more. In that series, she now has five stories published (including the prequel novella) one more finishing up revisions, and one more percolating. She also has several more ideas for the characters of Hazel Hill, North Carolina. The Knoxville FBI series will continue with a prequel novella and three more stories after this one. Liz also has numerous other series forming in her mind!

Liz is a member of ACFW and ACFW Louisville Chapter. Her heart longs to live in North Carolina (where she was born) or Tennessee and that is why she set her stories there. But, for now, she and her husband live in Southern Indiana where she homeschools their three daughters.

Made in the USA
Coppell, TX
29 March 2023